The Chiswick Chauffeur

The Eighth Catrin Sayer Mystery

ALLAN JONES

THE CATRIN SAYER MYSTERIES

The Chinese Sailor
The Scottish Colourist
The Falmouth Model
The Carnforth Double
The Powys Deacon
The Stratford Hunter
The Thornham Copyist
The Chiswick Chauffeur

OTHER NOVELS

Canons

*All novels are released as ebooks
and Kindle Direct Publishing paperbacks*

CONTENTS

Chiswick (pronounced CHIZ-ik) was an ancient parish in the county of Middlesex. [It] became a popular country retreat and part of the suburban growth of London in the late 19th and early 20th centuries. *Wikipedia*

UCAs [undercover advanced operatives]
are trained to undertake deployments involving
higher-level infiltrations in a leading role
with the ability to withstand intense scrutiny.
Undercover Policing Guidance, consultation document, 2016
College of Policing UK

PROLOGUE

In the casino in London, Jemilah Kohli was known as Ronnie; a twenty-six-year-old from a Punjabi family background.

"Better than Rohina," she would quip heartily, when away from the gambling tables, if anyone asked if Ronnie was her actual name. "I'm not a tree, I'm a woman. That's what Rohina means - a sandalwood tree."

'Ronnie' enjoyed her gambling nights with a girlfriend, and there were no male companions or family members in sight. She was a rebel against her traditions, it seemed.

It was an act, a cover. Jemma, as her family knew her, would say nothing like that in her parents' home, nor admit to a lifestyle involving casinos. But women gambling alone need a tough front.

Lisa Gardener, her partner in crime, was known as Carol in the same place. She was good at the tables but kept her private life under wraps. Jemma knew little about her. Apparently, they were the best of friends together in the casino. In private, in the car transporting them to and from the casino, Lisa was taciturn and uncommunicative.

It was work, not pleasure.

Jemma and Lisa had been brought together by Steve Jarrett for a common purpose; to be a core part of the team used to gamble away chunks of the Bolan gang's money.

Michael J. Bolan, known to all as 'Mikey J.', ran the drug operation covering much of the east side of London and parts of Birmingham. But insiders and the police knew that his dad, now in Wormwood Scrubs prison, still ran the show. Michael Bolan Senior had no nickname, nor needed one. Being referred to as 'Mr. Bolan' was his expectation of others and he got that respect, one way or another.

In London, the women played the roles of wealthy divorcees.

"We had the same solicitor. Now our ex-husband's pay for our nights out. We win; it's ours. We lose; it's theirs. You can't beat it."

It was their story, and they held to it consistently. They used it with enough humour, anger and bitterness to frighten away men in the bars or restaurant areas. Jemma was never sure whether these people were trying to hit them up or were casino security employees doing the occasional background check.

Both women were good-looking, polite rather than friendly, and serious about their gambling.

Besides the London work, they were taken out of the city every two to three weeks for a Friday night to Sunday morning working weekend. Once a month it was a Birmingham casino. Sometimes they had weekends in either Brighton or Manchester, without much prior warning.

In Birmingham they portrayed themselves as neighbours; bored housewives with rich husbands always away from home on planes. In Brighton they claimed to co-own a successful day-care nursery franchise. 'It's a lot of work, but everyone needs a little fun in their life', Lisa would say.

They didn't isolate like professional gamblers but gave the appearance of wealthy women wanting a good time. Their covers were simple and didn't require a lot of depth; they let no-one get that close to them.

They would turn up with cash, between one and four thousand pounds each for a night and change it into chips. What they had to gamble with was dictated by Steve, who provided their stakes. He told them once that it wasn't even his decision. Somewhere, a computer algorithm calculated the number. Everything was focused on blending into the crowd.

Who Steve took his instructions from was never stated, but they knew that further up the command chain there was a man called Arkady. He called the shots on everything for the money launderers of the Bolan gang.

Steve had explained it at the beginning once he knew of Jemma's gambling addiction and her struggles.

"You'll be debt-free, your creditors paid off, and you can gamble all you want. You get paid well and there's no risk."

It sounded so attractive.

She responded indecisively, "But its drug money; I could get caught."

Steve laughed. "Jemma, you have two types of dirty money. Rob an ATM or do anything where they can trace the serial numbers, it's a risk. But this money comes from the druggies. It's as legal as the cash in the dry-cleaning business."

Jemma's day job was a van driver for a laundry and

dry-cleaning company, one with stores across London. Between her day job and her casino work, she didn't have much free time for anything, she said.

She asked, at the beginning, "So why not just bank it? Instead of this?"

"For Mr. Bolan and the others, they have no logical, legal source for the income. They are rich; they have legitimate investments and so on, but they need untraceable ways to get a lot of their earnings into accounts they control."

Steve had coaxed her on to the Bolan payroll, but it was this Arkady who set her work schedule.

"He's obviously Russian," pontificated Lisa one night, feeling talkative for a change. "Russians don't mess around."

Jemma had no wish to test that theory. She was a competent poker player, but knew her limits. Her experience included enough time at poker tables with pros. While working for Steve, she would win big occasionally, but part of her instructions was to spend equal time at the roulette tables. There, she mostly lost.

The women knew it didn't really matter. The incentive to win was that Steve would let them keep five percent of their net winnings. Those, and the clothes they wore, were bonuses on their pay. He covered the cost for their dresses and accessories. They had to look the part.

In Jemma's day job she could move these on 'as nearly new', for more ready cash. Steve insisted that they didn't wear the same outfit to the same casino twice.

By two in the morning or earlier, if they ran out of money, they would finish and cash in their remaining chips. Two to eight thousand pounds between Jemma and Lisa, depending on their fortunes at the tables, would have moved from the world of street drug sales into payout slips for their winnings or receipts for the chips bought and lost. Either way, these would be in Steve's bag as they drove home. Jemma's focus was on sleep; her delivery van had to be out on the road at 8.30 a.m.

Many branches higher in the money laundering tree, at a level where Jemma and Lisa would probably need supplemental oxygen, their gains and losses merged with those of others. People in the casino side would smile and press computer keys as they transferred money to off-shore accounts of the people at the top. As Steve said repeatedly, it didn't matter if Jemma won or lost; to the bosses, that is. A five percent bonus from a sudden two grand winning streak mattered a lot more to Jemma or Lisa.

In the language of the drug trade they were smurfs, named after the cartoon characters. Mules and smurfs. Drug mules moved the drugs. Money mules, the smurfs, moved the proceeds. Jemma was happy not to be a drug mule. Being caught with money wasn't as bad as being caught with drugs, she reasoned. Her daytime job gave her a legitimate basis for a steady income.

She told family and friends who complained that she didn't visit enough, or spend time with them, that it was her day job that tired her out.

She wasn't sure who gave her the genes for the gambling addiction. If Steve hadn't pulled her in, she would be in a lot of trouble. As it was, she got to play regularly and have the thrill of the bet without the consequences. Importantly, it gave her a small apartment and independence from parents and uncles who would still treat her as if they ran her life, given half a chance.

Image was important. That was why Steve dropped them off in the BMW. It was silver, and he wore a suit and acted deferential. Which was ironic, given the reality; he was their boss. He had six other people in his string working the casinos, the dogs and the horses.

Millions of pounds of street income were laundered into legitimate money streams every year through Steve. If there were more like him on Bolan's payroll, Jemma didn't know, and no-one talked about it.

She had a better understanding of the crews, the street gangs selling the drugs, because Steve would prattle on, describing their current successes and failures, often bitching about the way the cash was treated. Stained with spaghetti sauce or beer on occasion, and always smelling of stale cigarette smoke, it was the worst part of the job for him.

Thankfully, it wasn't either Jemma or Lisa's job to clean the money, at least physically. Steve and his wife had someone who did that. They just received bundles of new and used notes to exchange for gambling chips each evening they worked

They were all smurfs in a sense, beavering away for Mickey J. and his dad, but it wasn't anything resembling the happy characters in the cartoons.

PART 1. KNIFE

1 RIVALRIES

The Southern Breeze Casino, located on the Brighton seafront, was formerly a hotel. Decades earlier, it had been built as the seaside mansion of a Scottish industrialist, Sir Theobald Cameron.

In his later years, for warmth and sunshine, Cameron moved as far south as possible without leaving the British Isles. His money derived from mining interests in the British South Africa Company, but he disliked travel and rarely went abroad. The French Riviera was as exotic a trip as he would undertake, relying on his more adventurous cousin and a lifelong friend, an accountant, as his agents in Africa.

The owners of the casino now made the most of the building's history by presenting Cameron's life story in the plaques and paintings in the foyer. People with more interest in gambling than history gained the impression that Sir Theo had been Queen Victoria's gift to the poor and downtrodden of Africa rather than a pillager of its lands and resources.

The main entrance to the casino had been impressively restored. At night, albeit indecently gaudy by the drab anonymity of most buildings on the Brighton seafront, people arriving there could 'make an entrance', particularly if they arrived by taxi or chauffeur car.

Kes Laird, a third ranker in Burcu Dogan's gang, with his girlfriend Trish, parked and walked to the casino entrance, dressed as if they were going to a wedding. He was twenty-six and had lived his life just north of the River Thames, so Brighton was 'foreign parts' to him.

Ask him what he knew about the town, his focus would be on stories of the battles between Mods and Rockers and, still earlier, the Brighton razor gangs. The Prince Regent, the Wilds architecture and the Royal Pavilion would not be in his vocabulary.

As he approached the entrance, he stayed alert. His livelihood and safety were tied to the area of London that he and his mates ruled. If he trespassed into other London boroughs where the drug trade was in the hands of other gangs, he was in danger of losing life or limb.

Kes viewed the world a little differently from the regular, go-to-work and pay-your-taxes citizen. He kept an eye out for his enemies; all of them, all the time. He didn't want a fight, just to steer clear of trouble; particularly if, in defending himself or his reputation, he could fall foul of the law afterwards.

Survive a confrontation and if you are a known member of a gang, the police and the court system will be out to get you. He would get no hearing of the truth; that if he had not defended himself, he would be the one propped against a wall, holding his guts from protruding through the knife wound, waiting for an ambulance.

As Mr. Dogan said repeatedly, when it comes down to the coppers and the Queen's Bench, there isn't any justice for his people. The Turk would also say, though, 'Despite all that, if you are called out, you don't back down. You give it to them, good and proper'.

When Kes saw Steve Jarrett in the full illumination of the Southern Breeze entrance, he stepped back into the shadows.

"Wait."

His girlfriend was part of his world, so she didn't flap about or raise any objections.

"Who is it?"

"He's Steve Jarrett, one of Mikey J.'s people, acting like a chauffeur, the prick."

They stood still. Trish watched Kes watch this man Jarrett. She, too, was conscious that they were here alone and they needed to avoid trouble.

As Jarrett opened the rear curbside door of the BMW, two women got out; an attractive, slim Indian woman exited elegantly whereas a blonde, beefier woman did a bottom shuffle across the back seat to follow her partner. Jarrett exchanged words with them before he walked around to the driver's side and re-took his seat.

"Classy," said Trish, taking in the women's clothes and movements.

Kes had his eye on the BMW now, not the women. Jarrett didn't park the car. Instead, he drove out to the road and turned left, heading into the centre of Brighton.

Thank God for that, Kes thought.

They followed the women inside, acting naturally. Trish was excited to be here; she had only been to casinos in London three times and this was the first time at one in Brighton. Jarrett's women headed directly to the cashier wall.

They are buying their gambling chips there, thought

Kes, so they don't flash a wad of bills at the tables in front of others. They knew what they were doing. These two weren't here for the food or the show.

Kes whispered to Trish, "Change our money behind them."

He passed over three hundred pounds in twenties and moved out of the line to one side, waiting for his girlfriend. The Indian, he took in, now held some higher denomination chips. The blonde passed over two bundles of twenties and fifties, worth around two thousand, he estimated.

After the women changed their stake money into chips and Trish returned with hers, Kes said, "I'll hold these; the two with Jarrett went into the women's. Go check them out, but carefully. See what you can dig up."

Trish smiled and gave him their stack of chips to hold. "They must have been in the same tailback near Crawley; it's hard on the bladder to crawl along in traffic when you are getting excited about having a good night. I'll powder my nose."

Kes thought Jarrett's women didn't appear to be excited. They had a sense of purpose.

Trish came out of the women's washroom five minutes after the Jarrett women, chatting with another woman. She was older, grey-haired and giggling at some comment. As they reached Kes, Trish said, "Sorry to take so long. This is Eleanor; we just had a girl's natter, a few of us doing our make-up."

Eleanor waved to an older man, her partner or husband, who walked over, obviously not wanting a conversation but get on with something else.

Trish continued, "Eleanor was talking with two other women from around here. They own a daycare franchise, apparently, and make a fortune at it."

She kept her expression neutral, but Kes knew who she meant.

The older woman laughed. "I could have made money raising other peoples' kids instead of my own."

Her husband, now introduced as Vic, gave her a look. He whispered, "Elly, we need to move on. Janet and Hugh will have a table in the restaurant by now and they'll be waiting on us."

As they made their goodbyes, Kes exchanged glances with Trish and said, "Let's get you started and then I'll give Nicky a quick call."

All Nicholas Jordan, Kes's boss, wanted when he heard the name Jarrett was Laird's location.

"Brighton, at the Southern Breeze."

"Not mixing it up with the other one, the Ballantine, are we? They are side by side almost."

"Give me a break, Nicky. I haven't had a drink yet! We are staying at The Old Ship tonight; it's Trish's twenty-fourth today. We thought we would go here first and try the Ballantine tomorrow afternoon, before driving home."

There was a pause. Kes wondered about Nicky's mood. He could be hard to read over the phone.

Kes had joined the Dogan gang from the Carlton Street Crew two years ago; 'graduated' so to speak. He thought Jarrett's appearance would be of interest to his boss. The 'Limmies', formerly TLF, 'The Limehouse Firm', was now part of Kes's responsibility. Steve Jarrett's name was dirt with them, for joining Mikey J. and his gang.

"Say happy birthday to Trish and buy her a bottle of sparkles on me as a present. If you see Jarrett later, don't see him and, if possible, don't let him see you. Get my meaning? But have a good time and, tomorrow, stay away from the Ballantine. Take her to another one. The Ballantine is off-limits."

"Well, thanks, boss. She'll like that. We'll go somewhere else, then."

He paused, wondering whether to ask why the Ballantine was a no-go area, and thought better of it.

Later, Nicky Jordan called Burcu Dogan.

"Kes Laird is with his girl, gambling at the Southern Breeze in Brighton. He saw Steve Jarrett dropping two of his women off for their shift, by the sound of it. He wonders what is going on, as his girlfriend overheard that the women are claiming to be local business owners, a kid's daycare set-up of some sort. I just told him to steer clear of Jarrett and the Ballantine."

"He doesn't know why? He's not starting something with Jarrett, I hope."

"No. He's steering clear of any trouble, he told me."

Burcu knew that Laird had two crews to manage in the East End and one of them, the Limmies, hated Barrett with a passion.

"Leave Kes in the dark, then. Thanks, Nick."

As Burcu Dogan closed the call, he thought Mikey J. may use the Southern Breeze for cleaning his money, just as he used the Ballantine casinos, both in Brighton and in London. As much as he hated the man, he didn't need trouble there. Laundering money was running smoothly at present. Any retaliatory action from Mikey J. for some stupid error by one of Burcu's people wouldn't help the bottom line. There was enough trouble fighting over drug sales.

The Limmies were currently in the thick of it with Mikey J. and under orders from Burcu to make a dent in the Liverpool Street Station area trade.   Spitalfields, Whitechapel and Mile End had become the battleground.

Keep it there, Burcu mused; keep the violence away from the casinos.

~~

Strangely enough, that same issue preoccupied the mind of another gang boss, one who had no business dealings with Dogan at all.

Dominic Connolly came from Glasgow, but currently he was serving a prison sentence in Her Majesty's Prison, Shotts, in Lanarkshire. If Burcu had known of Connolly's interest, it would disturb him far more than any inadvertent encounter between Laird and Jarrett.

Connolly still ran the drug world on most of the west side of Scotland. Earlier that day, he had been in a business meeting with Michael Bolan Senior. Located in Shotts and Wormwood Scrubs, respectively, it took place as usual via illegal mobile phones.

The two gang leaders had worked supply routes together in an arrangement that had lasted over a decade now, largely undisturbed by others. Undisturbed, of course, was a relative term. Their businesses always suffered skirmishes over territory.

As their business matters wrapped up, he asked Michael for a moment or two more, to talk about another issue.

Bolan could spare all the time in the world, in a sense; he was staying in prison. Dominic was not, he had informed Bolan at the start of the call. He would be paroled. The paperwork was now being processed. Michael received the news with mixed feelings but, nevertheless, he congratulated the man.

"It's not good, Michael, what I am hearing. We both know that the Dog has been eating into your business, but he is also creating problems upstream with our key people. They are saying we are going to have to deal with it and I'll be out soon."

Bolan sighed. "I hear Mikey complaining about the Turk, too. There's too much visibility with his crews focusing on the younger addicts and all the knifing incidents."

Burcu Dogan, 'The Dog', had appeared on the scene four years ago. His top people were hard as nails, chosen as much for their macho charisma as anything else. Dogan's crews tended to be young, impressionable and focused on sales largely in the same age range.

Dogan persuaded the younger members of his crews they were invincible. When arrested, the 'soft' juvenile sentences imposed became a rite of passage in their career with 'The Dog'.

Connolly responded emphatically. "You need to be out and back in charge - and you've a parole hearing due soon."

"We're working on it, here with the screws and their reports on me. Donald is dealing with the application and the world outside. It had better not get messed up, as it did last time. Jalaj Ranjani and his wife screwed that one up for me."

Donald Killam was Bolan's long-time solicitor.

Dominic knew Bolan's plan. He had trod that path himself, to appear squeaky clean and a reformed character.

His response was, "Could you send Mo up for a weekend to the Castle, with Joanie? I've got something to suggest."

Maureen Bolan was Michael's wife. In years gone by,

the Bolan and Connolly couples spent some time together, once at the Fonab Castle, near Pitlochry. Dominic liked the place. Whatever the proposal involved, it was clearly too sensitive or complex for a phone call.

Sensing the understated importance, Michael just said, "I'll call her, get her to contact Joanie and set up a girl's weekend together. They'll enjoy that."

Their wives were experienced in their businesses and trusted. Michael perked up, interested in what this meant and how it linked to his forthcoming hearing.

As one of Michael's team took the phone from him, to hide it away, the memories of the run-up to his last parole hearing flooded back. All had been going well until Jalaj Ranjani, his lieutenant in charge while Michael served his sentence, screwed up royally. Jalaj ran the operation well - almost robotically well - but he and his wife indulged in a dangerous and bizarre pastime; they were a pair of occasional killers for hire. Both were talented marksmen.

The fees paid for assassinations had supported Nirupa Ranjani's passion for expensive art. When the police discovered that lethal sideline, Michael's parole application went belly up and he needed a new person in charge of his business.

It was worse for the Ranjani couple. Nirupa ended up dead on her living room floor. Her loose comments during two police interviews, coupled with her potential to be rearrested, made their assassination syndicate act to protect their interests. Jalaj fled the country and now worked for the syndicate in other parts of the world.

Mikey J. stepped up and into Ranjani's shoes. While he was a Bolan, Michael knew his son was not as effective a leader as Jalaj had proven himself to be. Mikey was too hot-tempered, too keen to retaliate in battle, rather than win the fight without the opposition becoming aware they were already beaten.

It all tied in with Connolly's observation.

"Tea, boss? We've a fresh batch of your special Earl Grey brought in this morning."

Jolted from his thoughts, he thanked the man for the offer. He may be in prison, but his people looked after him well.

A little later, as he sipped his tea, his mind returned to that time. He remembered a conversation with Dom about the irony that the same person, an art cop called Sayer, had been part of Dom's comeuppance years earlier and, more recently, involved in the Ranjani investigation. Strange, that; uncanny. Michael and Dominic's businesses had nothing to do with art, so why would an art detective be such a thorn in their flesh?

He would give his wife a call; get her sorted for a mini-break in Scotland.

2 GLOCK

Streets between the Aldgate East and Old Street Tube stations form the historical area of Spitalfields, London. With the neighbouring boroughs of Hackney and White-chapel, the area makes up part of the old 'East End' of London. Buildings there are now largely upmarket multi-story apartments or businesses, many being the renovated original structures still crowding the narrow streets.

You can walk in seconds from busy traffic and pedestrian clusters into quiet residential dwellings set back in alleys and courtyards. On misty nights, a nervous individual could well imagine a horse-drawn hansom cab turning the corner on to a cobbled alley. If they did spot such a vehicle, it wasn't a phantom; rather, it was probably a movie being shot by one of the entertainment companies busy in London these days.

Catrin Sayer's home, a ground floor apartment, lay between the Spitalfields Market and The Blind Beggar pub, where Ronnie Kray shot and killed a rival gangster in the nineteen sixties.

For an artistic woman who grew up in South Wales surrounded by green hills and valleys, you would suspect the location could be confining or oppressive. Both Sayer and her husband, Chris Treneer, were settled and happy there.

Catrin had lucked out in finding the apartment years ago. The sole occupant at the time had just split up with her partner and needed another woman around her age to share the rent. When she later found a fiancé, she moved on and away and Chris then moved up from Cornwall to be with Catrin. The apartment and the surrounding area worked for them, too. Now with a baby, Chris was wondering whether they needed somewhere bigger. Catrin was not convinced.

Neighbours knew that she was a police officer. For most of them, this was reassuring; for others, it made them wary. Over the years, there had been occasional appearances of brightly marked police cars and men and women in uniform, either dropping Sayer off or picking her up at odd hours.

So, on a blustery damp day in March, the appearance of a Metropolitan Police Vauxhall Astra driven by a portly older officer caused some stares but wasn't a complete surprise.

"Harry Stephens, it's been quite a while!"

Detective Inspector Sayer beckoned the older, uni-formed constable into her home. He had steel grey hair and a bit of a pot belly now, she noticed, but still had a weathered, smiling face. The officer had called that morning, needing to follow up on a firearm report, he said. Could he visit her at home?

"It's good to see you, ma'am. Enjoying the leave? And how is the baby?"

"Come and see. She's awake and playful. Another face will be welcome. And it's Catrin, remember? Unless we have to be formal about this."

Constable Stephens had been a firearms instructor located at the main firing range for Metropolitan Police officers, at Gravesend.

Several years ago, he had been transferred to New Scotland Yard, in a role which made him less welcome with his colleagues. He was now the firearms expert assigned to the internal investigation unit, the Office of Professional Standards. If there was a problem with a Met officer and a firearm, it usually involved Harry at the technical level.

He looked at Sayer, comparing her now with his recollection from her training courses and the refreshers at the range. She looked different. Her dark blonde hair was longer. It had always been collar-length but now it was styled and down to her shoulders.

Her most characteristic feature was still a faint line, a two-inch scar on her left cheek. She was looking fit, he thought, but her bust, waist and hips reflected that she had been through childbirth.

Some women show it, others don't, he reflected. Sayer looked more mature, more a mother, in an intangible sense. He had seen the same transition in his own wife after their first child was born. He still found it magical, almost mysterious. For a minute or so he focused on the baby.

She asked, "So what's it about?"

He pulled out the file from the document case he carried and examined the cover sheet.

"A Glock 17, serial number 010245MPU7."

She said, "Sounds familiar; it was one of mine, if you are here."

"Issued to you for the last three months of your time with Assistant Commissioner Hunt. You turned it in when you left that role."

At his prompt, she recalled doing that, returning the firearm.

She had been Sandra Hunt's security officer for two years, as a uniformed sergeant, before returning with a promotion to plainclothes duties in the Art and Antiques Unit.

"Catrin, I'm doing a formal check with all users who had been assigned that specific firearm. Do you recall any problems with the Glock misfiring while assigned to you, reported or not?"

"An ammunition misfire; a failure to fire? They are so rare an event. No, I never had that happen with any assigned weapon."

Stephens continued. "How about any unintentional discharge with the Glock?"

"Again, no. Not with that or any other assigned fire-arm. If I had, it would have been reported immediately. Is this the perennial Glock safety debate?"

He didn't respond as he wrote her answer on the form before looking at her. He nodded.

"Final question. Do you recall a specific problem of any sort with the assigned firearm during the period you used it, reported or not?"

She thought back for a moment. "Not with that Glock. The only thing around that time I remember was an ammunition recall."

He murmured the answer. "That was a hot-fire issue, a claim of a sub-standard batch, never substantiated. We changed it out; we had no choice. Thank you, ma'am. Could you read through the sheet and sign and date, please, and I will witness the signature."

As she did that, he explained. "Yes, the Glock issue. An unintended discharge in a multi-storey car park search in pursuit of a bag snatcher wielding a knife, one of those moped thefts. The officer blamed the weapon. For the OPS hearing, we have to check with prior users about its earlier behaviour."

The internal review by the Office of Professional Standards.

"Was anyone injured?"

He shook his head. "No, thank God. In fact, the suspect gave himself up, thinking they were prepared to shoot him."

They looked at each other. Catrin didn't make a further comment.

The issue of the safety locks on Glock automatics was a longstanding debate. The weapon has a three-point safety system preventing handling misfires or a discharge if dropped, but each of these link to the complex, two-part trigger. There is not a separate safety lock.

An itchy trigger finger could lead to an unintentional discharge, so the investigation most likely arose from the officer denying his or her responsibility.

But Sayer was all for the Glock 17, as a firearm of choice for the Met, Harry recalled. He knew her story better than most, as he was one of the few to hear it directly from her.

Other than basic firearms training shortly after joining the Met, Catrin had initially opted out of any further involvement in a specialised firearms role. Her first use of a handgun in the line of duty was unexpected and life-saving, occurring during a trip to Kuala Lumpur with a Foreign Office bureaucrat.

During an unexpected encounter between the Malaysian Police officer accompanying them and a criminal with a grudge against him, the officer had been wounded. In the seconds of the event unfolding, he had passed his Sig Sauer automatic to Catrin. She had taken down the assailant.

Her ability to do that was based on two key elements. First, her accuracy while under fire. People in the Met had noted it. In time, it led to her security role with Assistant Commissioner Hunt.

Only Harry and some other firearm experts had heard the second reason; the realisation that the weapon design had saved her life. It had a two-action safety, a double pressure pull on the trigger for cocking the weapon followed by a single pressure trigger repeat. No other safety release was needed, and if it had been, she would have been killed.

Having no prior experience with a Sig, she had simply pointed and fired repeatedly, not even noting the trigger pressure changes. It saved her, the Foreign Office official she was accompanying and two Malaysian police officers.

She liked the Glock for the same reason.

She picked up her baby. "Mair, meet Harry, say hello and give him one of your smiles."

He asked, "Maya, is it?"

Catrin responded, "It sounds like it, doesn't it? It's Welsh, my grandmother's name."

She spelled it for him. Mair Jenifer Sayer Treneer had been born in November, four months earlier.

Harry played with the baby's fingers a little, then said with a sigh, "I'd best be going; I still have a few more people to see on this one."

They both knew it was a futile exercise; that the Glock was not the problem.

"When do you return to work?" he asked, as Catrin

opened the front door for him.

"In just over a week."

"Why don't you give Jocelyn a call soon and set up your re-certification at the range? When you get back, you will be up to your eyes, no doubt, so it would be a good idea to be slotted in already, ahead of the game. We can't have someone like you dropping off the AFO list, can we?"

AFO, an authorised firearms officer, in the jargon of the Met.

Catrin Sayer was a trained personal security officer, one with front-line experience, his expression conveyed.

Catrin gave it a moment's thought. "That's a good idea, Harry. Thanks."

He smiled, "I'll give her a heads up, tell her I've seen the baby, it will make her jealous. You won't be taking Mair to the range, but you'd better have photos on your phone!"

It was only later that Catrin mused on how different her life was these days. From a security officer to an art detective to a mother; from carrying a Glock firearm to being on the lookout for disposable nappies on sale.

But she didn't miss the security work or the more violent incidents of her career, where art crime investigations had crossed paths with organized crime. Art crime was the right area for her now. It was technical work and a little bit of a specialist backwater area of Met activity.

She cuddled her baby and thought about the reality of getting back to work at New Scotland Yard and the nagging problem; how to balance police work, a baby and her passion for ceramic art, a creative partnership with her friend Jean Hughes.

Friends from childhood in Pontypridd, South Wales, they lived minutes apart in Spitalfields. Jean was the co-owner of The Cwmbran Kiln, a boutique pottery in Spitalfields Market. She, too, had a baby daughter. Now the two artists had similar decisions to make around work and life balance.

3 CASTLE

When Joan Connolly hired Eric Knight, she was her normal blunt self. She told him that her husband was in Her Majesty's Prison, Shotts, and that they had legal business holdings and 'other interests'. She chose not to define whether that meant illegal businesses or a passion for darts. He could read the rest on the internet, she said, assuming he wasn't stupid.

They wanted a high-end driver, one who would not be involved with anyone on the dodgy side of things at all.

"You drive, that's it. And the pay is time and a half over the hourly that any contract agency chauffeur makes. Yes or no?"

"Yes."

"You keep your nose clean, ultra-clean; a spotless record in driving and anything else. And you will work any or all hours, OK?"

"At that pay rate, of course I will. And I don't need to research the internet, Mrs. Connolly. The terms are excellent. I'm glad to get a regular job."

Joan looked him over. "Is that your work suit or one

for this interview? How many do you have?"

Eric replied, "Well, this is my best and only. I have some formal black pants and white shirts for warmer weather. I could buy another suit, I suppose."

"You didn't have to buy your uniform when you drove for the city; you don't with us. Dom's tailor is Willoughby's, on George Street. Get two suits, and they will be top quality; bespoke. I'll let them know. You should look as good as the new car. We are celebrating my Dom coming home soon, but your first big trip will be north, to Pitlochry."

The Fonab Castle Hotel & Spa in the Highlands of Scotland offers its guests five-star accommodations and a comparable visit experience. Its client records have to be meticulous. A returning guest should not be greeted as if they were a newcomer. If a guest chooses to return, they must have been happy enough with the first stay. The second visit should be a foretaste of the future.

Angela in the Client Services Centre was an expert with the booking system and diligent as anyone would wish for.

"A Mrs. Joan Connolly, Gordon. She and her husband stayed quite a few times years ago. They are flagged as top-tier clients but have not stayed with us for a few years now. She is insisting on two Castle Signature rooms adjacent, but with only one occupant in each. We are nearly full that night, so should we tell her the selection is not available? Or can I move a provisional booking made last night, one that is still pending a credit card hold?"

She relied on him a lot. Gordon had worked at the Castle for a long time and knew more about many of the past guests.

"From Glasgow?"

"She is, yes. And the second room is a Mrs. Maureen Bolan from London. They are reserving a third room for their chauffeur, a Mr. Knight, but he's for a regular Loch room. That one's no problem."

Angela could see Gordon staring at the screen, pensive. He pressed a key that moved the details to the address section for a moment and then back again.

"Give Mrs. Connolly what she wants."

He remembered the Connolly couple from years ago. Lavish spenders but polite. Occasionally they reserved multiple rooms or suites, required transport to and from the golf courses in the area and took sightseeing trips for the family, on the occasions they brought their children.

Mrs. Connolly had particularly enjoyed the amenities, he recalled. Mr. Connolly was less effusive, preferring quiet walks or golf with other men also staying as their guests. What transpired then, no doubt, was business. Not any business Gordon would want to know about.

But he couldn't fault them as guests.

He recalled that around the time of their last visit, Dominic Connolly had been arrested, tried and convicted of a series of drug crimes. Found guilty after one of his gang had turned Queen's Evidence, he had been in jail for years now.

The weekend visit of the two women passed without incident or anything remarkable. They arrived with a young, smartly dressed man driving a new Jaguar limousine. The women visited the spa, dined together and clearly enjoyed the visit.

It was a coincidence that Gordon, on duty on the Saturday evening, delivered an urgent message to some American guests dining at a nearby table; one of those 'you don't want to give or get this bad news' deliveries.

He needed to get them out of the restaurant and into a private area to let them speak to their daughter in Tennessee, now waiting on hold.

After leaning forward and talking to them softly, he stepped back a little to give them time to absorb that there was a serious problem. Their fine meal would be ruined, he knew.

While standing waiting, he heard one person at the Connolly table behind him say, with conviction, "It should be this Catrin Sayer; don't you think? Given the Welsh woman's track record. Get her to give the sod the kiss of death."

It was an English voice. The response by her companion, Mrs. Connolly, was a low chuckle and, "It would be appropriate, wouldn't it? You and your superstitions, Mo!"

It was only after Gordon had overseen the arrangements for the distressed Americans that he had a quiet moment. His mind went back to the comment overheard in the dining room. The name Sayer was Welsh, he thought. He wondered if it linked to the Connolly drug business he had read about. The 'kiss of death', indeed.

Did Mrs. Connolly mean that figuratively or literally? Was this Sayer some gang member, perhaps, a violent woman, possibly a killer? It beggared belief, the violence in that world.

As the American suddenly spoke to him, thanking him for all the help they were receiving, his mind turned to the immediate problem and he put his speculations about drug gangs from his mind. It was not his world. He wouldn't want to cross paths with this forbidding Sayer character, became his last thought on the matter.

~~

Her Majesty's Prison Shotts is positioned between Glasgow and Edinburgh, near the town of the same name. It holds male prisoners in a maximum-security environment. The main entrance area is reminiscent of many ancient, cylindrical Scottish keeps, belying the modern prison setting behind.

Prisoners released at the end of their sentence, or with long-term or day parole, generally exit into the large car park, seeing their friend or relative waiting by a vehicle. Those less fortunate, without friends or money, walk a few more yards to the bus stop on Newmill and Canthill Road.

The immaculate, dark blue Jaguar XJ drew up and waited near the entrance exactly as Dominic Connolly appeared. If you mistook him for an overweight, middle-aged lag tired of life after years in prison, you would have missed the muscles beneath the fat and the strength of character in his face. He was a powerful man, physically and mentally.

In smart casual clothes, he walked across and climbed into the back seat, to be greeted with a hug and kiss by his wife. She gave one look, an icy stare, at an unmarked police car parked some distance away and said something to the driver.

Eric Knight was dressed in a smart suit and collar and tie. He exited the vehicle, moved around to the boot and retrieved a black leather briefcase. With the Prada motif visible, he opened the rear passenger door and passed it to her. Then he, too, looked at the police car, returned to his seat and, within fifteen seconds, the vehicle drew away smoothly.

The police car didn't follow them. It had no need to. They were there to check the chauffeur, in case either Joan or Dominic, in a fit of sentiment for old time's sake, had arranged for Kevin to drive, his long-time former driver. They had no illusions that would happen, but you never know.

Kevin had a criminal record and Connolly's parole conditions proscribed any contact with people with prior convictions linked to organized crime.

That the couple had bought a new car for the event registered with the officers from the organized crime group in Police Scotland. The purchase signalled that Connolly had returned to his business. During his years in Shotts he hadn't really been out of it, but it reinforced the message, as did the waggle of the £2000 Prada briefcase, probably containing nothing but today's newspaper, a can of lager and a cheese sandwich.

They were now running checks on the chauffeur. He turned out to be new and had no known criminal involvement, they discovered.

As the Connolly couple headed back to Glasgow, they talked of anything other than the business, with their new driver in the car. Connolly spent a few minutes talking to the man, checking him out, seeing if his wife had chosen well. He seemed satisfied.

"What's your best part of the job so far, Eric?"

The chauffeur thought about it a moment, to give his new boss a serious response.

"I like it all, really. Not having the bureaucracy of driving for the city is perhaps the best part. I take care of the car and make sure I give excellent service, or try to. Perhaps the drive up to the Fonab Castle Hotel last week with Mrs. Connolly and her guest has been the best so far. The weather was gorgeous, and it's lovely around there."

Joan smiled. "He's nervous, Dom."

One of the most powerful drug bosses in the UK leaned forward, making nice. "Call me Dom, Eric. We don't stand on ceremony unless we have company. It's easier that way. Once I get some easing of my parole conditions, who knows where we will drive to in this car?"

Maureen and Eric's thoughts turned to places they would like to visit. Dominic Connolly's mind, though, was on his business and, as part of that, his instructions to an old friend for a meeting in London.

4 MOORE

The day after Harry Stephen's visit, Catrin suddenly awoke from an afternoon nap as Mair cried out from the adjacent bedroom. She was tuned into her daughter's demands, day or night, even to the mysterious small cries caused by her daughter's dreams.

As she sat up on the bed, she realised that her doorbell had also just rung; she had the subliminal memory. Now someone was knocking there. Her phone was on silent mode, but it also buzzed. She glanced at the screen and saw that several calls had come in and the current one ringing was from her husband.

She answered as she went to see her baby, who was smiling at her now.

Chris said, "I'm on my way home in a police car. Commander Moore has been trying to get you, her assistant says. I called a minute ago."

Treneer was a computer specialist, a civilian employee with the Metropolitan Police. He worked on e-crime cases, having the job to intercept and document criminal activity using the internet.

She replied, "There's someone at the door. I'll answer. Hang on."

More alert now that Commander Moore's name had surfaced, Sayer picked up her daughter and moved to the front door of the apartment, seeing the shape of a police officer's uniform through the mottled glass panels. As she opened the door, she saw a female officer and, behind her, a Met police car with a driver at the wheel, waiting.

Sayer spoke into the phone, "It's one of us. I'll call back."

As she closed the call, the officer said, "DI Sayer? Constable Williams, ma'am, from Bethnal Green. Can I come in, please?"

Bethnal Green was the closest Metropolitan Police station to Catrin's home. Ironically, her closest 'nick' was a City of London Police station at Bishopsgate, but Commander Moore had no authority there.

Sayer nodded and smiled at her daughter, now looking wide-eyed at the visitor. The woman in uniform was dark-skinned and her resonant voice exuded competence. She didn't seem ill at ease with a more senior officer. Catrin wondered what was going on.

Seconds ago, as she picked up Mair, her most pressing need was to change her daughter's nappy.

She responded, "Come in. I was asleep; I nap a bit in the afternoon when my daughter does, if I can. What's this about? And what's your first name?"

The officer smiled. "Lila. I've been there with my own. I know what you mean about 'sleep when you can'. Commander Moore is trying to reach you, ma'am. She sent us round when they couldn't get through. Do you have the number? I have -."

She watched as Catrin thumbed through her call list, seeing the Met numbers pop up.

"I see the one, but I need to change my daughter first, though."

"I'll do that; point the way to the changing mat."

Catrin smiled, handing her daughter over. She wondered how Mair would react to an officer in uniform changing her instead of Catrin or Chris.

She called the number and, surprisingly, connected immediately with Commander Moore.

Karen Moore was a Mancunian by birth and accent, with a northerner's directness. She was young for her position as a senior officer, now one rank below that of an assistant commissioner. But Moore had been young, by Met standards, for every post into which she had been promoted. Nothing seemed to stand in her way, least of all more junior officers.

From the occasions on which Catrin had crossed Moore's path, her energy and decisiveness had been impressive.

"Catrin, how are you? Does Mair like the blanket I sent?"

Good God, thought Sayer, all this, and she is asking if her blanket was a suitable baby gift; surely not. And four-month-old babies aren't choosy about blankets.

"She likes it, ma'am; thank you. We use it all the time."

"Good. Your husband is on his way home to relieve you. And PC Williams there now is magic with babies, I am told, unlike me. She can hold the fort. Could I borrow you for an hour or so, please, rather urgently? Gerry and I would like a brief chat and some help over the next day or so. There's a car waiting for you."

"Yes, ma'am. I'll -."

The line went dead. The opener about the blanket had exhausted Moore's social skills. Probably the woman was annoyed that Catrin hadn't answered when she first called her.

The only 'Gerry' that Catrin knew in Moore's sphere was Superintendent Gerald Lauder, a senior officer in Organized Crime Command. If it was him, something significant was developing.

The world of Catrin Sayer, mother, and Detective Inspector Sayer, Metropolitan Police officer, had collided a little sooner than she had mentioned yesterday to Harry Stephens.

Then she heard Mair cooing at the unfamiliar person in her sights. It must be the uniform; my daughter will be one of us at the Met.

Catrin put on a suit jacket but was still in jeans. She hastily applied some make-up during the drive from Spitalfields to the Embankment, where New Scotland Yard was located. As she arrived, Chris phoned her again; he was now home.

"Lila is making us a nice cup of tea and asks is there anything you want her to do; laundry or something?"

He was enjoying passing that on. Staying on top of the laundry was a constant battle for them.

"You mean PC Williams? She's a police officer and needs to get on with her job, not hang around playing nursemaid to you."

"She was told to stay here until you get back and be useful in your absence. Her sergeant told her that came down from the top."

Five minutes later, she found herself in Commander Moore's office. The 'top' was addressing her across the meeting table, sitting next to Superintendent Gerry Lauder.

"Sayer, thanks for coming in. We are sorry to interrupt

your leave, although you've been gone so long, I'm sure you are raring to get back."

She didn't sound sorry at all, thought Catrin. Moore sounded enthusiastic, always an indicator that something was happening. From experience, it also signalled that her teams may not be so keen about whatever wonderful idea had emerged.

Moore looked at Superintendent Lauder with a 'Gerry, you kick off' look.

Lauder nodded.

"What do you know about Operation Undertow?"

Catrin recalled her last case working with Lauder, the Ranjani couple. He is straight into the deep end, as usual. Her first thought was that she was present when the Undertow received its name. But she stayed silent.

A memory from several years earlier of Assistant Commissioner Hunt flooded back. George, Hunt's driver, and Catrin, her security officer, had been in the front seats of Hunt's assigned car, driving back from a meeting. Hunt and Superintendent Frederick Roscoe, now Commander Roscoe, were in the back.

"It was a good discussion but lamentably slow progress, if I may say so, ma'am, for a second meeting."

"We are talking about money, big money, Fred. That takes time. The principle, turning the tide and stop chasing the small villains up the ladder to catch the big ones. They've bought into it, at least. It's the cost."

"Tide, ma'am, would be a good operational name, come to think of it. Better than a project code on a strategy list."

Hunt shook her head. "No; there have been other operations called Tide and, for what we want, tides are too visible an image. This is more like an undercurrent at the beach, an undertow. No-one sees one of those until the tow sucks them under. That's what this is about. Arresting the top people with no warning."

It had been Roscoe's concept, but Karen Moore had inherited the project. Right up to her retirement, Sandra Hunt had supported the addition of the new team to Serious and Organized Crime Command.

Catrin recalled that the people assigned to Operation Undertow were based in Battersea, not New Scotland Yard. It had a separate suite in the Lavender Hill Police Station.

Catrin responded neutrally, "Nothing really, sir. Word in the corridor before I left was that Undertow is focused on organized crime figures, but it's not run out of here. People transfer in, but what it's doing now; nothing."

Moore gave her a penetrating stare. "I know what the corridor talk was and is now. Did Sandra Hunt mention Undertow to you?"

Catrin replied, "If she did so while I was on her team, that would be covered by standing instructions to AC Hunt's staff. I could only discuss it with her successor or another officer of equivalent rank. With all due respect for your positions, of course."

You may be far more senior officers than me, a commander and a Superintendent, but you are still a rank or two below my permission level, she was saying.

Catrin waited apprehensively. She got on with Commander Moore, she believed, but the woman was a dynamo. People who crossed her or failed her expectations got chewed up and spat out occasionally.

Moore responded with, "Good. No-one blabs about Undertow; remember that. Let's continue."

Lauder said, "I want your help. Undertow has two

operational levels, Core and Focus. If the task was Undertow Core, you would be assigned full time; people go on to the team and so far, haven't come off, as you said. It's a quick Undertow Focus task we need you for."

Catrin perked up visibly; this task sounded interesting.

The senior officer continued, "I met earlier today with Donald Killam. Do you remember him?"

"Bolan and Ranjani's lawyer. Yes, I do."

~~

Lauder and Killam had met in Ilford, close to the solicitor's home, not in Central London.

Killam began with, "Mr. Bolan has a parole hearing coming up. Last time, the Met spoke against parole, citing prior crimes and fresh evidence all linked to the Ranjani investigation."

He paused, gauging the police officer's reaction; and got nothing.

"It was the primary persuasive input that denied Mr. Bolan his parole. We want assurance this time that the Met will not raise similar objections. If we have a sign of that, we may have some useful information."

Lauder was expecting something like this. Killam had been evasive on the phone about the purpose of the meeting, other than that he had information to pass on.

"It would need to be good."

"It will be. And if so, we want an explicit statement at the hearing that the Met has no objection to parole, not simply a silence or a convenient hiccup over a last-minute inability to appear. After your intervention last time, the Board will expect something from you."

"If the information assists our enquiries and is new to us, we will take note and act accordingly. I won't go further than that. But I will honour my side of the deal. So, what's this about?"

"I've not been told. But you will get a call offering information within three days from midnight tonight."

"I get calls all the time. How will I know if it's linked?"

"The caller will insist on speaking to that art detective, Sayer; the one who interviewed Nirupa Ranjani."

Lauder hadn't thought about DI Sayer in two years. That aspect was a surprise.

He responded carefully. "Jalaj Ranjani is still on the loose and resentful that Sayer broke through Nirupa's silence during the interviews. I don't like the sound of this. The man is an assassin."

"My client expected that complication, as well; that you may suspect some set-up, some payback thing. Obviously, it isn't. Michael wants to be out of jail, not provide a reason to keep him there. The goodwill item I can give you myself is this; Jalaj Ranjani was in the city of Sao Mateus, Brazil, only ten days ago. If he is there now, we can't say. But I suspect that the Met and Interpol don't have a clue where he is."

Lauder took the man more seriously now. That was a major piece of information, the recent location of a wanted murderer.

"If this other information is as good as you suggest, then we will speak at the parole hearing, to register no objection. I have nothing else hanging on Michael Bolan at present that I can prove. He'd better keep it that way because if I get it, this deal is off."

They read each other, recognizing that they had arrived at an understanding.

As they stood, Lauder said neutrally, "If Michael is granted parole, he will need to keep his nose clean. If he breaks parole conditions he'll be back inside."

"Understood." There would be no future favours tied to this.

"Pity, in a sense," Lauder added. "He'd run the business better than Mikey Junior does with his spats over territory with Burcu Dogan. It's messy out there these days."

Sayer was on leave, he suddenly recalled, trying to think who had mentioned it, but failing to do so. They needed her back.

As he drove back to the Yard, he gave that task over to Commander Moore.

~ ~

Lauder continued, "You will receive a call from a confidential informant. Why you, we don't know yet. Either it's one of your own informants or someone else who knows you. We don't have a name. Once you learn who it is and whatever information he or she transfers to you, you brief only only the commander and me."

He reached into his pocket and pulled out a mobile phone. "We have given them this number. You returned your service phone when you started your leave, I take it?"

She nodded.

"If the person is not one of your current CIs that you trust, call me before agreeing to meet. Even if they are, I want the name also, before you meet. I know CI's identities aren't shared, but this time it is an order you'll follow. Understood?

"I'll call you once they make contact."

He pressed on. "The rules agreed are, no recording of the discussion and no others present. I gather that whatever nugget of information you will receive will be that;

small and valuable.

"We have a team you can contact for security or babysitting even, you name it. It's lead contact is on the phone, DI Ed Franklin. He heads the Digital Intelligence team in Undertow and will be the one following up on anything we learn.

"With two years as an assistant commissioner's security officer, you should still be as good as anyone at assessing personal security risk, so don't agree to any venue or timing where you feel vulnerable. And my direct mobile number is in there. Any questions?"

She asked, "Do we know anything else?"

"Nothing that I can tell you. No."

So there was something, but Catrin wouldn't be privy to it. She wasn't classified as Undertow Core.

"Once I meet and hear whatever this person wants; what's next?"

Moore jumped back in. "You call Gerry immediately. He will meet personally with you to debrief. If it's significant, I'll sit in, too."

There's a comfort, thought Catrin.

5 THATCHER

Catrin received the call a day later on her new mobile at 11.10 a.m.

"DS Sayer, as was. Do you recognize my voice?"

It flooded back to her.

"Yes; from a warmer location, I recall."

"That's right. Could we meet at 1.00 p.m.?"

"Where?"

"The National Portrait Gallery. It's not too far for you; and is in public. By Margaret Thatcher, the Rodrigo Moynihan painting."

She knew the location well. "I'll be there."

As she closed the call, PC Williams was looking at her apprehensively.

Catrin said, "Well, Lila, it looks as if you are baby-sitting while I go to an art gallery. But I need to call Superintendent Lauder and report in first. Alone. Can you watch Mair for me, please?"

"Yes, ma'am; this is all quite the thing."

Williams sounded excited. All she had been told was that DI Sayer may receive a call, after which she would need to leave at once.

John Dalton was an elderly man, a forger who had served prison time both in the UK and Europe. He came from Glasgow and had been a friend of Dominic Connolly's father.

Catrin had met Dalton a decade earlier, during an art crime investigation tied to a major drug bust called Operation Finisterre, which had led to Connolly's arrest.

In the middle of forgery scam that Dalton had undertaken for Connolly, Dalton saw that things were going awry and fled to Spain. Ironically, his freedom arose from Connolly's bitter enemy, a lawyer and former friend of both men, Niall Irving. Irving had turned Queen's Evidence and betrayed Connolly, but in doing so, had made Dalton's involvement part of his own immunity deal.

The forger was a free man.

Dalton was watching out for Sayer, standing in the gallery by the painting of Margaret Thatcher. He was in his late seventies now, Catrin recalled. While he looked older than during their last meeting, in Minorca, he was nicely tanned, apparently healthy and well-dressed.

The forger said, without preamble, "I have a table reserved in the restaurant here."

He looked at the portrait. Margaret Thatcher, with her prim and regal pose, gazed back.

"Someone asked me once to paint a copy, a legit copy. On a smaller canvas, of course, but I turned it down, as I never liked her. Shall we eat and talk?"

He didn't wait for an answer, instead he turned towards the exit to the corridor. Catrin wondered if his comment on Thatcher contained an embedded message; a dislike of women in authority, perhaps.

She had met Dalton only once, at his condo in Cala en Bosc, Minorca, years ago. She had just been promoted to the position of detective sergeant.

Dalton had kept in his possession several paintings by an artist called Alistair Gault, long deceased, each one to have been the base work for a painting in the forgery scam. Sayer traveled to Spain to retrieve them, as she knew Gault's paintings and wouldn't be fobbed off by imitations if Dalton try to substitute one of his own copies.

In fact, he had been co-operative and hospitable, more so than she could stomach, given his role in the crime that led to her facial injury.

Their table in the National Portrait Gallery restaurant was by a window. Catrin chose a seat with a view of the room.

As they sat down, she said to the waiter, "Separate bills, please."

It made Dalton smile. She looked at him and waited, keeping her expression neutral. Would he get straight to the point or meander?

They spent some time on the menu selecting their lunch as she waited for him to say something.

Catrin, her security training now back on full alert, had been monitoring the people around them and others in the queue waiting to be seated. A family with a teenage girl and a bored looking younger boy had been the only ones placed near to them. One group waiting in line was a younger couple, who spoke to the server and pointed, not at her and Dalton, but at an empty centre table. Once there, they seemed preoccupied with themselves or the menus. Catrin wondered about them, just as the same waiter came over to take their order.

Once he left, Dalton took a breath and spoke softly.

"Do you know the works of Juris Martinov? He goes by his first name only on his paintings."

Catrin replied, "No, not really. Juris? He's the Latvian painter, I recall, having some commercial success with a series of paintings about gambling. Dice and playing cards a metre high, that sort of thing?"

Dalton nodded. "You aren't wearing any recording devices, I take it?"

She responded, "This conversation is not being recorded; that was part of the understanding. If you have a lot of detail I need to take back, I will have to scribble on a napkin, unless you want me to use my phone to record it. Is there?"

She was also to be alone, Lauder had said, but she glanced again at the couple.

After a moment to consider her answer, Dalton continued. "No, no details at all, I'll just give you the big picture. Martinov's younger brother, Peteris, is big in the drug business there. Your people and other police forces in Europe will have information on him. Juris and I got to know each other when he visited Minorca on holiday. He saw my work. We had a drink or two together. Well, more than that. He got drunk."

"You are still doing the street art thing?"

When Catrin visited Cala en Bosc, Dalton had secured a street license to sell paintings to tourists. His Picasso-style canvases were popular.

He shook his head. "No, my paintings now sell in two of the better tourist shops and a local gallery. I was in the gallery having a natter with the owner, a friend, when Juris entered."

Lauder had told her to listen but get facts that could be corroborated.

Catrin asked, "Can you give me a date for this meeting?"

"Not the precise day, but early in September, during the first week. In my world, the days are pretty similar then, nice temperatures and good light for painting.

"Juris had no idea about me or my background. I didn't enlighten him; I was just an old Scot, an expat who likes to paint in better light and warmer weather. He enjoyed a discussion on art, spoke of life in Latvia and became quite garrulous with enough wine inside him, including a description of his brother's world. At one point -"

He stopped. The waiter was approaching, carrying their plates. After he served the food, Dalton continued.

"Juris shared a little of his anguish; his brother was all money and no morality. Not morality related to criminal activities. Screw the Establishment, Juris said, on that point. But his brother had lost the perspective of being ordinary; he was obsessed with his elite status. That irritated Juris."

Catrin said, "And this political discourse led where?"

"The previous month, Peteris had bought one of Juris's more popular works, one of a series that sells well, for an English businessman as a gift. He paid the gallery who represents Juris's art the top price, no questions asked, not even a request for a brotherly discount. Apparently, it was a hit with the recipient. He would hang it in his office in London, he told him."

He paused.

Catrin said, "So this Englishman; is he in the same line of business as Peteris Martinov?"

"The same line exactly, I am led to believe. Moving money, cleaning it."

"Money laundering? He told you this?"

"No. The same business as Peteris, he said. I asked someone in Glasgow, a person from my old days. Don't ask who."

Connolly or one of his people, Catrin surmised. They were still in touch, she assumed.

"People who work for Peteris Martinov meet the Englishman regularly at various executive flight centres in airports in the UK, smaller ones such as Newcastle, never the big ones. That's how they transferred the painting, too. Peteris brought it over in person and presented it there as a gift of appreciation. No-one has heard of the Englishman, I gather."

"Do you have a name?"

He smiled. "That's where it gets tricky. I'd rather the police do their own leg work, thank you. You need your own papertrail for any follow up. I'm not far off eighty and I like my retirement life in Minorca. I have immunity for what I did to cheat the Colombian woman and no wish for yet another person wanting me dead."

Catrin nodded, seemingly accepting it. She worked away at her salad for a while.

She asked suddenly, "OK. Why now? I take it you are doing this as a favour for Dominic Connolly? But why?"

Dalton responded carefully. "Because I am here now. I'm not touching the rest of the question. It's not my job to tell you why you are here today."

It was his turn to say nothing.

As they finished eating, Catrin pressed him again. "Then why did you choose me? It's not a case about art at all, really."

He seemed prepared for that one. Dalton had no intention of revealing it was Bolan's wife's request, although Dominic had passed that on to him. He had his own reasons for seeing Sayer again.

"When you visited me years ago, that scar was not fresh, but it was a lot newer. And, you are aware, I'm sure, that it gets livid when you are angry. You were angry at Dominic, Neil and me, I could see that. I wanted to tell you then I was sorry you were injured, but I couldn't, nor would you agree to have a meal together, as artists. You declined that also.

"So now I'm having lunch with you, in the National Portrait Gallery, of all places. Occasionally, I look at your gallery website; check out your recent works and their prices. You are doing well. And I can now tell you I am sorry you were hurt. And, frankly, it's safer for me to meet with someone I already know by sight than an unknown copper that your colleagues would choose."

For the first time, Sayer smiled. "I was angry then, I admit it, even a year after the injury. But that is water under the bridge, long gone. And Miriam? I liked that portrait of her you were finishing."

Miriam had been a friend that John Dalton had made on arrival in Cala en Bosc. She had been terminally ill during Sayer's visit to collect the paintings. For a few minutes, they discussed art and the island of Minorca.

It was time to leave, she felt.

She asked, "When do you go back?"

"Right now. I head to the airport from here after collecting my bags from the hotel. I spent a few days in Glasgow, catching up on family and others."

"And with the Connolly family?"

He shook his head. "Mr. Connolly's parole conditions are clear. He can't meet with an old lag like me, can he?"

She couldn't read from his expression if that were true, or a deflection.

As they left the restaurant, she noticed that the couple

at the other table were drinking coffee but had already settled their bill. They had paid her and Dalton no attention at all.

6 DISMISSAL

On Catrin's return to New Scotland Yard, Super-intendent Lauder was deep in thought about the inform-ation received from John Dalton.

"You didn't push him on the name of this money launderer, I take it?"

"No, sir. It would have been counterproductive. You told me to take it easy with Dalton when we found out he was the informant. He was very close to Connolly's father, I recall, and to Dominic Connolly, too."

Then Commander Moore appeared.

Lauder summarised the feedback and Moore took Catrin through it all over again.

Moore concluded, "So we need to check quietly on any flights of this Peteris Martinov or his associates into the UK. Then what? Did this 'Englishman', as he referred to him, drive to these airports or fly in himself? We should check CCTV, aircraft and passenger lists at these executive centres."

Catrin interjected, "Perhaps the first place to check is with Customs & Excise, for any declaration of paintings by Juris arriving at these airports. I'm assuming they brought it into the country as a gift. At around £8,000 a painting, it's big enough to attract a customs officer's attention. Someone having much bigger money issues to cover up may well be glad to have a legitimate item to declare."

Lauder was nodding at the suggestion. It appealed to him.

She continued, "Sergeant Obi should check -."

Moore cut in. "No. No, thank you. In fact, we appreciate your assistance in doing the meeting and for that good suggestion, but this goes back into Undertow Core now."

There was a finality to the statement. It surprised Catrin, but she saw it to be both Lauder and Moore's position.

Moore added, "I think we can leave it there."

The abruptness of the dismissal caught Catrin un-aware. She said, "Well, I'll be going, ma'am, if there is nothing else?"

The senior officer nodded as Lauder added his 'thank you'. Moore observed Sayer consciously controlling her irritation at being excluded. As she reached the door, the commander called, "Sayer!"

Catrin turned around as Moore asked, "Remind me. Did you complete the economic crime primary or advanced module at Hendon in your DS training?"

"Primary, ma'am; but I took a more advanced art crime short course in DC with the FBI which was financially focused. It tied into the Art Crime Task Force meeting there a year after I qualified as a detective sergeant."

"Right. But this discussion makes me think. Professor Lister from King's is giving us a one-day seminar on recent developments in money laundering networks soon.

Can you attend it? On my authority and budget. It's a good one to get under your belt."

Catrin took it to be a token reward for the support given and the subsequent abrupt dismissal.

"Thank you. I'll check the details and let them know. With so much art crime tied to organized crime these days, an update could be useful."

After she left, Lauder gave his boss a long look. "Lister's course is oversubscribed. I already have two officers on the standby list if there are cancellations."

He suspected that Moore was fully aware of that, but she ignored the implication.

"Did you see her react when I chucked her out, though, Gerry? Hang on a minute and we'll get back to next steps."

Moore walked to her desk and pulled up something on her computer monitor as she picked up her phone and spoke to her assistant.

"I'm looking at the attendance roster for Lister's course at Hendon a week next Tuesday. It's full. I see DCS Cole has put a consultant, an Ivor Earnshaw, on it. I know they are working on the Joffrey case, but I'm not having us pay one bloody consultant to sit in a training course we are paying another to give. Earnshaw's off the list. And put DI Sayer on it, not any of the back-ups."

She closed the call without a further word and returned to the meeting table, lost in thought. "Now, let's make a decision on the next steps."

Gerry Lauder said in a monotone, "For the follow-up on the new lead, or for DI Sayer's career development?"

It brought a rare smile to Karen Moores' face.

~~

Over the next few days, members of the Undertow team followed up on several lines of investigation to track the Juris painting, starting with HM Customs and Excise and the UK aviation authority.

Separately, through a DS Leo Jansons brought in for another Undertow Focus task, there was a discrete discussion with the Latvian Police about the criminal activity of Peteris Martinov and a check on his brother the painter.

Jansons, whose parents were Latvian, maintained a working relationship with the authorities there; his uncle held the rank of captain in the force. As they got off that call, DI Franklin, the Undertow team member assigned to the task, asked him, "Who's Maris?"

"That's me. It's my middle name, after my grandfather. My uncle calls me that on my visits over there. His second son is called Leo, too."

Franklin responded, "Well, it ties in, doesn't it?"

Particularly Dalton's lie, he thought, but that name hadn't been shared with Jansons.

"Well, Leo or Maris, we appreciate the help. I'll go brief my boss."

Then DS Jansons was dismissed with the same haste as Sayer.

The declaration of the painting as a gift occurred when Peteris Martinov visited the UK eight months earlier, at the Executive Centre in Norwich Airport. The Customs & Excise officer who signed off on the import certificate recalled the declaration.

The concierge on duty also observed the transfer of the painting to the recipient. It was accompanied by a little celebration, with a toast in champagne. The recipient had made a light remark about the need to declare the gift to his accountant, as an unearned asset.

That provoked further laughter, as the man was an accountant himself, Martinov told the concierge.

But it was above board, the concierge thought. They had the customs document.

The identity of the recipient of the gift was a casino executive. Mr. Howard St. John-Leer was the Finance Director of the Ballantine West Casino in Chiswick, West London, just off the M4 motorway, conveniently situated for motorway arrivals and the West London punters. It also attracted international gamblers coming to the UK through Heathrow.

The Ballantine Entertainment Group ran two casinos in the UK; Ballantine West and Ballantine South, in Brighton.

Casinos were hot spots world-wide for money laundering, with the amount of cash used. Under UK law, you can't buy gambling chips directly with a credit card, so a lot of ready cash was required. ATMs kept busy supplying it and every casino turned the cash into gambling chips, at the tables or the purchase counters in the building.

Mr. St. John-Leer's name was flagged four or five times a year as an international airline passenger, travelling in business class to the United Arab Emirates, where the Ballantine Entertainment Group was headquartered, or to a holiday destination with his family.

His name came up far more often on the passenger lists of an air charter company called ECExec, with whom he flew to destinations across the UK and sometimes to Northern Ireland. He travelled with them several times each month, from either Luton or Biggin Hill airports, usually returning the same day or the following morning.

The only inconsistency in Dalton's story turned out to be the alleged visit of Juris Martinov to Minorca and his supposed conversations with Dalton. No record of that visit appeared on flight lists around the date given to Sayer, nor was there a record of any hotel stays in Minorca by the artist. Juris could have entered illegally on a sailing vessel, but why? The man was an artist and has no criminal history.

The Undertow team concluded that wherever Connolly or Bolan dredged up the information on this money launderer and the painting, they wanted the leak to be well away from them and their source. Connolly must have called in Dalton to do the job.

Operation Undertow consisted of four teams reporting to Lauder. When he met with his team leaders, they all realized St. John-Leer was into significant money laundering for one or more criminal organisations. An interception on one of his trips could bring him down.

He had no criminal record. Perhaps under questioning, they would get him to reveal the names of others involved, or his computer records would do that. Fast and neat. However, they knew it wasn't the next step, nor was it Undertow's purpose.

St. John-Leer laundered the money, but they wanted the people using him, the drug gangs. Whoever was using St.John-Leer was obviously no friend of Dominic Connolly or Michael Bolan.

At the end of the meeting, a DI Andrew Collard was instructed to give a member of his team, Detective Sergeant Ian Under-hill, the liaison role with an undercover police officer assigned to get close to the target, St. John-Leer. That person would not be a member of Undertow or even a Metropolitan Police officer.

DI Collard and DS Underhill then organized a meeting with an investigator called Sheila Lansing at the National Crime Agency, located in Tinworth Street, in Vauxhall, West London. Lansing managed a UK-wide interchange system of police officers, people trained for undercover roles.

Superintendent Lauder had been very specific about this approach. A few years earlier, the Met had been involved in a scandal associated with a long-term undercover operation. Members of the Special Demonstrations Squad, in undercover roles, had established relationships with women locally.

When it emerged that the men were not who they claimed to be, the women and children involved were devastated.

While the undercover operation focusing on St. John-Leer was not expected to be long term, it could require an officer in place for weeks or several months. Lauder wanted someone outside the Met, a skilled police officer who would do the job well, but one who would evaporate into the ether afterwards and be untraceable.

7 ASSIGNMENTS

"Well, there will be different decisions to make next week from those I have been making over the last year, that's true," responded Catrin, to a comment from her boss, Detective Chief Inspector Tim Wetherby.

He laughed. "Besides... not in place of, I think."

Wetherby and Sayer met up on the Friday afternoon, in a café just south of Spitalfields Market, as a precursor to Catrin's return to work the following Monday. She left Mair at the Kiln with Jean and Melanie. The prospect of returning to work after a year's absence was a big change.

He had selected the venue. "It gives me a chance to get out of the office," he had told her.

Formerly a borough copper, Wetherby found his headquarters role somewhat stifling these days.

He hadn't seen Sayer for nearly six months. He and his wife had received an invitation to the christening of her daughter but were not able to attend. They were on holiday, away.

And he only found out after the event, from his own boss, Superintendent Harrison, about her call to assist

Operation Undertow earlier in the week. That news hadn't made his day.

"Well, at least you are getting back to work as the weather gets nicer, hopefully."

It had been drizzling for the last hour and now the sky was turning ominously dark.

Catrin had been telling him how her husband was taking paternity leave now, both the legal entitlement plus a month's unpaid leave. They were still sorting out plans for childcare arrangements thereafter. Both wanted to return to their careers.

Wetherby was a 'list and notebook' man. Even in the café, he kept his notebook out, open, consulting it. His next item for the briefing was staff updates.

He continued, "Howlett has decided on her retirement date, it's in four months. She said she talked to you?"

DC Isabelle Howlett was the most experienced art crime investigator on the Art and Antiques team, someone who had steadfastly resisted promotion.

"Yes, she called to inform me. We had a good chat. Her partner Morley is now set up in a apartment near Paris. Her concern is for her long weekends until retirement; she wants to be in Paris every third weekendobvious if she can. She works all hours, so I don't see a problem."

Isabelle had met Morley Kerswell in Paris during an Art Crime Task Force meeting that Catrin had made her attend, as her substitute. A former FBI agent, he had retired earlier than Howlett.

Wetherby responded, "I think Nkrumah rides her coattails too much; him being new, her being the veteran. Derek will need weaning, to become more self-directing. It's a small team."

She nodded, accepting the assessment. She brought Derek Nkrumah in from borough work in anticipation of her extended medical leave. The officer was keen but inexperienced. She would make her own assessment but accepted that Wetherby may be right.

They had already discussed her most senior officer, Detective Sergeant John Obi. He filled in for Catrin during her absence, leading the little team. Initially he struggled a bit, but overall, it had worked well.

Obi was to take a holiday soon after Catrin returned. He deserved it.

"And how are you doing?" she asked during a pause.

He appeared slightly surprised by the question. "Everything is working reasonably smoothly. I wish at times I was back in Camden, though, back in borough work."

He looked at his list and pursed his lips. Another item.

"I'd like you to get up to speed on a recent development in the Syrian statuettes case. Senior Agent Klintz at the FBI called me last week. I have not informed Obi of the discussion; I left it for your return."

She responded, "We passed on Neville Coltrane's tip-off to the Americans, I understand. We've been after Masud for years, so his arrest is good news."

Her former boss, Neville Coltrane, constantly surprised her.

He was let go during the last major reorganisation of the Met after refusing any assignment other than art crime. That led to Catrin's appointment to the lead position for the Art and Antiques Unit.

Independently wealthy, after mooching around for months, he took a job with the United Nations. He had connections there and spoke French and Italian fluently.

Multilingualism is always an asset in a UN environment.

Coltrane now held the position of a deputy director of UNODOC, the United Nations Office on Drugs and Crime, with a special liaison role with UNESCO, the United Nations Educational, Scientific and Cultural Organization.

When Catrin worked her way through the mouthful of acronyms and blurbs, she found that Neville now chased stolen antiquities, currently focused on crimes associated with the conflicts in the Middle East.

The arrest of Jon Masud linked directly to the theft of two small statuettes from the UNESCO World Heritage Site at Hatra in Iraq. They were intercepted in transit to the USA. It was an audacious gambit for the art smuggler, as he transported them personally in a private aircraft rather than use an accomplice, his normal method.

The French and the US authorities already had two smugglers serving sentences for other thefts linked to Masud.

Now an informant close to Masud would be killed if they identified her. The value of the art wasn't the issue; betrayal of Masud meant death, the primary reason why the two hapless associates in prison stayed resolutely silent about their links to the man.

This time, Masud had been over-confident.

The statuettes had been 'adjusted' to make them appear as fine copies. Only curators and restorers could identify them as originals. Masud had transported them as souvenirs, a gift to his wife while they were travelling, to be carried home to Florida as part of their luggage.

At Bristol airport, the executive aircraft had refueled, changed its flight crew and been serviced for the continuing journey across the Atlantic.

Like other private jets for hire, its clientele were a

combination of the lead passenger group and the ancillaries, business travellers with executive jet travel cards. The lead passengers, Masud and his wife and daughter, were art dealers in Miami. They set the end-to-end routing and had the choice of the seats. Of the other passenger seats, three places were filled on the Damascus to UK segment and all four on the Transatlantic leg.

The aircraft's final destination was Miami, Florida, but its flight plan called for immigration and customs clearance to take place at an executive jet centre at Charleston International Airport, South Carolina. It gave the VIP occupants traveling the whole route another chance to stretch their legs and the taller ones an opportunity to stand up straight. One of the tag-along passengers planned to leave there as well.

While the jet flew over the Atlantic, Neville Coltrane called DS Obi.

"John, I have information received in a personal capacity of a crime in progress that will require immediate action," he began without ceremony.

The Art and Antiques Unit had, in turn, informed the FBI.

The Charleston Executive Centre area appeared quiet as the passengers completed the routine immigration and customs check. After the apparently bored but efficient customs officer had received from the passengers the official declarations of goods on board, agents in black tactical gear emblazoned with FBI across their back appeared.

People were detained and the aircraft searched. In a regular suitcase, in foam supports, they found the two statuettes, declared as souvenirs, copies bought for $1500.

They weren't copies. They were priceless, in the sense

that a price had never been established for them as they were not for sale.

Masud and his family were taken into custody and processed.

Tim Wetherby continued, "Some problems are emerging now. Masud's defense lawyer is suspicious about the timing of an air traffic control transmission verifying the flight coordinates over the Atlantic. The check appeared non-routine, not at a regular reporting point for the flight.

"The American air traffic people are dismissing it as insignificant; such occasional checks happen all the time, they say. However, the FBI has been informed that the lawyer wants a more detailed statement from the Met. Specifically, they want to know the date and time the informant first contacted us."

"It is in the incident report provided, I expect."

He spoke carefully. "The report gives everything that happened through official channels."

She paused a moment. "I don't think I should ask the obvious question; I know Neville too well."

She now realised that Coltrane had earlier knowledge of the crime and waited until Masud's plane entered US airspace before alerting the Met. He timed the official communication so Masud could be arrested in the USA.

"Quite. Now the defense is suspicious. They requested a representative of the Met to appear as a witness next week at the trial. You are the head of Art and Antiques, so that is your first big task. You can repeat the contents of the report."

He added, as an afterthought, "I made sure the test-imony will be given by videolink from a room at their embassy. It's not justifiable to send someone over to the

USA for this triviality. It's too costly, financially and in absence."

Tim Wetherby was a budget-conscious man.

Catrin felt as if she had returned to work.

"I'm jumping in at the deep end, I suppose. How does it link to any defense strategy? Did David Klintz say?"

Wetherby nodded. "FBI persecution. He thinks Masud will claim that they were only away from the plane during the stopover in Bristol. They will suggest that someone swapped the real statuettes for the copies they bought, to set them up."

"Trials," said Catrin, musing on it. "All you have to do is sow the seed of doubt to give a jury a reason to throw out the charge. And I can't give them Neville as the informant; it would lead back to others."

"Fall back on the Police Act on that one. It's untouchable."

"I will. But I'm not looking forward to this one, so soon after I return."

Wetherby smiled. "Welcome back. I said that already, I believe?"

He looked out of the restaurant window. "It's brightening, and the rain has stopped. It looks like a good time for me to head back to the office, and for you to get home."

8 UNDERCOVER

Sylvia Johnson was a first-rate field hockey player, they agreed, but she would never rank as core team strength. The Selection Committee played her whenever it worked, but she displayed talent and versatility rather than dedication. Skill alone doesn't make a team member capable of winning a championship cup. You need the drive, the determination and the team commitment. With Sylvia, the commiment wasn't there, unfortunately.

She worked as a police officer, true, but that was hardly the issue. Look at Hilary Cramer, also a Bedford-shire Police officer, and based in a police station. Sylvia said she drove people around, being based at head-quarters. It sounded like a pretty straightforward role for a copper. Yet Hilary wouldn't miss a practice or a match for love or money unless there was a crisis at the station or at home.

Any serious field hockey team could live with that.

Sylvia was a regular player for weeks at a time then missed games at a critical point for the team. Her paltry explanations then didn't cut it with the committee. That was a pity, given her talent and personality, as she could light up a conversation or say the right thing when a game ran into rough spots.

She had an expressive face and friendly eyes, June said; that's what did it. Sylvia has a bright mind, said another committee stalwart, in rebuttal.

Whatever the reason, her rating this year again would keep her a second-tier player. It bothered them but, if Sylvia had been a fly on the wall during the upcoming season's strategy meeting, she would silently accept their conclusion.

Rasheed Fulton was older than he looked, but not by much, Sylvia decided. He sounded like an academic finding himself in the strange world of crime prevention. On the rise in the National Crime Agency, Sheila Lansing had told her Rasheed was still inexperienced. In the NCA, he probably had plenty of opportunity for development.

Sylvia's contact since the inception of the program had been Sheila, an older woman and a skilled bureaucrat. Rasheed seemed to be one of a new generation of NCA investigators.

He asked, "It's four months since the sudden curtailment of the Harmony Road operation. How did you feel about that winding up only a week after you started?"

Sylvia had completed the post-assignment report and filed it. She got the impression he was aware of its contents.

"It could have lasted a month, they said, but that's the nature of these operations. You can't predict the end point easily. I'm glad to have contributed. I got back to normal life and it gave me the chance for more hockey games, at least."

He smiled. "I saw that you are a player. As am I."

"I know," she responded. "Your boss told me when she called."

"So, are you up to another job? This one is in the London area with the Met, and possibly for as long as several months. Are you and your partner on board with a longer assignment?"

Sylvia served as a headquarters-based driver with the Bedfordshire Constabulary and her partner was a tactical unit officer there. He had one of the 'drop everything and respond' roles. They understood each other and their respective career needs.

Fulton was checking her personal situation as a routine element of the selection process. An undercover role gave limited time for the officer in place to break their cover role. In the one the Met had defined he could foresee her having only occasional days for personal commitments.

Fortunately, Bedford and London were only an hour's drive apart.

She just nodded. "What role?"

"A contract chauffeur; it should be right up your street. The liaison is a DS Ian Underhill, part of a section called Operation Undertow. He has an exemplary track record as a handler."

Fulton added, "It's linked to taking down a drug gang."

He knew her profile, she saw.

"I'll stand for it if they want me. If so, I guess I will miss a lot of hockey for a while."

He smiled. "It takes another player to understand that sacrifice. Thank you. I appreciate it. I'm still finding my feet in this job."

She didn't comment or ask why.

He continued, "They are still in the early planning of

the infiltration phase but have just had a break. I don't think it will be very long before you get a call."

He stood, and they shook hands.

"When I go back, we will formalize the arrangement between the organisations, as usual."

This was now a new undercover assignment, her third as part of a group coordinated by the NCA. Rasheed would sort it out with the Bedfordshire Police and the Met. Her own direct boss, a Sergeant Morris, knew of her role and that he might lose one of his fleet drivers suddenly, no questions to be asked.

As she pondered the next steps, a text came in on her mobile. Could she play left midfield against the University of Bedfordshire next Saturday? Lorna has an ankle injury and can't play.

She took some time composing the answer to that one; after all, it could be her last game for a while.

9 SPITALFIELDS

The following week, Chris Treneer's phone rang just as he turned into Brick Lane pushing the baby stroller. He was glad that Mair had settled at last.

"How's she doing now?" Catrin asked, clearly in a hall-way or somewhere similar, one that was reflecting the sound.

"I have taken her out for a while and she's OK. I don't know what it is, but she wouldn't settle after her bottle. You think after last night, she would be zonked out. The way she is biting down, she may be teething, but I can't feel anything coming through. Now she's quietly watching the sky and everything else passing as we walk."

They had bragged how good a sleeper Mair had become until the last week, having experienced several broken nights where their baby wouldn't settle for any length of time.

Catrin suggested, "Well, pop into the Kiln, perhaps, if it's on the way. Between Melanie, Jean and Lili, there will be plenty to occupy her attention."

He smiled, "That is part of my plan, to round up the

troops. I should be there in ten minutes."

"I just wanted to check on her before my phones have to be switched off. They'll call me soon, I hope."

"Well, good luck in court."

They closed the call.

Three-quarters of an hour later, Jean Hughes automatically increased her stride as she passed a group of men.

Now she was the one pushing Mair in the stroller, this time along Commercial Street, just a little east of the landmark Hawksmoor-designed church, Christ Church, Spitalfields, across the road from Spitalfields Market.

Wafts of organ music carried faintly to the street as Jean realised that an organist was preparing for the lunchtime recital. With the Market and her shop nearby, it was a regular feature of her world.

Jean and Mair were returning to the Kiln and needed to cross the busy main road at the pedestrian crossing. Mair, still grisly and, to her and Melanie, definitely teething, had settled again as soon as she was back in the stroller.

Twenty minutes earlier, Jean had been working on a set of bowls for an hour at the point Mair started crying again. Jean needed a break and Lili was ready for her nap and needed quiet.

"I'll get some air, walk my little Myfi for a bit," she announced.

Myfi, short for Myfanwy, had been her pet name for Mair from way before she was born and baptized, as Jean anxiously watched Catrin, day by day. After two miscarriages, her best friend had monitored closely the third try by Sayer and her husband.

Chris, left alone for half an hour in the company of

Melanie, his phone and a sleeping toddler, had sung Jean's praises. As Melanie smiled at a customer entering the pottery, he retreated into the back, to make coffee.

Jean was moving at an angle to pass the group of males. They were in their late teens or early twenties and not one of them was showing any sign of courtesy, giving ground to someone with a baby stroller. They were voluble, swearing and haranguing one in their midst about something. She wanted Mair, finally blissfully unaware as she slept, well away from the noise and profanity; that was all.

She had just passed two delivery vans. From one, a young woman was unloading an armful of dry cleaning in their individual plastic wrappers, to take into a shop. A man from the other vehicle called out to her. They knew each other, from their exchange. But it was peripheral; the voices of the group had Jean's attention.

She didn't feel threatened. Not at all. They were just obnoxious, was what she told the police officer later. She hadn't seen if they had come out of The Ten Bells pub or not. There were lots of pubs around, but she had fleetingly thought beer might fuel their argument. But she hadn't picked up a beer smell.

Her focus was on getting to the pedestrian crossing by the church and back to the Market; back to the Cwmbran Kiln. It was only yards away.

And a world away, it turned out.

The scream behind her was female, piercing and cut off suddenly. As Jean spun round and the stroller turned with her, she saw a woman, the one from the dry cleaning van, bent over, collapsing on to the pavement. She fell to her knees, with one hand to her chest and the other reaching out to the stone slabs. The dry cleaning bags had spread out on the pavement, the slippery plastic aiding their spread.

The teenagers were now running, fanning out in different directions. Two were dodging traffic on Commercial Road, causing honking horns and squealing brakes. One of them ran past Jean as she turned. Another, holding a knife and with his back to Jean, was striding away. He had just reached the corner of Brushfield Street and, as he turned the corner, she saw that he broke into a run and disappeared from view.

The man from the van in front had run up to the injured woman, pulling out his phone and calling for an ambulance. Jean hurriedly pushed Mair back to them, arriving on the scene confronted by the woman now on the ground, apparently in shock, with spurts of blood on the paving slab beneath her.

It was well over a decade, nearer fifteen years, since Jean thought of her First Aid training with the Girl Guides, but it came back at once. The blood was bright, arterial, so they needed pressure to slow the bleeding. She put the stroller facing towards the shop window, set its brake and said to the woman, "Can you roll over and lie down? We have to stop the bleeding."

There was no response other than a nod and an acknowledgement in her pain that she understood, as she rolled over on her back. The stab wound was now visible; a rent in the uniform top and her slip underneath revealing a puncture slit in the skin that was leaking blood, pulsing.

Jean pulled a disposable nappy from the pack on the stroller tray and placed it plastic side on the woman's chest firmly as she said, "I'm sorry if it hurts more but I need to put pressure on it."

Her first thought was to use the absorbent side to catch the blood. Somewhere in the recess of her mind, her training told her she had to seal the wound if a lung was possibly punctured. It didn't absorb the blood, but the plastic side would seal the slit in her chest more effectively.

Other people in the vicinity crowded around. Some had their phones out, taking photos or video. It irritated Jean, but she couldn't do anything about it as she focused on the woman and tried to keep Mair in her sights. One older lady had moved forward and was talking softly to Mair, now awake; saying how bonny she was, sensibly keeping her attention.

Most other people were adding to the confusion.

Jean concentrated on maintaining the pressure and watching the blood leak out of the nappy edge. The injured woman's breathing was becoming irregular. In the background, she heard the other van driver talking, giving information and asking how long the ambulance would be.

I don't know how I should deal with this, Jean thought as she started to panic.

The woman turned her head slightly and said to her, "I will be okay, won't I?"

A question for someone else to give her reassurance, it seemed. It stopped Jean's own panic in its tracks. They had both just heard a siren. Hopefully, it was an ambulance, not a coincidence.

I don't know; I hope so, thought Jean. How can I know? There is so much blood. She replied, "The ambulance will be here any second now; you'll be in good hands."

Suddenly a man pushed through the growing crowd

and knelt next to Jean. He said, "Harder, press harder in a moment; I'll get my finger underneath the pad and try to push into the incision. I want to stop the flow, hopefully, if it's an artery near the surface. Then press harder still in the area around my finger."

He concentrated on what he was doing and said to the woman, "I'm a medical student."

The injured woman gave a gasp, a short phrase delivered with a painful smile. "Going to be a doctor?"

He smiled back, "I hope so. Sorry, I know this is hurting more, but it's for the best."

Two police cars arrived together and officers took charge. The crowd of onlookers was suddenly moving, voluntarily or by command, Jean heard. The sirens merged into a cacophony as other emergency response vehicles also homed in on the incident site.

An ambulance arrived. Knifing and terrorism attacks in London had emergency response teams well trained. Two paramedics in uniform quickly took over the care of the victim. Jean listened to the staccato, cryptic conversation between the medical student and the older paramedic as Mair started crying again.

The other paramedic said to Jean, "We'll take this now, love; you did well."

The injured woman, the paramedics and the student moved into the ambulance, his hand still pressed on the woman's chest as the gurney entered the vehicle. In seconds, it and an accompanying police carr disappeared from sight.

Jean stood there, her pants soaked in blood around the knees.

As she turned to her goddaughter, the woman who had been keeping Mair occupied said, "Best wash, first. You never know."

Her eyes were on Jean's blood-covered fingers and palms.

A police officer, an older woman, one the police officers around her, took charge. "Come sit down, over here, please. My colleague will bring your daughter; she's safe. You can tell us what happened. And we can get you checked out."

Jean replied, "It's my goddaughter. Her mum is at work. She's with your lot."

"The Met or us?"

Then Jean realised that she was a City of London Police officer.

"The Met. Her name is Catrin Sayer, she's a detective inspector. But Mair's dad, Chris, is across the road."

"And you are?"

"Jean Hughes. I own the pottery shop in the market, across there. That's where Mair's dad is."

The woman nodded. "The Kiln, I've bought things there. Now you sit, while we get people to help you. You were great, but it's been a big shock, I can see."

As Jean slumped, suddenly feeling tired and shaky, the officer stood over her and called for a blanket. Her head tilted as she spoke into a radio. Two other uniformed officers, one with a foil emergency blanket, came to help Jean and Mair.

Jean looked around. Half in a daze, now that she had nothing to do, she saw another ambulance team converging on her. A few feet away, she could overhear the delivery man who made the 999 call talking with another officer.

"Our routes often meant we stopped here about the same time; her for the cleaners. Jemma, she calls herself, but it's Jemilah in full, I think she said once, but I don't know her last name. She's nice, friendly. I can't think why anyone would do this. It's horrible, horrible."

He couldn't stop talking, Jean realised. And she could hardly speak as she looked at Mair but couldn't touch her.

That's how Chris and Melanie found them several minutes later. They had heard the sirens, but as they became louder and there were more of them, both became concerned. Chris had stepped out to see if Jean was close by, just as a police officer jogged towards the Kiln door.

On her arrival, Melanie called to Jean, cried out more, really, and were allowed through to see her. As the women hugged, Chris picked up Mair, who in her innocence was now happy as anything with all the activity and attention.

They had cleaned Jean up a little, at least her hands and arms.

"I have to wait, to be checked out again and talk to a detective, as I was a witness. Take Mair - and where's Lili?"

Chris replied, "Asleep still, with a police officer watching her and another one in the shop."

Jean started crying. "Go back. Keep Lili and Mair away from this. I'll call when I know something or when I can come back to the Kiln."

Melanie glanced at Chris and saw the same expression of concern.

He said, "Stay with her. I'll look after Lili and Mair."

Melanie nodded.

He added, pulling out is phone, "I'll call Catrin as well; to tell her. It's her world, all this."

Jean said, "I think they may be on to her already; I told them Catrin was a copper."

But Detective Inspector Sayer wasn't answering her

phones. Chris's call went to voicemail.

He suddenly realised. "She's in court as a witness; her phones are off."

He looked up a number and made another call.

"DCI Wetherby, Chris Treneer here, Catrin's husband. There's been an incident, a stabbing. We are fine, I mean me and our baby, but if Catrin hears… yes, a knife attack in the street. By Spitalfields Market. Our friend Jean was walking Mair and had to give first aid to the victim. Can you… Thanks, I'll leave my phone as clear as I can. Yes. Thanks again."

He closed the call.

"Her boss will get to her as soon as it's possible. She is currently on the witness stand or, at least, in front of a video camera, he said."

10 WITNESS

"I remind you, Detective Sayer, that you are under oath and, effectively, you are in a United States jurisdiction at present.

"I will rephrase my question. Is it possible that your informant could have directly placed the statuettes in the plane in which my client was travelling during its refuelling stop in Bristol?"

Catrin sat at a table staring at a video camera. She was in an ordinary-looking meeting room in the United States Embassy in Nine Elms, south of the River Thames.

The trial of Jon Masud, accused of illegal purchase and smuggling of two priceless artefacts from Syria, was underway in a courthouse in South Carolina.

In front of her were two screens, one showing the defense attorney asking the questions, the other giving a general view of the courtroom three thousand miles away.

Over the video link, the face of the defense attorney, a Mr. Harrison Fancourt, showed his exasperation.

Catrin responded evenly, "Detective Inspector, not detective, sir. And I can only repeat what I said previously. We provided details of the flight, and the tip-off that it carried statuettes on board, to the FBI Art Crime Unit. This is consistent with normal interjurisdictional arrangements.

"We cannot identify our source for that information in any manner under UK legal provisions, including the 2005 Police Act. Therefore, I can give no location information about the informant."

"I'm having difficulty, Detective Inspector, not only with your answer, but with your accent. I take it you decline to rule out the possibility the statuettes were placed on my client's aircraft by the informant during its stopover."

Catrin saw the prosecution lawyer, an assistant district attorney, bounce out of his seat, about to make an objection. He had no need; the judge intervened.

"I must direct the jury to ignore that interpretation of the response from this witness as an inappropriate conclusion. Mr. Fancourt, Detective Inspector Sayer did not say that. Moreover, sir, her evidence has been presented clearly, despite your comment on her accent. I insist on good manners in my courtroom and you are very near the limit of my tolerance, sir."

He turned his attention to the jury. "May I ask if any member of the jury has had any problem understanding the witness, so far? The accent is Welsh, I might add."

He paused. Catrin got the impression that any juror raising an objection might also incur the wrath of the judge. After a moment he said, "Mr. Fancourt; you may proceed."

"I apologise for my inappropriate comment to the witness. The difficulty must be mine. I thank Your Honor for that guidance.

"Detective Inspector Sayer, your department called the FBI at a point in time that ensured the apprehension of my client by United States officials. If you had called half an hour earlier, the aircraft would have been recalled to the UK. Was the delay by the Metropolitan Police a deliberate act?"

Catrin kept her expression neutral. "We acted within a few minutes - less than ten minutes, in fact - from receiving the information ourselves. It is in the record. My sergeant reported to my immediate superior, and he advised him we should inform the FBI. They made the call to Senior Agent Klintz together."

"You were not involved directly, I gather?"

"No, I was not on duty."

She hoped that the lawyer would change track again soon. She saw the direction the questioning was heading. While it was to be expected, she had to be exceedingly careful in her response, for the record. She felt on a knife edge.

On the screen showing the courtroom, Catrin saw a man in a suit approach FBI agent Walkley Ballard, one of David Klintz's team, now sitting in the row behind the assistant DA. He whispered something to the FBI man and he, in turn, said something to the assistant district attorney. The attorney stood, interrupting the process and spoke up.

"Your Honor, colleagues in London have just in-formed us the witness is urgently needed elsewhere. We request that she be excused."

It surprised Catrin, coming out of nowhere.

She thought the defense attorney, Fancourt, would protest, but Ballard had already moved forward to brief him, as a court officer simultaneously whispered to the judge.

The defense counsel said, "No objection, Your Honor. But we reserve the right to recall. We have not finished with the witness."

The judge gave his agreement to the request from the defense and added, "Detective Inspector Sayer, you are excused for now, with our thanks and good wishes."

As Catrin sat back and looked around, somewhat astonished with the stroke of luck that that defense lawyer was not pressing the point further at present, she saw the two screens go blank; the link with the courtroom had disconnected. She wondered what was going on, then realised that Isabelle Howlett, who had been sitting nearby, had left the room. Howlett was visible through the glass in the doorway, talking on her mobile.

Something was wrong, she realised. A military-looking man in a suit had entered. He waited nearby, out of range of the camera until the screens darkened before he approached her.

"DI Sayer, I am Andrew Von Ryan, with Embassy Security.

"There's been an incident near your home, across the road from the Spitalfields Market. Your husband and daughter are safe, OK?"

"What -."

"They are safe. Take that in first. A car is waiting for you now. It will take you over there directly. DC Howlett is on the line with your DCI Wetherby, I gather. He wants to talk with you directly. Ms. Howlett will go with you, she says."

Her home. Her husband and child. Her friends. The pottery. Everything tumbled around in her mind with the word 'incident'. Chris and Mair had gone to the market, to the pottery, she knew. She had spoken to him before entering the embassy meeting room.

With that, he led her out of the door, away from others tied to the case in the courtroom and, with a final wish of 'God speed' from the American, within a few seconds she and Howlett were in the back seat of a Metropolitan Police Peugeot 308. Its lights started flashing as they set out. The vehicle markings showed it to be a dedicated incident response vehicle; one with a driver who knew how to cross London rapidly.

~~

During the journey north-east over the river, after speaking with her boss and then with her husband, Catrin's anxiety level dropped and she calmed down a little; but not much. Her daughter and her best friend had been caught up in one of the ever-increasing knife assaults in London.

She said to Howlett, "Find out where they've taken Jean, will you? Chris is really worried; she looked in shock. Melanie went off with her in the ambulance but is not answering her phone. Jean did well, he said, on scene. He's looking after Mair and Lili now, back at our place."

She closed her eyes and lay back, trying to absorb it all as Howlett made a call and waited. Then she was transferred and put on hold again. Finally, she bitched at someone, threatening him with the wrath of Commander Moore.

As Isabelle waited again, Catrin said quietly, her eyes closed, "You shouldn't do that, invoke Moore without her permission."

Isabelle dismissed the point. "She bought you a baby blanket and came to the christening. How do you think she will react? Probably give me hell if I didn't. Hello, yes. The Royal? Right, thanks."

She closed the call. "Jean is at your old stomping ground, in the Royal London Hospital, in the ER department being checked out. They want her under observation during the prelim interview by one of the investigation team assigned to the knifing."

Catrin had spent time in the hospital during her last miscarriage. It was also the Royal where she gave birth to Mair.

They asked the driver to head there.

Jean said, "Mair was good, Catrin, the entire time. I think it was the people. A woman fussed over her, which helped. But it was terrible. The poor woman. I'm sorry we got caught up in it."

Catrin had just returned to the treatment room holding Jean after sending Howlett back to the office, to arrange for someone to collect her car at the embassy and park it at New Scotland Yard.

She finished hugging her friend. "I talked briefly to the City constable outside, the one who brought you in. You did superbly well, she said. You and a young guy, a medical student."

Jean responded, "In the fiasco, with the people around us, he was the one to help the most, him and the woman looking after Mair."

"She said that. Now, she's waiting here with you until one of the investigating team arrives to take your preliminary statement. I'll wait, too. Chris says Mair and Lili are fine and a friend of yours, Chloe, is now at the Kiln, wanting to help. The officer there called Chris, to check if he wanted to talk to Chloe directly."

Melanie had been quiet so far, watching her partner intently. She spoke up. "I'm sure she is. She would enjoy the chance to help with the little ones."

The name clicked with Catrin. "Chloe is the woman who made the gender change. I just remembered."

Catrin had met her only twice, at the Kiln. She was part of Jean and Melanie's LBGTQ community. Catrin had noted how Chloe was changing; how the hormone therapy was feminizing her facial features.

The door opened and the City of London officer came in with a man who identified himself as DC Meadows.

He got straight into it. "I am here to get your preliminary statement, Jean, if that's okay with you right now. I must tell you also that we will ask you further questions as we piece this together. You were right there, and this is a rough moment for you, but everything you recall can help us."

Jean asked, "How is she doing? The woman attacked?"

Meadows' face revealed the truth.

He said softly, "I'm sorry, she didn't make it. We heard a couple of minutes ago and the news isn't out there yet. Her heart gave out, the doctor thinks. You and the other chap did what you could, but this is now a murder investigation."

Melanie moved forward in front of him to hug her spouse; she had read Jean's response sooner than anyone else.

As Jean cried, Catrin whispered to the officer, "Give her a few minutes, please. I'm her friend, Catrin Sayer, but I'm a DI at the Yard. Art and Antiques."

He pointed at the door. She followed him outside.

"It's rough for her, ma'am, but she needed to know, so I thought it best not to put it off."

Catrin nodded. "Agreed. No issue there. I'm sure she'll try to help as soon as she gets herself steadied. It has been an enormous shock for her. Her life is home and the pottery. Who are you with?"

"I am based at Bethnal Green, ma'am. But I was sent

over because I'm on the Knife Crime Task Force. A DI Hudson from the Organized Gang Crime Unit is to lead the murder investigation locally. I will be the Task Force liaison on this investigation."

Catrin slowly nodded, understanding. "DS Mark Harper is on that Task Force, I know. He used to work with me."

"Yes, he is. But he is away on leave at present. The report says your daughter was with Ms. Hughes. Is she OK?"

"She's with her dad and he says she is fine. She is only five months old. Any ideas what this was about?"

"It looks to be a random attack, but it's too early to say. And, if you will forgive me, I shouldn't say anything, anyway. But how are you doing with this, with your baby being involved?"

"How do you think I am doing, DC Meadows?"

"Well, my read is that you are being calm and professional on the outside, doing what you can to help your friend, but you are mad as hell inside."

Catrin smiled. "Too right. Shall we go back in?"

Meadows ensured that the interview was brief and dealt with the key points of the attack. He was primarily building a relationship, she knew.

Tomorrow they would want Jean to be interviewed at the police station. They would take her mind back to the incident and try to deal with faces, clothing and conversations. At some point, they would take her over the violent act itself and her actions. Beforehand, people would work late into the evening, reviewing the data gathered so far and prepare an interview plan for each key witness.

It was later, as they were leaving to go home, that

Catrin saw media people waiting outside the hospital entrance. She stopped Jean and Melanie.

"This way," she said. She led them down other corridors and out through the maternity area entrance, a familiar route. Jean said they could walk home, it was only twenty minutes away, but Catrin just said, "You look worn out; we go by cab."

Her intuition about the media was right. Two reporters were waiting outside as they arrived at the Cwmbran Kiln, making a brief stop there to close the shop properly before taking Jean and Melanie to Catrin's home.

Catrin guided Melanie and Jean ahead of her into the pottery before turning to speak to the reporters. She didn't want any coverage at all, but the gate was wide open on that one already, she was sure. The news was out on the internet that the victim, a Jemilah Kohli, had died despite the best efforts of the ambulance service and local bystanders to help her.

She identified herself and said calmly, "My friend has had a traumatic experience today. Please respect her privacy. We are upset about the events that occurred near here and are so sorry for the person so viciously attacked and for her family and friends. We offer them our sincere condolences at this tragic time."

She turned away to go in.

"Was it your baby with Jean, Inspector Sayer?" asked one reporter. "She was walking her goddaughter, we understand."

Catrin glanced back and said nothing. She regretted that later.

The evening media coverage of 'local heroes in knife attack' showed a photo of Jean and Melanie as they approached the pottery. Separately there were photos of the medical student, an Andrew Young, and a shot of Catrin as she looked back from the Kiln doorway.

They could have used any photo taken during her impromptu statement. She would have appeared professional and even-tempered. But no, they used one with Catrin looking back angrily, with the caption, 'Detective Inspector Catrin Sayer, Metropolitan Police, escorting her friend and artistic partner Jean Hughes. Her daughter was with Hughes as the incident unfolded.'

"Blazing mad at someone, more like it," said Chris, sounding proud, when he saw it later. They were watching their daughter sleeping evenly, with the occasional small sigh. Both hoped Mair was dreaming of milk and toys, not the events of the day.

~~

Commander Karen Moore was shown the same article on a trainride back from Manchester, from an interminable day of meetings there. Her companion on the trip was a DI John Leigh. He wondered what the commander would say. Adverse media coverage was enough to send his boss into a hissy fit, he had found from experience, and it had been a tough round of meetings today. If he was tired, she would be more so, as she had led the Met participation in the meeting.

After a moment, Moore looked out of the window. Leigh saw reflected what he took to be a slight smile.

"Sayer did okay, I suspect," was her initial comment.

She paused, thinking something through.

"Superintendent Lauder is updating me on the Undertow case next week, the monthly status review."

"Yes, next Wednesday ma'am. You are participating in

Commander Roscoe's operational review of the overall investigation a day earlier, you said."

"Can you arrange for Sayer to be in my office after Lauder's update? I'll let you know if the timing needs to change."

He seemed a little surprised. Reading his thoughts, she said, "Whenever I call her in, she always thinks she is in for a bollocking. You can do it nicely. Tell her I want her help with something."

He nodded, pulling out his phone to send a text.

As he typed the message, he heard Moore speaking with Superintendent Lauder. What surprised him was that during their discussion she specifically mentioned DC Bo Digsby in a reaction to something Lauder said. It sounded like she was questioning it, but ultimately demurred to Lauder's judgement.

Digsby was a member of Operation Undertow, but he was a systems expert in the Digital Intelligence Unit. Leigh thought Digsby was probably one of the sloppiest-looking officers in the forty thousand souls that made up the London Metropolitan Police Service.

11 INFILTRATION

DS Ian Underhill met Sylvia at King's Cross Station, at the pre-agreed place, a shopfront under the moving light array that was part of the McAslan ceiling.

They had met once previously, at a café off the A6 between Bedford and London. He gave her the preliminary brief there and they had a chance to size each other up.

Now she was arriving by train to start her undercover operation, without a personal car to park or the possibility of being traced through a vehicle. She had one large suitcase and one small bag. Anyone would think she was a traveller to London, a tourist or a relative of the man meeting her.

PC Sylvia Johnson from Bedfordshire had changed into Alison Fuller, an ex-army driver, with four years' post-service employment with a wedding and funeral limo service in Peterborough. That company had shut its doors. After a lean year and a half on minicabs, she was giving the impression she was keen to obtain any decent chauffeur job.

After King's Cross, there was a prearranged visit to a local hairdresser in Marleybone, then Ian drove her to a hotel in Hammersmith. She had a one-night reservation there.

He had been watching her unobtrusively, checking her readiness. As they arrived at the hotel, he said he would wait in the car while she changed.

Sylvia went up to the hotel room carrying the small case. Her larger bag was now in the boot of his car, to be stored temporarily by him.

She placed the bag on the bed, took a deep breath, then removed its contents before stripping to her underwear, carefully placing everything she had worn or carried from her normal life into the case. Clothes, her shoulder bag and, with the same hesitation as on previous assignments, her wallet purse with family photographs and the leather folder containing her warrant badge.

In the empty purse she took from the bag, she placed the driving license Underhill had provided, with a matching Peterborough library card and a debit card in the name of Alison Fuller.

The only thing she kept on her person from her normal life was the engagement ring, which she wore. Ian would keep this bag in his possession while she went to the interview at the casino.

She looked in the mirror at the haircut and styling she had just received, at the strange streak of blue in the new jet-black hair in its short style. It wasn't her at all, which was good. Her background profile, the hairstyle and clothing, had been carefully chosen, considering both the chauffeur uniform she would wear and her cover story.

She had to stand out enough, but also needed to fit smoothly into the chauffeur group of the Ballantine West casino; the balance was crucial to the success of the operation.

As she dressed in the unfamiliar colours and garments, she sensed the change in her role, her personality. This may be the third undercover assignment she had taken on, but given the target and the plan, it may be the most comfortable one so far.

That could be deceptive, she knew.

A luxurious casino could be as dangerous a venue as the small apartment next door to a woman believed to be harbouring a wanted terrorist.

In that case, it had been a week in Doncaster, without incident. They caught the man in Grimsby when another officer doing surveillance saw the suspect leave his uncle's house. If she had been identified as a police officer by the man, the transition from safety into imminent danger could occur in a second.

It played on the nerves.

Downstairs in the car park, she met up again with her lifeline, Ian. Handler and undercover officer, they were now a team; only time would show if their relationship would work or not.

Underhill said, "We have a practice timeslot at the driving centre. And I have checked out the way in which Frank Loomis usually tests his chauffeurs' defensive driver skills. It'll most probably be a handbrake turn and a straight exit out; he likes that."

She nodded. That wasn't a problem.

Underhill looked at her. "But no guarantees on that; he may not even bother."

She responded, "It's logical. I doubt he would choose something riskier in a limo. These days, with electronic parking brakes, you can't do them anyway."

"Well, if he takes you out in an older model, watch out for it."

For a half-hour she practiced in an older Audi SUV with a Met driving instructor. They used pylons to lengthen, shorten, broaden or narrow the turning zone; the point at which the handbrake locked the rear wheels as she took the vehicle into a slide that reversed their direction.

She crushed only two pylons.

It was near noon when they finished. Ian took her to a café for lunch. He had continued monitoring her, sensing the tension in her.

Sylvia just needed to succeed in the interview. If the casino hired her, she was undercover; if not, she was back to the hotel to change and rest before heading home later today or tomorrow, to have her hair fixed as best as they could before she returned to her regular job.

That's the way infiltration phases unfolded.

If the Southern Breeze Casino in Brighton showcased its aristocratic past, the Ballantine Group carefully avoided mentioning the origins of their UK facilities. Both in Brighton and West London, they successfully bought out buildings under construction from companies that overreached their financial dreams. In the case of Ballantine West, it had been an award-winning design for an office block, transformed into a functional and attractive three-story casino, with restaurant, theatre and parking facilities.

It was later, as Sylvia approached the casino, when apprehension gave way to acceptance. It was beginning. The wait was over, and she became calm. Ian picked up on it and found it reassuring. In their line of work, they mistrusted people who were easy-going and calm until the reality hit and the tension took over.

"Good luck, I'll see you later" he said, as he got out of the little Honda they had given her at the hotel.

As he climbed into another vehicle waiting for him, she drove into the casino parking lot and found her way to the desk inside, identified as Ballantine Chauffeur Services.

"I'm Alison Fuller. Mr. Loomis is expecting me at one-thirty. I'm a bit early," she said to the smiling assistant on the desk.

"The new driver?"

"I hope so. I'm here for the interview, at least. A bit nervous, really."

"I'll let him know, he's with another driver, back with the vehicles. Just a 'heads up'; Mr. Loomis doesn't do 'across the desk' interviews. He'll get you on the road immediately and talk as you go. And you'll be driving."

Alison, as Sylvia had become, responded, "I'll do my best."

"Well, good luck. I'm Viv, Vivian. We've never had a female chauffeur. It is about time, if you ask me. We are getting more female VIP players here. I'm sure that some women would be happier with a woman driver."

They were on the Great West Road in a seven-seater Ford SUV; one with a handbrake, she noticed, as she adjusted the seat. Telling Loomis that she hadn't driven this specific vehicle, she took time familiarising herself with the layout of the controls before setting off. He just watched, showing no sign of impatience or approval.

Frank Loomis was in his early fifties, a little over-weight and easy to talk to, almost paternal. Dressed in a light grey suit with 'Ballantine Casino' stitched in a charcoal grey copperplate text along the top edge of each lapel, she saw it was a distinctive uniform without being 'over the top'. With a casino logo signboard and the client's name, punters arriving at airports could be sure he was a casino employee.

He hadn't commented on her driving, although he had given her some challenging route elements. She had just completed a sudden route change, crossing three lanes of traffic to turn right instead of left. No-one had even honked at her, the way she had finessed it.

"We'll go down here, Alison, and turn on to Cutters Lane. It was a lane. Now it's a dead end. When we get there and, assuming it is quiet, I want you to perform a handbrake turn, if you would? Then head back out again."

He checked her response.

"You are OK with that? Defensive driver training was listed on your resumé."

"I'm up to it, Mr. Loomis. It can be hard on the car, though."

All she said as she turned into Cutters Lane was, "Tell me when."

"It's coming up. You'll see the bit I mean; it has an open gravel area on one side of the road and grass on the other, so you won't hit anything."

If I screw it up, she thought.

The lane worked, but it wasn't easy, the paved width allowing for some error, but not by much. Sylvia took the speed up higher than Loomis asked for because she wanted to make her skills visible. She worked the handbrake, gearshift and the steering wheel and, as she did so, the back wheels locked as the car went into the swing and the slide.

It had enough whip to make Loomis grab the dashboard. As she compensated and used the front wheels to realign the direction of travel, she released the handbrake and slipped back into drive. The maneuver completed, Sylvia took the power up gradually as they faced the outbound direction.

Her prospective boss said nothing for a moment as she reduced speed, awaiting further orders.

"Did that in the army, did you?" he asked.

"I trained to do that there, yes. But no. I didn't need it during the piece of action I was in."

Her expression made him ask. "What did you do?"

"I was in a Wolf; they were in Fiat. I hit them on the front right bumper and went with the turn, gunning it. I pushed them off the road and they rolled into the ditch. We got out of there fast as the officer I was transporting reported the incident. A patrol got two of them and both were armed, so we were lucky."

A Land Rover Wolf, a military utility vehicle.

He said, "Or well trained. I won't be testing you on that manoeuvre, I tell you. The insurance rates are bad enough. Anyway, Alison, you drive very well. Danny Bell vouched for you and said you were a good'un so the job's yours. The others will be happy.

"We need a break, to let us have more time at home and, I tell you now I'm hiring you, the candidates we've seen in the last week or two have been less than stellar. You know how you can tell, I'm sure. You feel a professional driver in charge from the first minute or so. I saw that in you. So welcome aboard."

She made the right noises of happiness and appreciation and seemed thrilled when Loomis talked about the uniform for the fleet. He was sending her straight to the tailor they used. The shop had a fast turnaround.

"Now when can you start?"

"Whenever you want; as soon as possible from my perspective, I need the money."

"Well, come in tomorrow at five p.m., for a seven-hour stretch. Black pants, white shirt or plain blouse and, do you have a blazer or jacket of some sort?"

"Yes, a dark wine-coloured blazer."

"Wear that. We'll send you on regular runs with clients we know already and are comfortable with. You'll need the uniform more for the image with the jet-set gamblers and the casino executive team when you settle in. The tailor will have you fitted in no time."

It was later, alone, when she called Ian.

"I'm hired; I'm in."

It wasn't the punters she was targeting; it was the executive team trips and one particular person there. She needed that uniform.

"Good. Well done. Now that's over, forget the hotel. We have an apartment for you, a one-bedroom unit in a block overlooking Ealing Common. Well, your apartment doesn't have that view, it faces another road. It is a nice area, and you have a parking permit for the Honda. I'll meet you with your bags and you follow me over there. It's only a couple of miles from the casino."

"How do I explain getting a place like that so fast? It's really hard finding rentals in the west London area, I read. But I like it, for the privacy. I thought I would need to start off in a cheap hotel, or something."

Ian said, "We thought of that. A captain in the Grenadier Guards owns it and we are building the links for your backstory now. I'll brief you there."

"Well, it's convenient, at least. I'll be spending a lot of time on the Chiswick flyover or under it, finding altern-ative routes. And going to Heathrow."

He laughed, "And crossing Kew Bridge to Biggin Hill airport. And out to Luton, I hope."

She understood the reason from the briefing. Her target frequently used the Biggin Hill and Luton Airport executive centres for his business trips within the UK.

12 HARPER

Catrin met DS Mark Harper at the St. Stephen's Tavern in Westminster late in the afternoon, a week after the knifing. The tavern was busy, but the MPs must be in session, she thought, taking in that it wasn't packed. It was the closest pub to the Houses of Parliament, other than the many watering holes inside the Palace of Westminster itself.

She had spent time talking with Jean every day since the incident, seeing her reaction to the crime and the follow up. Like others in her situation, it took its toll and, being her friend, it was harder for Catrin to deal with also. It was three days after the incident that Jean raised the issue.

"DC Meadows gave me a special number to call anytime I felt something was wrong and suggested that I don't go anywhere alone. Just in case, with it being a violent crime and the perpetrators still at large.

"It's a bit frightening. I'm worried about the girls mainly."

Catrin had expected Jean would be advised about

routine security. It took her back to times when she had felt threatened, knowing how helpless she felt.

"I'll look into it a bit, see how we can help," she had told her.

The first thing she noted was Harper's eyes. As an artist, she could be quite analytical about changes in facial features. What passed through her mind was the same set of thoughts she had on seeing her face in the mirror years ago, a week or two after the Kinnington Church attack, once the bruising had cleared and the dressings had been removed.

She had been told that Mark was away on leave. For a while.

Harper reached out to shake hands and said, "It's good to see you."

She held on to his hand and said, "You feel like shit, don't you, Mark?"

He looked surprised, then amused.

"Am I that easy to read? God! I was feeling better... same old Catrin; get right to it."

She was right; he was on medical leave, and from his eyes she thought it wasn't a physical injury.

She smiled. "Who are you seeing?"

"A Dr. Perry. Louise Perry. She works in the practice that your guy, Dr. Herrington, started; it's grown. She's good; good for me, anyway. I'm past the stage of insisting I need to be at work, that I'm needed."

Catrin nodded slowly, recalling her own experiences. "Work with her; that's my advice. And you will come out the other side stronger and better able to handle the job, I assure you."

"I am. I plan to."

He asked after John Obi, Isabelle Howlett and Neville

Coltrane, then apologised for missing Mair's christening. She let him lead the way; she had the time. She remembered how precious the occasional chats with colleagues had been when she was on stress and medical leave.

After a while, he moved on to the subject of their meeting. "So, you want to talk about the attack in Spitalfields, I gather. That's what Jim Meadows said."

"Just the big picture view from an expert; not the details."

He paused.

"We know that the attack was made by a member of one of Burcu Dogan's crews, the Limmies. You are concerned for Jean, I take it?"

Catrin nodded. "She's really hit hard by the death of the woman, Jemma Kohli, but she's a witness. I want to know how serious the risk will be with this gang? It's years since I worked the drug scene at ground level, so I don't want to fool myself."

He grimaced slightly. "You were on the drug squad in Brixton, I recall. The crews change a lot but not the big players, but you know that.

"If her evidence is crucial for a conviction of anyone in the Limmies over the age of seventeen, then she's definitely at risk. Dogan prides himself on keeping his crew chiefs and command team out of trouble, at any cost. The crews themselves and any minors, he wouldn't bother about those that much. They fight the charge but take the sentence and get straight back into Burcu's world."

He stopped and took a breath.

"But the crews are tight, violent and unpredictable. Even without Dogan's say-so, they could go after anyone they see as a perceived threat. They may try to scare a witness off before anything worse, providing they are not high themselves on something. If they are… there's no telling to their logic or limit to their methods.

"Sorry that I can't be more positive or clearer. It's a different world of policing to what we used to do; that you still do, I mean."

Catrin said bluntly, "You were clear enough. It's frightening, but clear."

He shook his head. "It's all this way now and getting worse. We ran some numbers, projections. We are sliding towards the status of US cities; murders won't be newsworthy, they will become a routine."

His eyes lit up; there was an unhealthy energy there. Catrin asked herself whether meeting Mark was as good an idea as she first thought.

"One of my last cases, an apparently trivial one. Lonnie is seventeen. Two months ago he needed a fix and for that he needed money. He'd been charged twice for minor dealing and given a Youth Referral Order.

"So, he sees a bag left on view in a car parked in a neighbouring road. He is so focused on his craving that he picks up a brick to break the window, oblivious that the car is alarmed. He gets the bag, runs like hell and it's all caught on CCTV, too. A man sees him, yells out that he is a thief and Lonnie, in a panic now, turns the corner, running at full speed.

"His sister's boyfriend is there with a mate, but Lonnie only sees two guys blocking his way. In a panic, he pulls out a knife to get past the pair and slashes wildly.

"Now we have a twenty-year-old young man who has an arm that is nearly useless unless surgery can repair the damage. Lonnie's family is in crisis and he is in remand and will serve a custody sentence. The woman's car contained only a bag with two library books. At fifteen,

Lonnie was drug free, a good student and played soccer for his school. He volunteered with a local charity, as I recall."

"Multiply his case by a thousand, even, and you'll be minimizing the issue. Schools are becoming war zones, between parents, teachers and staff trying to keep kids clean and the drug crews trying to get them hooked so they can grow their customer base."

Mark had quickly forgotten, it seemed, that Catrin had years of this in Brixton. She didn't cut him off but, as she saw the stress building up, she reached out and touched his hand.

"Sorry," she said, "I probably shouldn't have come and stirred it, bothering you."

He smiled. "No. It's me. Louise is working with me. I have to stop carrying the world on my back."

He paused. "I was better at handling the theft of that Tompkins clock."

A case they worked on together when he was a sergeant in the Art and Antiques Unit. They had recovered a valuable English antique mantel clock.

She laughed. "That was the easy part, telling the couple we had recovered it!"

He laughed too. Glad to move Mark away from the topic of knife crimes, she added, "Their niece, the one in the wheelchair who came home before we left, she was a peppy one, a schoolgirl making smart remarks to you. She was full of go."

He smiled, remembering.

Catrin continued steering the conversation to safer ground. "Isabelle retires in a few months. She and Morley will live in Paris. Fulfil a dream, I guess. We have Derek Nkrumah - remember Derek? I seconded him to us temporarily when you were there. He is full time now, added to the headcount while I was on leave. He'll stay, he's settling in well."

Harper smiled, but his face changed as he said, "I've no real advice for Jean that you can't share with her, given your time with Hunt. Don't be out alone, carry a personal alarm, have her put 999 and your numbers into her speed dial, that sort of thing. My read of her, from the couple of times we met, is that she is not someone to fight back. She'll panic or try to reason with the person, seeing a kid, not a gang member high on something."

Catrin nodded silently, then added, "She will, unless Lili is threatened. Melanie though, may be different. She could pick up a vase and brain the little sod as soon as he threatened them."

It was Mark's turn to smile. "Tell Melanie to stay close then. I'll call people, we'll do what we can to keep a closer eye, or at least be immediate in any response."

"I talked with DC Meadows again, asking that, already."

Mark gave her a look. "He probably takes your interest to be a concerned friend. Me, well, it's our area. It may help."

Later, as she left Mark, with the well-meant promise on both sides that they should keep in touch, she was worried what the future may bring for Jean. Burcu Dogan's crews were out there and any trial, if they made an arrest, would be months away.

On the way home, Catrin went to talk to Jean and Melanie. She wasn't sure how to play this; not wanting to increase their anxiety, but equally wanting them to take steps for their safety.

She wasn't the only one worried about that, she found out. Chloe and another friend, a tall, solidly built man,

Paulo, were already there.

Catrin joined in the conversation, hoping to get time to speak with Jean and Melanie alone, but also wanting to get home to Mair and Chris. Somehow Melanie tuned in-to it.

She said, "The issue is how do we keep Jean safe? Chloe and a few others are worried. They plan to help."

"Funny you should raise that," said Catrin.

Jean said, "They want to make sure I don't go any-where without one of them being with me. And they will try as much as possible to have someone at the Kiln, regularly."

Paulo, who turned out to be a Brazilian, spoke. "It'll mainly be Chloe or me, I think. I work part-time on the door at The Crimson Goat."

He worked door security. The Goat was a well-known gay pub.

Catrin nodded but looked at Chloe, a little surprised.

Catching on, Chloe said, in explanation, "I'm from Liverpool. I've had a bit rougher upbringing than most down here." She smiled and added, "We play tick with hatchets, as the song says."

Now it was Paulo's turn to appear lost.

Melanie explained. "She's referring to a local song there, called, 'In my Liverpool home'. You know, the game of tic, it's the same as the American game, tag. But it's just a song, Paulo."

The Brazilian gave Chloe a long, suspicious stare, which made her laugh. "I'm joking, right?"

"With you? Okay, if you say so."

Catrin thought his response showed more about Chloe than the Brazilian's unfamiliarity with British slang.

At home, Catrin mused on the life of her friends.

Although they socialized with her and Chris a lot, particularly now they each had a child, Jean and Melanie's involvement in the gay community was a big and support-ive part of their lives. They were always helping someone or other. Now they were receiving help themselves. How practical or useful that would be, she wasn't sure.

Tomorrow she was scheduled to see Commander Moore. She wondered what that would involve. Not art, for sure.

13 MADONNA

Commander Moore was at the meeting table in her office when Catrin was shown in by Moore's assistant. DCS Lauder and an unknown and surprisingly unkempt younger man were seated there as well. Copies of the same file marked, 'Undertow Confidential' sat on the desk in front of each officer, closed.

Moore began with, "Superintendent Lauder has another Undertow Focus task for you, Sayer, a follow-up to the lead you got from John Dalton. And you'll want to do this one, I assure you. Especially after I saw your face in the news last week."

Catrin looked surprised. "The money launderer; is he linked to the murder in Spitalfields?"

"I didn't say that. Life isn't that simple. Just take my word for it."

"Yes, I'd like to help, ma'am."

"Then sit down."

Lauder said, "Sayer, it's good to see you again. This is DC Bo Digsby."

Digsby was an English name; Bo was a nickname, or it

could be an Asian name, she surmised. The man appeared Eurasian in facial features.

As Catrin smiled an acknowledgement to the Superintendent, she took in the young constable, concluding that he must be an undercover officer.

She said hello. His response was a monosyllabic mutter. His uneasiness in being in the room, probably with Commander Moore, was obvious. He was intrinsically good looking, but nothing about his appearance bolstered that.

Lauder swallowed a brief smile, probably at Sayer assessing his team member.

"The Ballantine Casino in Chiswick. There is a painting on a wall in the executive suite; the Juris painting that you heard about from Dalton. That is the area where the senior management of the casino and its sister operation in Brighton are located.

"We want you to follow up on an investigation in the executive area, one that you will invent as a reason to justify your access there. It is vitally urgent that you examine the painting, is the line we want you to follow. How you build that story is up to you, but it needs to stand up to solid scrutiny from an art perspective. You will need to speak with a man called Howard St. John-Leer, the Finance Director, in his office area and nowhere else.

"We are currently finding out more about the casino and the painting location, so this is a heads up; to start you thinking up the story you want to use to give us access."

So I'm right, concluded Catrin. This guy Digsby is in an undercover role, probably at the casino. They have an investigation underway there.

Moore couldn't resist butting in. "DC Digsby needs to

be with you as an art team member; he needs the access and some time to study the area. You will need to prep him to appear as a genuine Art and Antiques member, to look and sound right. He's in the same line of work as your husband but operational within Undertow -."

DC Digsby interrupted Commander Moore; at his peril, Catrin thought, from Lauder's look.

"That's Chris Treneer, right?"

"He's my husband, yes," responded Catrin.

Moore swept on. "As I said, Digsby has to come over as genuine an art detective as you or anyone else in your lot. That's important. He looks artsy to me."

No-one got the impression that Moore was giving Digsby a compliment.

Lauder continued, "Nothing you do must suggest a link to any casino activity; nothing at all. Now, in principle, do you see any problems?"

They watched Sayer's reaction.

For a moment she seemed lost in thought, before focusing on Digsby, taking him in.

"What art are you familiar with, in general?"

He looked surprised, which, in turn, threw her; he knew he was being asked to pose as a member of Art and Antiques, so he should have already given it consideration.

"I like Anime; the Japanese stuff."

"And beside cartoon images and graphic novels?"

"I have a Madonna print on my wall."

"Which one?"

There were many paintings of the Madonna. She wondered where his art interest lay, if he had any at all.

"The leather hat and bubblegum poster, ma'am."

He sounded defensive, or surprised she had to ask that question.

"Oh, the singer. I see."

Lauder looked at him balefully. "Digsby doesn't talk much, though; truth be told."

That may be his only asset, thought Catrin.

Moore sat back, took a deep breath and said, to wrap it up, "So; if you need anything as you plan this operation, Sayer, let Superintendent Lauder know directly. We'll leave you and DC Digsby to become acquainted. In your office, perhaps. Once we have a little more information, we'll be giving you very little notice of its implementation."

She needed to move on, was the message.

As they stood to leave, Lauder was clearly planning a last word with Moore alone. Catrin said to him. "And if you could have someone find out the educational background of this man St. John-Leer, sir; what schools and university he attended, and if any Met officer here was a contemporary of his at any of them, that may help."

An idea to gain access was already forming.

Lauder smiled. "I'll assign one of my best officers for that task. He'll even find out the sports teams they played on, won't you, Digsby?"

Catrin added, "I'll need one of my team, probably Howlett with us. Obi is busy with Nkrumah on a Finsbury Park mugging of an antiques dealer. If Digsby needs time for whatever he needs to do, I need someone to talk to about the painting, with St. John-Leer or his people being there. Howlett can talk the hind leg off a donkey, art-wise."

She left unstated that an art conversation with Digsby wouldn't last ten seconds.

Lauder glanced at Moore.

From her first reaction, Commander Moore seemed about to object, then acquiesced before saying, "Send her along; Howlett and I can have a brief chat about confidentiality related to Undertow Focus tasks."

"Yes, ma'am," she responded.

I'll stay clear of that one, she decided, particularly when Isabelle emerges from Moore's office.

14 GINNY

Jean Hughes seemed to be back to normal, albeit a little quieter, as the days passed.

Catrin and Chris accompanied her and Melanie to Jemma Kohli's funeral, where they met Andrew Young, the medical student, and his fiancée. Chloe and Janette, an older woman who did front sales in the Kiln on two afternoons a week, were babysitting the children.

Jean cried once, but otherwise she was composed.

Like similar tragedies, the funeral was a large event, many people attending not being able to get into the body of the funeral home and filling the entrance and an overflow seating area in an adjoining room.

The family had reserved space for Jean's and Andrew Young's people.

The press took photos outside, but mercifully, given that it was a funeral, they didn't pester them with questions. The media focus currently was on two drug crew members now under arrest, with speculation around which one actually killed Kohli. At the end, as the crowd exited slowly, Catrin heard a Welsh voice, a woman, but on looking around, she couldn't place it in the faces she saw.

There was a visible police presence, and she recognized several officers, including DC Meadows and one of the duty officers outside. The last thing the Met needed was another knife attack during a funeral.

It was Melanie who mentioned that there were more patrols around the Spitalfields Market. That was enough for Catrin to give Meadows a call.

"It's just a precaution, ma'am. We are keeping an eye on each person who contributed to the arrest, given it's the Limmies."

Catrin asked, "Is Jean at a more elevated risk status, for some reason?"

"Not particularly. Her statement corroborated that of the other van driver. He's key; he saw Oswald Balogun pass the knife to the younger male, the one Jean saw taking it away around the corner, Jo-Jo. He wiped the handle before dropping it down the grid. They smeared the fingerprints, but the DNA of both crew members, Oswald Balogun and Jo-Jo Graham, were on the handle and we have both in custody.

"But Dogan's crews are unpredictable, so the increased presence is a precaution. You know it would be more than that if we had a specific threat."

"Yes, I've been there on that one in the past. I know."

At work, Catrin and DS John Obi found their team called out to a major robbery of an historic home in Kingston-on-Thames, one involving vandalism of the art left behind as much as the theft of valuable items. As they worked with the borough investigation team, particularly looking into outlets for the stolen pieces, it meant a fair amount of shuttling across London.

That, and the planning for the Undertow Focus task, resulted in long days for Catrin. Work and time with her family consumed the following two weeks.

~~

It was during a dinner with one of Catrin and Jean's most loyal collectors when the changes in Jean really hit home for Catrin.

Mrs. Eugenie Kowalski from Texas prided herself on her collection of ceramics. Catrin wasn't sure how often she visited London, but an annual dinner with Jean and Catrin, their gallery owner, Liz Marshall and her husband William was a regular event. Police work had made Catrin miss the dinner only twice over the decade or so of the relationship.

One thing Catrin liked about Ginny (they had progressed from several years of Mrs. Kowalski, to Eugenie and then finally to Ginny) was that she would be direct with them. You learned what she liked and why, what she didn't understand and, sometimes, what she did understand, but didn't like. And she had the precious ability to do that without raising hackles or resentments from the artists.

Jean had just explained a comment she made about 'less time' for their joint work with both bring up a baby, something Liz had passed on to Sayer-Hughes collectors. Instead of a sympathetic response about the challenges of working and raising children, Ginny asked Jean, "Is it less time or less motivation, do you think?"

Jean thought for a second and gave Catrin a glance before responding.

"There was an incident, a knife attack in the street. I

gave first aid to the victim, but the woman died later. Since then, the Market hasn't felt a safe place. Melanie tries to talk me out of it, but it is a bit of a struggle to stay on top of everything. So less time is one reason, but there is also too much tension. It's a distraction."

Catrin reached out and squeezed her hand.

Jean continued, "It's only in the last week that I have been able to pin it down, but... Ginny is right. I don't have the same focus, the same drive I once did. Sorry."

Liz started to make positive noises about the effects of time being a healer, but Kowalski interrupted her at the first decent interval.

"Jean, is it your safety, or your daughter's? Can I ask?"

From Jean's face, Catrin suddenly saw how incisively perceptive the American had been and how she had herself underestimated the level of anxiety and reaction in her friend. She blushed with embarrassment and looked down until the flush had passed.

Jean was saying, "I worry for Liliwen; and for Mair, growing up with things like these gangs, this violence all around us. And the drugs. We are settled in London, Melanie and I - and Catrin and Chris. But what's it going to be like for our kids growing up?"

Ginny responded directly, "Well, Jean, if I were you, I wouldn't give up my creative work. It is part of you and part of your friendship with Catrin. Equally, I wouldn't force it, either. You need to be kind to yourself.

"Let Liz deal with all the querulous, bad-tempered people like me looking for Sayer-Hughes pieces. That's her job; she can take the bruises. And it's William's, too; he doesn't bruise as easily as he claims."

Liz said humorously, "I'll remind you of that; it will come back to haunt you."

Catrin said to Jean, "I know there is extra policing in

the Market area. It helps, I hope."

Kowalski responded with, "Police work is largely after the event, after the crime is committed. Very rarely can they head off the perpetrator from committing the act. In Texas or here, I think, they deal with the aftermath."

There was something about her tone of voice which told them that the American collector had direct experience of that aspect of the police role. She didn't elaborate.

As the conversation moved on and Catrin and Jean exchanged glances, Catrin was hit by the fact, as a police officer, she had reached a cherished milestone in her career, heading the Art and Antiques Unit. It was only a couple of years since she had turned down a more demanding role within Trident, dealing with biker gang crimes and with an implied promotion, just to stay in art crime.

But in the area where her best friend's anxieties lay, in the fears for their children and their neighbourhood, she had been more valuable a decade or more ago, as a uniformed constable in Brixton.

The thought swept through her mind and didn't quite escape from the other side.

~~

For years now, St. Paul's Cathedral had been a special place for Sayer. It was somewhere she could find peace, meditate or just silently let go of problems. A mile southwest of her home, it had become a regular stop on her walks during her leave and, with Mair in her stroller, a stop on the exercise route that now gave her daughter time outside in fresh air.

Over time, she had become acquainted with a few

people there, ordained or lay staff, but her strongest contact with the cathedral was still her former boss. Retired Assistant Commissioner Hunt had been a lifelong parishioner and she was still heavily involved in the cathedral's activities.

She had been the person to take Sayer there soon after her face was injured in Scotland.

It was no surprise for Catrin to run into Sandra Hunt outside, in the gardens, a few days later. After years of being 'Sayer' and 'ma'am', Catrin still had to consciously say 'Sandra'.

After catching up a little, Hunt asked Catrin how it was, being back at work. She didn't sound wistful about it, as if she was missing it herself. Hunt had a plate-load of activities she was involved in, Catrin knew.

She was honest with her old boss about the pleasure of returning to art crime work now being marred by the recent developments after the Kohli murder.

As she explained her dilemma she concluded with, "Part of me was so looking forward to returning to art crime work and my team. I've really settled into the role and... now I am not sure."

She realised that it sounded lame. Not sure? About what?

Hunt offered no instant advice. She just absorbed it, keeping that intense gaze on her that Catrin remembered from the past.

After a silence, she said, "Sometimes being good at something isn't enough, don't you think? Take that Italian from the Art Crime Task Force; the one I met when you asked me to do the welcoming speech at the dinner, the night before it met in London."

Catrin recalled the meeting. Neville Coltrane had given her the task of organizing the event. She recalled that, at one point, Hunt had been locked in conversation with Major Vittorio Cuoco, an Italian art crime investigator with the Carabinieri.

"What about him?"

"He'll be happy as an art crime investigator until the day he retires, he told me. If he died the day after, he went on to say, he would tell St. Peter his life had been full and complete."

Catrin smiled, thinking of Vittorio; she liked the man a lot.

"The question is, Catrin, will you? Will you feel complete?"

It was so direct a question that Catrin looked away, unable to come back with an instant answer. Hunt gave her no time to concoct one. She reached out and touched Mair's arm, as the baby was waving it a little.

"This lovely girl is part of your completeness, we both know. Your growth as an art crime detective is also. You are a long way from being PC Sayer in Brixton. But the future will unfold when it's ready. Just be open to it. As each of us must be."

Hunt smiled at her and in the shade of the cathedral wall, the comment settled the doubts and indecisions milling around inside her from the dinner with Eugenie Kowalski.

15 CADWALLADER

From behind the limousine desk at the Ballantine West Casino, Frank Loomis walked across to Sylvia, who had just reported in. She was scheduled for a collection from London City airport.

"You know the ropes now, Alison. Your next job is to meet Mrs. Cadwallader, in the executive office. She manages the suite for the senior management. Stay on her good side, as she has considerable influence for someone in an admin role. She took a dislike to Malcolm. He gets none of the Exec work now, even if needs the overtime. Clear?"

"Yes, Mr. Loomis."

He smiled then reached up to his hairline. "You are ex-army, so a brief tug up here now and again doesn't go amiss.

"Up to the third floor and ring the bell. She'll give you a passcode to memorize for the keypad there, for future use. I'll send Kevin to the City Airport pickup now; you can do his Heathrow when you come back down."

As she turned, he said, "And if you think security

coverage is tight in here, it's more stringent upstairs. Be on your best behaviour."

Mrs. Cadwallader looked to be in her mid-forties and assertive; she was no pushover.

Sylvia took in the security camera on the wall across the foyer as she waited inside the entrance, let in by an assistant working at the reception desk. As Cadwallader approached, she pointed to the easy chairs in the open area. They sat across from each other.

"So, it's Alison, I understand. Welcome."

The woman sounded Welsh, Sylvia thought.

"Yes, ma'am. Alison Fuller."

Mrs. Cadwallader liked the 'ma'am' title; that was clear.

"Well, Alison, I am to give you a briefing about any chauffeur assignments of the executive team or their special guests."

Sylvia nodded expectantly.

"I will issue a pass code for the door here. Each time you enter, protect the number from others seeing it. You will then wait here in reception; do not go further in. You will first take any accompanying baggage they may have to the vehicle or arrange help to do that, as needed, with the casino services staff. Someone else will bring the bags to the foyer."

"I understand."

"Most trips will be to hotels or airports. I expect those will be straightforward for you. Mr. Suarez normally uses Kevin, so you probably won't drive him but if you do, it will be to Kew, to his home, or to Heathrow. He arrives here later than most of the management team and works later, keeping Spanish hours, I think of it as."

Mr. Suarez was the chief executive officer.

"Should you chauffeur Mr. St. John-Leer at all, he uses

119

Heathrow occasionally but mainly travels in executive aircraft. He is such a busy man. Make sure you are familiar with all the routes to Luton and these smaller airports. For him, particularly, if you are the assigned driver, your job includes checking the traffic advisories and letting me know of any need for an earlier departure than planned. Mr. St. John-Leer is very accommodating, but he hates to see us paying supplementary fees for delays with corporate aircraft.

"Also, he is a stickler for carrying his own briefcase, always. Sometimes it's a smaller one; sometimes it's a larger bag similar to those that pilots use. Even if he looks as if he needs assistance, leave it to him.

"The other executives working here generally need chauffeuring to airports or to events in central London. Occasionally you will need to make trips to the Ballantine South facility. Have you shuttled people to the Brighton casino?"

"Yes. Twice now. Two VIP couples."

Cadwallader nodded. "Finally, while you wait here for a client, you may use your mobile for calls or texts, but do not take any photographs nor make any attempt to connect through the executive server. It is monitored and has the same security settings as the casino banking section. One of your colleagues didn't listen."

That was Malcolm, Sylvia thought.

"Fully understood, ma'am. Thank you for the guidance. Being new, it is much appreciated."

Mrs. Cadwallader stood. "Welcome, then."

She passed a card to Sylvia. "Memorize this now. Don't write it in any little book or store it on your phone. It is now specifically assigned to you."

A 4-digit number. After a second she handed it back. "Got it."

She looked around taking it all in and deliberately gave a big sigh. The older woman smiled. "A lot to take in, I know."

Sylvia responded, "It's like entering the boardroom suite at the top of an office block. And that painting is eye-catching. I thought at first it was metal, with the sheen, but it isn't. I can tell that now."

Mrs. Cadwallader arched her eyebrows. "Goodness, I'm glad you noticed. You are the first driver to comment on it."

The painting showed three dice, cleverly done. They appeared to be tumbling out into the room.

She continued, "It's a Juris; a Latvian artist. It was a present to Mr. St. John-Leer from a service supplier. He has loaned it to the office as his personal contribution to the suite décor. The painting is quite valuable."

Sylvia had been told by Ian to look out for such a painting, comment on it, if possible, and note it as a reference point if she saw it. Why, she didn't understand yet.

"And I am glad to see you have an eye for art. It looks like a metal street sign, but the medium is oil paint on oak; an oak panel made from boards."

Sylvia gushed a bit, commenting on the finish and the artistic impression. She was happy she had struck a little chunk of gold; a bonding point with Mrs. Cadwallader.

The Welsh woman added, "The artist wants his work to last, for posterity. He says that in a century or so, he prefers a museum to pay a restorer using traditional techniques rather than someone removing rust from metal. He has a sense of modern taste but a passion for traditional materials. I hope we buy more of his work in time."

Sylvia moved away a step.

"Well, thank you for that explanation, too. Anytime I am here I can look at it as I wait; a little pleasure in my day."

Cadwallader smiled. "I'll let you get back, then. Still have that number?"

Sylvia smiled. "Oh yes, ma'am; the army makes you remember numbers."

It wasn't only four digits she had to memorize; it was everything about the encounter. At Heathrow now, not City airport, she would meet Ian and review the meeting with Cadwallader while it was still fresh. Then he would ask questions that occurred to him. She had a lot of experience with being debriefed.

16 CASINO

Catrin, Isabelle and Bo Digsby timed the operation for 1.35 a.m., two days later, a night of heavy intermittent showers keeping people off the streets.

It took a little time for 'Sinjun', as Howard St. John-Leer had become abbreviated to during the intense planning process, to answer his phone.

Both Digsby and Isabelle were looking apprehensive as Catrin dialed the number. The casino exective sounded only half-awake and annoyed for the first few seconds.

At least he answered. The alternative, seeing as they were in a vehicle nearby, was to bang on his front door.

"Mr. St. John-Leer? This is Detective Inspector Sayer."

"Yes; who?"

"I said, I am Detective Inspector Sayer, sir, with the Metropolitan Police Art and Antiques Unit at New Scotland Yard."

"Antiques; at 1.30 in the morning? What's this about?"

She put an officious tone into her response. "You are Mr. Howard St. John-Leer, I take it? Can you confirm that, please?"

"Yes. No, it's a police officer. I don't know… I am just explaining to my wife; she has woken up, too."

"We ask for your help in a confidential and urgent matter. You own a painting called, 'Dice Seven' by Juris Martinov, I understand?"

"Yes, it's mine."

"May we disturb you to examine it, please; now? We are just leaving Whitehall and heading to your home."

"It's not here; it's in the office where I work at the casino."

"Casino?"

"The Ballantine Casino in Chiswick. It's there."

"One moment."

They could hear him talking to his wife as they waited. Digsby was now smiling.

"Sir, if you could get dressed. A police car will collect you at home and take you to your office. We will head there ourselves; it will be easier to explain, face-to-face. The car should be there in about ten minutes."

The officers in the vehicle transporting 'Sinjun' had been instructed to say nothing but flash the lights a lot. Catrin set off, having a head start.

"See," said Isabelle to Bo Digsby. "Even a member of the top brass loses their sense of self-importance when you drag them from their bed at one in the morning."

St. John-Leer was of average height and unremarkable features, other than a neat moustache contrasting with his day-old stubble. The finance VP of the casino had dressed hurriedly, but still wore a striped dress shirt and formal dark grey pants, Catrin noticed. His only concession to informality was that he wore a waterproof windbreaker instead of a suit jacket. His hair wasn't as well-groomed as he would like, she expected, with spiky bits sticking up at the back.

After introductions, she said, "Let me begin by thanking you for coming here at this hour on a wet night. This matter is a criminal investigation, one which has nothing to do with you, sir, or your work of art. Let me immediately put your mind at rest on that point.

"We need to examine the painting, though, if we may, with a device that DC Digsby has with us. It shouldn't take long. The procedure is non-invasive and will not harm the painting at all."

Digsby was carrying two cases. One was a computer case and the other, a little larger, a hard-sided instrument case.

They had met up inside the still-busy casino foyer. In the car bringing him to the casino, Sinjun had called ahead to his on-duty security chief, a woman called Francesca de la Puente, a Spaniard.

De la Puente was in a dark trouser suit, with a face and figure to die for and an expression that suggested she was no pushover, whether they were police officers or not. Independent of the sight of the Met vehicle and the uniformed officer bringing the executive into the building, she insisted on seeing the warrant cards of Catrin and her colleagues.

Her examination was not cursory, either. Catrin could see her lips move slightly and silently, as she memorized the names.

She accompanied them to the executive area.

"Examine the painting, but to do what precisely?" de la Puente asked, once they were in the quieter office area.

Digsby spoke up.

"It's a portable X-ray fluorescence monitor. It shows the composition of the underlying paint and layout materials, such as charcoal. The instrument is like a body scanner at an airport security check, revealing images of materials underneath the surface."

Wow thought Catrin. Digsby sounded coherent, even knowledgeable. His choice of the security scanner was a good comparison for the security officer.

Francesca still looked concerned but spoke formally. "It does not present a radiation risk to people here or further way, in the casino, perhaps?"

"None at all."

"It does not connect to a computer?"

He shook his head. "Not to any of yours. It's an older model. It connects only by cable to the laptop we use to display the images. There is no connection to your network."

"Good. That would not be allowed. We allow nothing to connect to the casino executive system at all, as it is fully isolated. But I insist to be there during the process, assuming Mr. St. John-Leer agrees to you making this examination of his painting, of course."

Sinjun was looking bleary-eyed but agreed to the request. A waiter had just brought in a tray with coffee and tea for everyone. He said, "Thank you, Francesca. I am sure we can rely upon your capable support."

Catrin and Isabelle made a fuss of the painting as they took it down from its mount. Meanwhile, Digsby was setting up what looked to be a tripod topped by a large power drill. He pointed it at the surface and fiddled with controls on the back after connecting a cable to the laptop.

Isabelle began the examination of the back of the painting, calling out meaningless details to Catrin, who noted them down. They had rested the work across the arms of one of the lounge chairs at a height that worked for the tripod. As they turned the work around, so the image was facing the tripod, Digsby coerced de la Puente into holding one corner, 'to keep it vertical and assure its stability' as he moved the probe closer to the painting surface.

"The background, first," said Isabelle, pointing at a spot.

Catrin stepped back, pointing towards the inner office. "Mr. St. John-Leer, perhaps I could explain a little, in confidence, while my staff members carry out the test. I think I owe you that."

With his office door closed, he motioned her to easy chairs surrounding a small meeting table by the window. He said, "I saw your picture in the news a little while ago. That stabbing case. Your friend was a witness, I recall?"

"You are right, sir, you have a good memory. My daughter was with her during the incident."

"A sad affair, Inspector. It's not an easy time for you, if you are up tonight as well."

"This is a somewhat urgent enquiry, beyond our control or planning. In fact, it has more to do with your line of expertise than mine."

He sipped his coffee and looked a little more awake.

Catrin continued with, "This is confidential. A certain member of an important family has got himself into trouble in a private, elite-only, gambling group in Europe. At one point a painting, one of Juris Martinov's 'Dice' series, exchanged hands in settlement of a twelve thousand euro debt. It was moved on within their social sphere and its new owner is now claiming it is a near-worthless copy."

St. John-Leer asked, "An important family? You mean aristocracy, politicians, or what?"

"Both. They often are, aren't they? But I can't be more

open, I am afraid. Several people are potentially facing charges, including the person I mentioned. Embarrassing gambling losses are one thing, but if the painting is a fraud, it's a charge that will be very damaging to an important family at a sensitive time, once the media get hold of it. I'm sure you understand?"

He nodded, "I think so, although I haven't a clue who you are talking about. We hear of these sort of uncontrolled gambling clubs quite bit in our business. They often have disputes that tear them apart. But fraud, as well; I see. It has a different dimension to it."

Catrin responded, "You have the background, as much as I can share. Superintendent Murray said you would be on-board quickly."

St. John-Leer looked surprised. "Tony Murray? That's right, he is with the Metropolitan Police, I recall. I last saw him at the reunion two years ago. But he didn't know I had the painting. How did you, may I ask?"

She smiled. "We did a quick check on you with him before we called. He was woken up, too. He said you are trustworthy, a good man, which is why we called at such an hour. How we knew? Well, we checked the Customs and Excise database for any Juris imports. Your painting was both the closest in location to us and from the same series, so it was a fortunate find, given the time pressure."

He smiled. "A good man, Tony. We played First Eleven's cricket together, you know?"

Yesterday afternoon, Moore had spoken to Superintendent Murray. She had conveyed that St. John-Leer wasn't quite a 'good man'.

She smiled conspiratorially. "He didn't say that. Now, what's going on out there? Your painting is genuine. We have every reason to believe that. It is close in the output sequence of works by the artist to the painting that has just been similarly examined in Europe. If the underlying structure of each is a close match, in the choice of paints and the layout drawing style, it will be an indication that the painting in question is genuine, too. If it differs markedly from the one in Europe, well... that will show also. The charges, as I said, could make things more difficult for the accused.

"DC Howlett and DC Digsby shouldn't be too long. Howlett trained at the Courtauld Institute; she is very experienced."

She stood. "Shall we check on the process? Then I will have the car take you home."

As they exited his office, she saw Digsby standing back from the computer. He was looking around the room, somewhat bored, it seemed. Howlett was focused on the screen, absorbed in the image.

"Can we go back to the manganese spectrum, please?" she asked Digsby.

He bent over the device and pressed a button, studied a small screen on the instrument itself before turning a dial.

'That's good. Perfect, in fact," said Isabelle.

She moved the cursor around the new screen image on the laptop, although it was showing little resemblance to the finished painting.

Nothing was said for another minute or so. They all just watched Isabelle and the screen, other than the bored technician. He was now looking at an unreceptive Francesca sitting on an office chair by a computer at the reception desk. Clearly, she was already tiring of the process. Isabelle was saving sections of the image and separately making notes.

Howlett suddenly looked at Digsby and nodded,

saying, "We are done."

It sounded like a statement rather than a question, but Catrin knew it was really a check with Digsby whether he had finished. He nodded imperceptibly and turned around to switch off the equipment and began putting it away in its case.

Howlett approached them. "Ma'am…"

"Go on. It's Mr. St. John-Leer's property, after all," said Catrin, indicating that she could speak in front of the owner.

"Comparing it with the information from… our colleagues across the water, I think the two paintings have nearly identical layout styles and pigment sequences. It's a powerful case for both being genuine."

Catrin raised her eyebrows slightly at the casino executive. His face showed he understood.

"Thank you, Howlett. A moment."

She gently took St. John-Leer's arm and steered him back towards his office door a few steps. "It looks like our friend may have scraped through any fraud charge, at least. If so, I will make sure Superintendent Murray is aware of the assistance you and your staff provided."

"Thank you. I'm glad it's appreciated. But I thought Tony was in a general operational type role; logistics, he said. This sounds more… diplomatic-type stuff."

She smiled. "I can't comment further there, either, I'm afraid. But I'll make sure he is aware."

On the way back, Catrin drove. "Satisfactory?" she asked Digsby, once they were on the move.

"Yes, it worked for me. Thank you for all the help, ma'am."

Isabelle said, "That security person, Francesca, was monitoring us carefully the whole time. She wouldn't take her eyes off us."

"As was her security camera," said Digsby.

There was a lengthy pause. Then Isabelle asked, "So what, may I ask, did you do? I don't get it."

Digsby responded, glancing at Catrin. "I shouldn't say. So I won't."

Catrin nodded. "If it achieved the goal that Superintendent Lauder set, that's fine. I think I am ready to head home, get a little sleep before my daughter wakes for a feed."

Isabelle said, "I'll be in late, ma'am."

She looked at Digsby, challenging him to comment.

He muttered, "Can you drop me at the Hammersmith Underground? I'll get picked up there and head into the office. I have more work to do now."

His head burrowed into his phone as he contacted someone from Undertow by text.

17 CEMETERY

DS Ian Underhill and Sylvia parked separately near the South Ealing Cemetery, enjoying the fine weather. It was one of several locations they had chosen for debriefing meetings.

Ian, like most experienced handlers, wanted those meetings face-to-face in person, not by phone, whether audio or visual. He needed to read his partner; her mood, reaction and state of mind, as much as to give her instructions or process the information received for transfer to his team.

The meeting venues included South Ealing Cemetery, car parks near London City airport and Heathrow, a pizza restaurant at Kew Bridge and a café in King's Cross Station, if Sylvia was doing a drop off in Central London.

On pleasant days, Sylvia wanted to get some fresh air and walk as much as possible, now she was spending so much time driving a limo for the casino. Debriefing at the cemetery let her do that. The work hours of the little limo company servicing the Ballantine Casino were long and unpredictable, as Sylvia knew they would be.

There were delays associated with their client's arrivals at Heathrow, or a traffic foul-up that prevented another driver getting to an appointment. Every day, Frank Loomis had to adjust the schedule, often as not through Vivian on his mobile, as he was on the road himself.

The high-end cars and the uniforms made the service appear plush. In reality, it wasn't far from a shoestring operation.

Dating from the mid-nineteenth century, graves at the cemetery varied from ancient to new. As they walked, one or other of them commented occasionally on a particular gravestone or an inscription. At first glance, they could be taken by locals to be tourists.

She said to Ian, "I have been making a fuss about the lattes in the balcony coffee shop when I am between trips. They are expensive, so I mention it is my special treat and I make each one last. The tables there give an excellent view across to the Executive Suite entrance and cover a lot of the casino floor below.

"What I see ties in with the snippets of information gleaned from Frank and Kevin after they meet up with clients in the suite foyer, plus my own experiences in there. Only authorized staff members enter or leave, generally the line managers, the security manager and several people with treasury roles. And special visitors on business, of course.

"One employee was brought up and fired there, then escorted out of the building. His name is Zac or Zack; he's Asian, but I didn't get more than that. No reason was given in the gossip, but he is a table dealer."

"We'll look into it."

"My biggest break this week was that I took one of the

target's guests to Heathrow. His accent was from some-where in the Baltic; not Finnish or Swedish, as I know those accents. He's a Mr. S. Kryov, which sounds Russian. I don't know more about him and he wasn't conversational in the car, nor did he make any calls I could understand. On one call the word Humberside was mentioned, twice."

Humberside Airport thought Ian.

"No dates or times?"

"Not that I could understand. No."

Ian paused before replying, eyes on a gravestone.

"We'll have to fix you up with a recorder if you have access to calls like that. But it increases the risk. You know that?"

"I was trained; yes. I understand. I could be spotted, or the recorder could screw up in some way."

Ian added, "Or picked up on a mobile RF detector. They are smaller than mobile phones these days. It would blow your cover."

He was now watching her, judging her reaction. Sylvia said nothing for a moment then responded tersely.

"It goes with the job; there is always some risk."

Ian gave her a searching look. "And apart from that new wrinkle, how are you feeling?"

"A little frustrated. It's a waiting game, I know, but these are interminable days on the road with little information of use to us, I feel. I know I can't force the issue but… it is frustrating, as I said."

"Your next day off is Wednesday. Are you staying local, in role, or what?"

"I haven't decided."

"Well, take a break. Say you are away visiting your mother that day. Go meet up with your partner; pick somewhere and have an enjoyable dinner and relax, on expenses. We want you to mention your parents and their health problems, for one thing. It'll give you the opportunity to do that on your return. Some time spent away from the role should help you."

Her fictional parent's health was part of her cover, but linked more to the exit phase, she knew. She had got nothing of substance yet, as far as she was aware. Her face clouded over. The people in Undertow were keeping their options open, but they, too, were wondering if this undercover placement was meeting their needs.

Ian said softly, "There's no rush; it may turn around. Don't sweat it, take it as it comes. Anything else?"

She thought for a moment. "Nothing I can think of."

Ian said, "Again, don't dwell on the issue of progress. You do your job, I'll do mine. The bosses in Undertow have a bigger picture than either of us. Leave it to them to call the shots on our work."

He seemed so experienced. She was glad to be working with him.

18 ORANGE

At the end of the following week, Catrin inadvertently turned Detective Constable Derek Nkrumah into a local hero in Greenwich.

Well, for a few days of newsclips there, at least. Sayer hadn't exactly planned it that way. In fact, she was accompanying him on an enquiry in the borough to see how he performed, given the concerns raised by DCI Wetherby.

In doing so, she was taken back to earlier times in her work in Brixton and with those thoughts, yet another reflection on her chosen career direction.

DS John Obi had left on holiday mid-week. It was big trip; he and his family were visiting Kenya with his parents, a chance to meet relatives for the first time. He would be on holiday for nearly three weeks.

On the Friday, a call early afternoon from the station inspector in the Royal Borough of Greenwich had started the case. It was a request for assistance with a minor art theft, but one with relationship issues for the Met with a borough politician.

A painting by an art student, Janice Sowell, had been stolen from a temporary exhibition. She was the winner of a local competition. Four of her paintings were on display for a month at the Greenwich Centre, a municipal complex.

As the station inspector finished the report to Catrin, he added, "A councillor is now involved, and she isn't partial to the Met, so if we could deal with this with no additional aggravation, it would be very much appreciated. If someone from Art and Antiques turns up it will show everyone we are taking the matter seriously."

Catrin took down the details and walked out of her office. Both DC Howlett and DC Nkrumah were at their desks. She went across to Nkrumah.

"Derek, one for you, seeing as Isabelle is probably counting the minutes until she gets on the Eurostar to Paris. It's not chasing any Rembrandt, this one, but the Greenwich borough wants a little of our time. Here are the details; a theft, apparently."

Nkrumah gave a brief frown as he looked at the clock. It was a Friday; the weather was sunny and warm and he and his girlfriend had plans for a weekend away. He also lived west of London. Now he was being sent south-east, across the Thames. If this one dragged on, they would need to change his plans for the evening, at least.

Sayer caught the transient smile on Isabelle Howlett's face as she read the expression on Nkrumah's. She added suddenly, "Tell you what, it's a nice day. Why don't I come with you, see you at work and get me out of here? I've been in one office or another all week."

She couldn't read whether he was happy about that or she was adding insult to injury.

They made excellent time to Greenwich.

The Greenwich Centre is a modern complex, housing leisure and fitness facilities, a swimming pool and the local library, all located just down the road from the big tourist trap, the National Maritime Museum.

Once inside, a staff member took the detectives to a curved wall with three almost-similar orange panels, works in oil on canvas. Two were in sequence, then there was a space where the third painting should have hung. The fourth painting now looked like a lonely outlier.

"And the title of the specific item stolen?" asked Nkrumah. He was trying not to be judgmental. They had spent the last few minutes listening to Mr. Holland, so he could hazard a guess, but with his boss watching he followed protocol.

Holland's first words after meeting them had been, "Well, I am a librarian, really, not an art curator; I just take care of the display section here."

"Orange 3," Mr. Holland replied. "I don't know what we will do now. We are waiting on the artist to advise us, but she is not responding to our calls or texts yet. Her email account says she is on holiday."

"Do now?" Nkrumah responded.

"Whether we leave a space where it was or move Orange 4 over. If we do that, it will alter the installation dramatically. If we don't, it will dislocate the work; destroy the ambiance. People will lose the flow…"

Nkrumah cut across the speech. "Do you get many people through?"

"Well, it's a leisure centre. People use the library and many pass through this corridor, so yes. Quite a few people stopped to look at the installation. More came through on the first day, when the artist was here. She is personable; enthusiastic."

They had already established the timing. The painting

had disappeared during the previous evening, before closing.

Catrin had already pointed out silently to Nkrumah a student seen carrying a large portfolio case, passing by. The Centre was close to the University of Greenwich. If someone was in the corridor alone, they could have grabbed the artwork.

The librarian continued, "The news of the robbery seems to be out locally, now that Councillor Hewitt has expressed her outrage publicly, so a lot more people are looking as they come through. They say there is no such thing as bad publicity. But we can't show them the installation close up, with the roping off of the wall area. Visitors seemed to find the police tape to be fascinating; almost artistic itself."

The title of the exhibit was 'Day'. Canvases of streaked oranges, blues and yellows, with subtle differences in their tones, each with a white circle making its way in an arc from canvas one to canvas four.

"Sunrise to sunset," said Sayer, as she looked at it.

Catrin was waiting to see if Nkrumah wanted to bring in a forensic specialist; it wasn't a hard decision. A theft of a student painting wouldn't bring out the Flying Squad and a wall covered in fingerprints added nothing to the investigation.

"Where's the artist, this Janice Sowell?" Derek asked.

That is a good question, thought Catrin. To begin with, let's find out more from her.

Holland responded, "That's the thing; we don't know. She is still not contactable, and she should have responded by now; it has been nearly a day. The college says they left her a message and other students have been coming in. Even on holiday, with her biggest show yet, you think she would have called me back by now."

"Does her voicemail also tell you she is on holiday?"

"No. Just her email bounce-back. Her voicemail says leave a message, and I have left two."

Nkrumah said, "We'll follow up with her. Was anyone else involved in creating the work or assisting with the set-up; that sort of thing?"

He had the artist's contact information in the file.

Holland shook his head. "No, it was all hers. Her boyfriend, I think it was that, or a male friend, anyway, was with her the day she came to set up. When she found out about the theft, I expected her to be here in a jiffy, crying her eyes out."

They had enough details now, and a photo of the work that was missing.

When they were alone, leaving the building, Catrin asked, "What do you recommend now?" She wanted his assessment.

He grimaced and checked his watch; 3.25 p.m. "The locals want feedback on our observations, so they can say we were here. The theft is unrelated to the painting's value. It was personal, for spite, or an act by someone with an unhealthy fixation on the student.

"They will need to check with the boyfriend, the one who helped with the setup, if the artist is away; and follow up with her when she shows. But there is no art issue for us here, I would say."

He paused. "You'll need to head home and see to Mair soon, so I can call it in."

She waited him out. He looked at his watch again.

He continued, "But it worries me that the artist hasn't shown up. Her address is further south in the borough. When you leave, I may get one of the locals to drive me over there."

Catrin's face showed her approval. "Too right, we should check her out; an artist not responding to this news. I'll get plenty of time with Mair, probably at three in the morning. Let's go see her ourselves, at least, if she is home."

Janice Sowell's apartment was in Wickham Road, a four-storey, ordinary-looking block built in the seventies.

As they walked to the stairway, Catrin noticed that one lift was out of order, the notice said, and somewhere higher up, she could hear the doors of the second lift banging, as if someone was blocking their closure.

A group of teenagers in the stairwell examined them before moving over slowly and reluctantly, to let the two detectives turn the corner. One said something into a mobile; another climbed the stairs, two at a time. They had them typed at least, Catrin thought; police, or official-dom. She was sure that they were warning someone.

After they passed by them, the oldest teen, a girl, said. "Can I help you?" Her tone was balanced between politeness and insolence.

Another person giggled.

Nkrumah shook his head and smiled. "No, thanks." Then, on instinct, he said, "Janice Sowell lives on the third floor. Do you know her?"

The girl nodded. "The artist. Yes. She's OK. But I don't think she is there; we haven't seen her today, have we?"

Her question was to her friends, who said nothing, eyes on Nkrumah.

Sayer and Nkrumah turned and made their way up the stairwell.

They got no response from ringing the doorbell, or by

knocking. A neighbour further along the walkway came out of her own flat.

"You want Janice?" she asked.

Nkrumah responded, "Is she around?"

"I've not seen her. She is probably down at the college or the Centre; Janice has a big show… why?"

"She's not on holiday then?"

"Not as you would put it. She works part-time at the Tesco Express and took time off for her show. Is she in trouble?"

He asked, "Is it that obvious?"

"That you two are coppers? Yes, what do you think? That I talk to every Tom, Dick and Harry about the people who live here? Is she in trouble, I asked."

Catrin spoke. "Not that we know of. One of her paintings was stolen from the Centre and we are looking into it, but the email bounce-back said she was on holiday."

The woman's face showed her concern. "I don't know a thing about emails and bounce backs, love. But something must be wrong. She has been living and dying this show for two weeks now."

She moved forward a step or two and knocked on the front door of the apartment next to Sowell. An older woman opened it.

"Lucy, you have Janice's spare key, don't you? These two are coppers looking for her. It's something to do with her art going missing."

"She'll be at the show or classes."

"She isn't there. We need to check if she is OK, see if she is ill or something."

The older woman looked suspiciously at Nkrumah. "Can I see some ID, please?

Both Nkrumah and Sayer pulled out their warrant

badges.

The woman disappeared momentarily and reappeared with a key ring. She said firmly, "I'll open the door, if you don't mind."

Nkrumah said, "Be my guest." He looked at Catrin, who smiled. They didn't have a warrant to enter and they had insufficient reason at present to enter themselves.

Lucy led the way to Sowell's front door, pushed the key in the lock and gave it a heavy turn while muttering, "It's always stiff, this one."

The door opened and the woman called out, "Janice!"

Derek, who was behind her, saw the flash of orange on the floor; a broken painting frame, and a ripped canvas. He eased the older lady to one side by one arm and said, "If you don't mind… wait here."

They had probable cause to enter now.

He led and Catrin followed.

As Derek adjusted to the light change as he passed through the door, he saw that the painting on the floor seemed to be one of the series from the gallery.

"Not good," said Catrin, now just behind him, taking in the same sight. She turned to the neighbours. "Don't enter; wait here."

Nkrumah found the light switch and turned on the light, calling out, "Janice? Janice Sowell. It's the police."

Closer to the missing painting, Nkrumah could see that it had been hacked with a knife or some similar instrument.

As the two police officers moved further in, they could see no-one in the adjacent kitchen. They entered a short corridor with doors to the bedroom, toilet, and bathroom. No-one was in the bedroom, but a woman's clothes were on the bed, as if someone had just got undressed. It was Sayer who walked past Derek into the bathroom and found Sowell there.

Janice Sowell was lying in the bath in her underwear and a nightdress with a Wharhol soup can print on the front. Her legs were together, bent at the knees and rested on one side, her head resting on the bath edge on the same side. There was a red-brown mess around her left arm, with striations, tendrils of dark red stain stretching from mid-thigh towards her feet. For a moment, Catrin couldn't distinguish between the red of the soup can print and the blood.

She had apparently sliced her left wrist.

"She's here!"

As Derek's entered, Catrin pulled out her mobile and called it in.

Nkrumah's first thought was that although there was blood in the water, there wasn't enough; Sowell hadn't bled out. But she was dead, he thought.

For a second, he wasn't going to touch her but then he felt for a pulse on her neck. Her skin was icy, as was the water, but he found the pulse, weak and irregular. Closer to her head now, he could see that she was breathing shallowly.

He said, "She's alive, but really cold."

Catrin slipped off her jacket and pushed up her sleeves. "Let's get her out of there." She reached for the knees as Nkrumah, now also in shirt sleeves, got his hands under the woman's back and armpits before they lifted her.

Between them, they got Sowell out of the bath and carried her to the bedroom floor. They rolled her to the semi-prone position and checked that her airway was clear.

The cut wrist started bleeding again and Derek

grabbed a piece of clothing off the bed, a thin top, and bound it over the wound. Catrin retrieved the phone she had put down after asking for an ambulance urgently.

"She's so cold. Boss, get towels or something. Warm them in the microwave, perhaps."

Catrin walked the kitchen, grabbed two tea towels and threw them in the microwave. As the appliance hummed away, she took a stab at finding others, opening drawers. She could hear Nkrumah rubbing away with a towel from the bathroom, drying the woman.

As she returned with the warm towels, she found one neighbour had entered to help. The woman had grabbed a duvet; whether out of modesty to cover Janice up or to warm her, Catrin was not sure.

"I heard," she said. "Lucy has gone to call an ambulance."

I have done that, Catrin thought, and I am on the line. Instead, she replied, "No; these first," taking the warm tea towels and putting them on Sowell's back and chest under the duvet. "We need to bring her core temperature up slowly."

On the dresser, Catrin saw a water glass and two prescription containers, one empty and neither with the lid screwed on. White pills were loose on the surface. "Derek; it appears that she may have taken this medication, too."

Catrin spoke again to the emergency operator. She indicated that a drug overdose was possibly involved and started reading out the labels on the bottles of tablets she had found.

A few minutes later, two uniformed police officers entered, followed almost as quickly by an ambulance team of two paramedics. The room changed from being nearly empty to overcrowded, with voices on radios and Nkrumah briefing them about the steps they had taken. Catrin listened carefully; he did that well.

They withdrew afterwards to the front room, where they could examine the damaged painting. One of the officers came out and said, "Sorry ma'am, but could you wait outside now, please? DS Reed is on his way and is taking over the investigation."

"He's with your borough, right?" asked Catrin. The officer confirmed it. Of course, she thought, it is a crime scene, and this is the borough's patch.

They watched as the paramedics wheeled the gurney carrying Sowell to the lift. The two neighbours were comforting each other after the shock. Other people had appeared to watch, in response to the police presence.

Lucy said to the other woman, "He was very good, wasn't he?"

She was referring to Nkrumah, who looked surprised.

"The way you took charge. It's what we expect from a copper. Right, Anne?"

"Too right. Not having one of them picking on our kids."

Catrin's mind went back to the teenagers on the stairs, the phone call and the boy racing to warn someone. They were involved in drug buys, she concluded. That real-isation, with the discovery of a person unconscious or dead, took her back to her time as a uniformed constable with the drug squad in Brixton.

Wisely, both officers just acknowledged the somewhat backhanded compliment with a nod and said nothing.

Later, after Catrin dropped Nkrumah at a Tube station so he could head home, she thought Derek would make much better time on the London Underground than she would on the roads.

His last comment was, "She was lucky we got there when we did."

Catrin agreed. "And that she decided to end it in the bath, as well. The water cooled fast. It slowed the bleeding. Slitting the wrist is a tricky thing and many people muck it up, thank goodness. And the cold water slowed her metabolism, reducing the effectiveness of the tablets."

Nkrumah suddenly realised. "You've seen this previously."

Catrin nodded. "Brixton. I did two years in support of the Drug Squad there, remember? Yes. Now get on home, talk to Anisha and don't brood on it."

Derek was dating another police officer, Anisha Green, a nice woman from Conwy, North Wales. Catrin had met her twice now. Occasionally, she ribbed Derek about learning Welsh.

His comment about her experience made her think. She had helped save a woman's life, as Jean had tried to do for Jemilah Kohli. Yet, when she took the call earlier from the borough, it was an intrusion into the real art crime work. She had moved a long way from her policing roots. She loved the work, but something was starting to niggle away at her.

In twenty-four hours, DC Nkrumah had found local fame in Greenwich. His unpaid, unwelcome publicity team of Lucy and her neighbour Anne had given his name to the reporter from the local newspaper. Catrin was left out of the picture, something for which she was heartily grateful.

By Monday, the Greenwich borough officers had tracked down and arrested Janice Sowell's boyfriend for the theft of the painting from Greenwich Centre.

The follow-up with Janice, once she regained consciousness and stabilized, made it clear that the case was not complicated.

Resentment and envy at her success and her total focus on the exhibition had been the drivers, the boyfriend claimed. He had stolen Orange 3 easily enough and taken it to her home to confront her. He slashed the canvas and told her they were finished before he stormed out.

Inspector Royce in Greenwich told Catrin that the former boyfriend did not impress anyone during the interview.

"He showed no remorse, putting it all on to her. Nor did he accept any part in her subsequent suicide attempt. Yet he knew she had moodswings and had received treatment for depression. For a month she had been on a bubbly high, he threw back at us. He hadn't seen it coming, he claimed."

Catrin briefed Wetherby. "Nkrumah did well; it's noted on his file. I doubt that the magistrate will look leniently on Sowell's boyfriend. I hope not. But the case is finished, from our perspective."

That gave Wetherby some satisfaction, seeing a case closed.

Two weeks later, Janice Sowell visited New Scotland Yard with her parents, to thank Nkrumah and Sayer.

It was an easy meeting, really, with the expressions of appreciation, a lighter chat about art and the stresses of being an art student, which moved on to Janice asking them about their roles as art detectives.

As the family left the building and Catrin and Derek returned to their area, she recalled her thoughts on the drive back from Greenwich and the earlier insight provided by Sandra Hunt. She had enough on her plate balancing work and life at home, so she wasn't going to instigate any changes, but if the right opportunity came along, she would be open to considering it. As much as she loved her work in art crime, it surprised her that she was thinking that way now.

19 DREAMS

On her day off, Sylvia and her partner spent most of it at Felixstowe Beach, given the weather forecast. She didn't want to be seen around the Bedford area with her current hairstyle and it was a place they had gone to several times, the first time together for their second date. It was busy, but she didn't mind that, enjoying the anonymity in the people enjoying the day at the sands.

She was struck how strange it seemed, to be in a quiet coastal corner of England after spending so much time in London. When she was back in her normal role in the county, she wouldn't think twice about Felixstowe being small. Everywhere around her now seemed small, compared with London.

Aidan, her partner, had changed shifts to fit her availability; it was part of the arrangement with the Bedfordshire Police. They both made a special effort to enjoy the limited time together when Sylvia was under-cover and had these opportunities.

A year earlier, on Sylvia's first undercover assignment, they had met up and it had been a disastrous day. He was coming out of an incident that had gone awry, and their tactical unit was under internal review. She was tense from her new experience of undercover life. They had argued and left each other feeling worse rather than better.

Aidan had just come back from a swim and, on his way up the sand, kicked a football back to a child trying to recover it. The child had kicked it back to him and, for a minute, Sylvia watched him play football with the kid.

Whe he sat down on his towel, to dry off, she said, "It suits you, playing dad or big brother."

He smiled. "But would it suit us, I wonder?"

He looked at her, waiting. In the past, such a hint would have been met with a silence or a change of subject.

"One day. Some day, I hope. But not yet."

Not while she was doing undercover work, she meant, and he understood it that way.

She said softly, "I'm having dreams again. They are waking me up."

He nodded, understanding. It had happened during both of her earlier assignments. She had spoken with a psychologist about it, part of the requirement for her role.

"The strain is getting to you, then. It's been going on for weeks now."

She grimaced. "I know. There is nothing specifically threatening, no identified risk. But day after day playing a role…"

Aidan stopped looking at her and focused on the sea. "The psychologist you see told you that dreams like this were natural, a way the mind releases the tension of the role; isn't that it?"

"Something like that, yes. I will talk to my handler about it, let them know."

"Good. You should."

She pushed at his shoulder. "You fraud! Sal told me at the party before I left that they had to drag you kicking and screaming into Dr. Lehman after the incident at Santa Pod."

The Santa Pod Raceway; a drag racing track near Bedford.

He looked wide-eyed with feigned innocence. "Me? Me! I led the pack, I tell you, first of my team through the door. She applauded me for my proactive behaviour."

"Dr. Lehman: she applauds people? Not in my experience. Before we get too deep in the hole you are digging, how about getting changed and having an early dinner?"

Before they went on their separate ways, she implied.

"Fish and chips?"

"No, something fancier. And more expensive. I'm paying."

Or not. Ian had said it was on expenses.

~~

"Sorry to hear the news. What was her name, Jem?"

Dominic Connolly had been briefed but found it better to appear more distant in the conversation with Michael Bolan. He made it the first item on the telephone call.

"Jemmy, one of Steve's people. Good sort. Hard worker, good at the tables, pleasant. Mikey says Steve is heart-broken; he thought the world of the girl. And Arkady is hell-bent on getting the bastard who did it. It's all Mikey can do to stop the boys going after Dogan's people, but I am firm on that. There is a lot of visibility at present. I don't want us to be part of that. We'll bide our time."

"Do you know who did it?"

"It's down to two in the Limmie's. But the instruction to hit one of mine came down from Dogan. We know that, even his precise words. Give one of Mikey's a rupture, Burcu said, to be precise. So, for me, a lot depends on whether this fishing expedition with Lauder goes anywhere."

Dominic said quickly, "We won't know that until something breaks or there is a leak in the Met. And I'm sure you are thinking of your parole."

"I am. It's part of the reason for the instruction to Mikey to avoid retaliation. But I'm convinced something will happen; you saw that Sayer was involved in the incident?"

Now that surprised Dominic. He hadn't heard that.

"No. How?"

"Her friend was the one who tried to help Jemma. At the time, she was taking Sayer's baby for a bit of fresh air. It was in the Standard, the picture of them. Sayer, her friend and another guy who helped. Sayer wasn't there, but she looked madder than hell in the photo."

He paused. "You know Mo. She said its fate. Something's going to happen, so I am biding my time."

Connolly shook his head. "Sayer is an art detective. The baby issue is a pure coincidence, Michael."

"I agree, Dom; logically. But Mo has a feeling about coincidence, and I have a very good reason, my own parole, to wait it out and see if she is right."

Connolly was trying to find the right words to respond, but Bolan spoke again.

"But once I am out, if Lauder doesn't follow though on the tip-off, I'm going to take Burcu Dogan out of the game. Permanently. I don't mind competition. Well, I hate it, but I can live with it. But this nutter, he's gone, I guarantee it."

Connolly replied, "So, let's hope that someone else does that for you."

In the years he had known Michael Bolan, the man had come across as calm and calculating. His voice had hardly changed but the anger in the man had showed through today.

He continued, "Can we talk about the powder coke shortfall resulting from the seizure in Spain?"

It was a relief to get back to normal business items.

20 KEW BRIDGE

Luckily, there was one assigned parking spot free for the pizza restaurant, located below the Kew Bridge approach. Her BMW didn't stand out in the other vehicles parked around the large Sainsbury's store in The Hollows. These were high-end shopping locations.

Ian had a table upstairs, watching the bridge and the water. The level in the Thames was high at present and, to Sylvia's eyes, there seemed to be less room underneath the arches of the bridge.

Once she was settled, they ordered food and started the debrief.

She said, "I've got something, perhaps it's significant. Twice now, in the executive suite, I have seen the same man carry a folio case into St. John-Leer's office. He works in the casino cage."

The vault and the cage area, the more visible area where client's cash is exchanged for chips, were the financial centre of the casino, both focused on money storage and use.

"I have many of the employees identified now, by

sight but not their names. I took a photo of the individual afterwards, from some distance away, as he left the building. It should be enough to identify him if you need to do so.

"The second time, I was in the executive reception, waiting for a visitor. Kevin was there also, waiting to take St. John-Leer to an airport, Luton, to the private jet location, he said. Before my client was ready to leave, St. John-Leer came to the foyer for his airport trip a minute after the employee from the cage delivered the folio case. St. John-Leer had an overnight bag and a pilot's briefcase, as Cadwallader said. I don't know if the folio case delivery and his departure are linked, but they could be.

"Before Kevin took him out, St. John-Leer smiled at me and said hello, asked me if I was settling in."

Underhill acknowledged the insight. "That's good. We'll check out the image and see if there is anything to it."

As Sylvia worked through other elements of her report, Ian judged the moment for him to flag the changes.

"You said Kevin had asked questions about your experience driving a Wolf last week? We checked. He hasn't served in the military, but his brother did, and it seems that Kevin has a strong interest."

"Yes, I got through it, mainly because I could justify leaving the conversation for a pickup. Frank had mentioned it to the other drivers, I found out. As I said, I feel a bit thin in that area of my cover."

Ian responded, "Well, we want you to be pushier about the army background. To do that, you will need a deeper briefing. We have arranged for someone from the Royal Horse Artillery, a Captain Sarah Hollingsworth, to brief you, to provide a solid experience background.

Before then I have files from her for you to read."

Sylvia nodded. "She has been overseas?"

"Yes, two tours, the last one in charge of a ground transport services unit. She nearly lost a driver in that tour, I gather; he was severely injured in a roadside attack. Hollingsworth can cover other incidents involving the Wolf with you. And she has an idea regarding visibility of the supposed army experience. You'll need this."

He smiled as he passed over a small tubular device with a side-hook holding a covered blade, a Resqme escape tool. "Bright Orange, to be visible."

She knew what it was; a vehicle escape device, for cutting seatbelts and breaking tempered glass. It was connected to a white lanyard.

He added, "She'll probably tell you that they used the butts of weapons to break vehicle windows, not that. But it may help."

~~

The following morning at 7.45 a.m., Sylvia turned up at the Aldershot Garrison near Farnborough.

Captain Sarah Hollingsworth was in her mid-thirties. The army officer wasn't particularly tall, but she had presence, exhibiting an air of quiet authority as they walked and talked.

Sylvia saw that Hollingsworth's complexion had seen too much sun over the years, it was lined and weathered.

They walked from the reception building through an array of corridors leading to a parking area with three similar vehicles in military camouflage. She selected one of them and turned to face Sylvia.

"So, a Land Rover Wolf. It looks like a civilian Land Rover Defender, but it has several differences and is considerably heavier. Did you read the files I provided?"

"Yes, ma'am."

"You are not army, so why not call me Sarah and I'll call you Alison, I gather? You don't use ranks in your job at present. In you get; let's take it for a drive. The Met says you are a police chauffeur, professionally trained?"

Sylvia nodded.

Hollingsworth asked, "Have you ever used a diff lock?"

A differential lock fitted to the rear axle, to make the wheels move synchronously, particularly on steep and uneven terrain.

"On a tractor, yes, in my teens, on a farm. But I have never driven a road vehicle with one."

Hollingsworth laughed. "These days, I am surprised chauffeurs can use a clutch, with so many of them driving automatics. Let's go for a spin, starting out down that small road over there. Later on, you'll be wondering if any of the route will become level and solid ground again."

She climbed into the passenger side.

As Sylvia climbed into the driver's seat and adjusted the seat and mirrors, she thought, 'OK Captain Hollingsworth. I guess I am doing my driving test all over again, for you this time. Will you want a handbrake turn in this vehicle, I wonder?'

The trip turned out to be a far more interesting challenge than a handbrake turn. After a while, Sylvia found it enjoyable, putting the vehicle through its paces.

Half an hour later, they returned to the parking area. Sylvia was glad it wasn't her job to take the Wolf through a car wash; the mud coming off it would clog the drains.

Hollingsworth asked, "Feel that you can talk about the Wolf now?"

"Yes, thank you; it was very instructive."

The officer said, "You did well; even allowing for the fact that you are a trained police officer."

"Thank you. One question. This Resqme escape tool I received yesterday. I am told that you suggested that?"

"Yes, I did. I have one myself, a great little thing in a tight spot. After all, you can't exactly carry a standard issue bayonet around to cut through seat belts after a crash, can you? Not in this country, anyway. There are too many knives around as it is, if you ask me. But it is visible and it gives you the opportunity to strike up conversations where you can raise army driving skills, I hope. That's what DS Underhill wanted, I was told, a chance to pretend you were one of us."

She paused. "Sorry, it didn't come out right. I'm sure you have your share of the 'Oh my God, why did I sign up for this' heebie-jeebies, too."

Sylvia puckered her lips before responding. "You could say that."

As they parted, Sarah Hollingsworth shook hands and in doing so, said, "Good luck, and as I say to my team, 'safe one out; safe one home'. I know you are out there already, so I'll just wish you the best for whatever you are doing and a safe return."

PART 2. CASINO

21 TOOL

Sylvia closed the limousine door quietly. She had been holding it open for Mr. St. John-Leer to enter. As he settled in the back seat, she moved to the driver's side, entered and fastened her seatbelt. Next, she picked up the lanyard with the Resqme emergency tool and placed it around her neck before starting the vehicle, taking her time to do so, but being careful to avoid a glance in the rear-view mirror.

As the engine purred in the background, he asked, "Why are you wearing the lanyard? I saw you wear it on the last trip I had with you; I meant to ask then."

"An emergency tool, sir, for breaking windows and cutting seatbelts. It's perfectly safe. The tool has no sharp edges sticking out to cut anyone."

Leave it there, intuition told her. Checking her mirrors, she set off, catching that he was still focused on the lanyard. Good.

A few seconds later, at the stop sign, she added, "It was part of my training. So I bought one recently."

He sat back in the seat to focus on something he

planned to take from his briefcase and read in the car, but his mind was on the issue.

"The other drivers don't have them."

Thank God he commented, she thought; I don't need to press the point.

"Mr. Loomis and the others are very experienced drivers. They know London and its byways in more detail than I do. They are also trained in defensive driving techniques. Mr. Loomis put me through my paces on those skills when I was interviewed, to make sure I met the standard."

As she turned into Green Dragon Lane on a shortcut to stay clear of an M4 snarl-up, she reminded herself to keep it conversationally light. "The army taught me to a different level, though; that's why I wear the lanyard in the vehicle. It becomes a habit."

"A different standard. What do you mean?"

"Offensive driver training, sir. If, for example, someone threatens my client or myself while travelling, and there is no obvious escape route, I see my job is to protect us. That mean ensuring the vehicle safety cage remains intact, as far as possible. The rest, well, we are in a two-ton weapon. If events deteriorate to that stage, there will be a lot of damage. I can't be messing about looking in a glove box for something to extricate us then, can I?"

"No, I suppose not. And hopefully will never need to use one."

"Yes sir, I hope so, too. But as you know, sir, some of our VIP clients carry large amounts of cash to and from the casino. Best be prepared, I was taught."

She could see St. John-Leer musing on the remark. All he said was, "Thank you for the clarification."

She let the matter drop, for him to mull it over.

At the airport, as she pulled his overnight case from the boot, St. John-Leer asked, "That thing earlier, the defensive, no, I mean, the offensive training; did you ever have to do that?"

He stared at her intently. Clearly, her message had stayed in his mind during the drive.

"In training or for real? I did it in practice, sir. For real, well, I can't say much on that, I'm afraid, even if I am a civilian now. But once, yes, I did, and got my passenger and me out of it in one piece, thank God. Mr. Loomis asked me about that, too. Have a pleasant flight, sir."

Two days later, Frank Loomis called her into his office. "I'm glad you seem to have made a hit with Mr. St. John-Leer, Alison. You, not me or Kevin, can do most of his airport runs from now on. You'll be out day and night, from our experience; he's as bad as the worst of the punters for anti-social hours. The man's a workaholic."

She smiled, "Well, Frank, that was why you hired me, to take on part of the load and get you set for retirement, you said. I thought he would go with Kevin or Howard though, them being here longer."

"No he specifically asked for you. Kevin is Mr. Suarez's driver, when he needs one. He has been Suarez's primary chauffeur for several years."

He mused on the news he was conveying, deciding whether to say something else.

"I don't think Mr. St. John-Leer is after you; at least I hope not. He always appears very proper. You never know, though. So stay alert there; for you and our little firm. I don't want any problems. If anything worries you on that score, bring it to me, OK?"

She smiled. "You've got it. I'll do my best for you, I

promise."

But I will take any problems I have to someone else, a man called Ian. And if what I have to do next causes those, I'm sorry, but that's my job.

~~

Bo Digsby had secured access to an exact model of the computer he had seen on the desk across from the Juris painting during the night visit with Sayer and Howlett.

Identification of the model, the assessment of the distances for the planned wireless contact, the checks on ways to insert the transmitter; all had been part of the reason for the art hoax perpetrated to get him inside the executive suite.

He and Ian Underhill had improvised the rest and had practiced the move themselves before 'Alison' was summoned to a meeting. She had just completed a drop-off at Heathrow and needed to return to the casino shortly.

The Undertow officers were waiting in the room at the Airport Hilton as the chauffeur knocked quietly on the door.

"Here's one idea we thought of; a suitcase tipping over would distract anyone watching the camera. Like this."

Digsby demonstrated the move, his knee catching the weighted suitcase at the top, tipping it before he could pull up the handle.

"As you kneel to retrieve it, use your left hand to grab the handle and the right to steady yourself on the desk. You will have already palmed the USB stick. As you stand, your back should conceal your right hand from the camera behind you, giving a second or so before you need to move away with the suitcase. Push the stick into either of the two USB ports here. It's a simple push, press the button and pull. The sleeve will stay inside."

"Is this like a regular USB drive, only inserting one way up?"

"No. Either way will work. Just make sure that you insert it all the way before you press the button."

She rehearsed the process for ten minutes, getting the flow right.

Ian said, "If it's not a first time hit, pull back or withdraw it without pushing the button. The sleeve will stay with you. Try again another day, with a fresh approach, if you see one. This is an exercise in situational opportunity."

He made it sound optional, a simple decision with no pressure. She wasn't to know that once she inserted it, they would reorganize the schedules of a bunch of police officers and associated personnel in London and East Anglia.

"I'll give it a go."

Ian smiled. Digsby looked as serious as ever as he spoke. "Now, give me back the stick. Ian will arrange to deliver the computer to your flat, to let you practice the move."

She seemed surprised but complied. He took out another identical piece of plastic and handed it to her. "This is the actual thing."

It took a week for Sylvia to find both the opportunity and confidence to complete the task.

In several visits to the executive centre beforehand, she had mentally rehearsed the move, thinking about potential opportunities. Tipping the case over was only a possibility if either Mr. St. John-Leer or his visitor had a suitcase. More often than not, they didn't.

But Eve, the receptionist, was always there until five p.m. After that, if it was a late pickup, Mrs. Cadwallader may be in her office or passing through reception.

On one occasion, Sylvia found herself alone, waiting until her client appeared, ready for the off. Even in a deserted office, she had the security cameras to consider.

She made a point of being pleasant to Eve, but not overdoing it. It turned out that the receptionist was a fan of C. J. Archer novels. Sylvia ran the alternative idea by Ian, who agreed it was worth a try.

The following day, she arrived early for a 3 p.m. pickup and found Eve at the reception desk.

"C. J. Archer; you like her books, you said? Have you read this one? It's her latest but…"

She paused in mid-sentence as she approached the desk, holding out the paperback with her left hand, the right apparently supporting her on the edge of the desk behind the computer as she reached over to pass the novel to Eve.

The receptionist focused on the novel. "No, I have it on hold at the library, though."

As Eve intently examined the book, Sylvia said, "It was left behind by a client I dropped off yesterday at Heathrow. She had finished it and didn't want to carry it back on the plane. That, and a conference folder giveaway, the reason she was visiting the UK. It's not the first time I've had clients do clear-outs of their carry-on bag in the back seat of the car on the way to an airport. But seeing this book made me think of our discussion. So, enjoy."

"It's nearly brand new, too. She must be a fast reader. Thanks, Alison, that's fantastic of you."

Sylvia smiled and looked up, seeing Mr. St. John-Leer

emerging from the internal corridor. She moved back and stood still. But by then the rest of the device Digsby had given her was back in her pocket.

She said, "Traffic is looking fine for the run, sir; as of five minutes ago."

It was only when she had dropped him off at Luton that she could let Ian know. And breathe a sigh of relief. She wasn't finished yet, she knew, in terms of tricky bits, but she had achieved a milestone.

It was a DC Amelia Tilson who had the job of confirming the range of contact between the tiny insert now resting in the far end of the USB port and her phone.

She had been all the way up and down the public staircase in the casino, the one that mirrored another labelled 'authorised staff only'. Oblivious to the sound carrying to others nearby, it was evidently an argument on the subject of her gambling. How much she spent was her affair, she hissed loudly into the phone; it was her money.

It was intense enough to make people stay away from her and, near the bottom of the staircase, she turned around to give whoever it was some more not-so-private feedback as she retraced her route. Half-way up she stood still. After a minute or so of silence and sobs, she angrily closed the call and headed for the nearest women's washroom.Anywhere above the halfway point or higher was in range of the computer, her phone told her.

The insert was now powered by the host computer, but they had made no attempt to penetrate the system. When that took place, Digsby and other members of the Digital Intelligence Team would be responsible for reaping the benefit of all the effort put into the operation so far.

22 NOD

On Saturday, Chris was happily away for the day, playing in a five-a-side football match in Welwyn Garden City. He had less time for practice sessions these days.

Catrin took Mair to the Cwmbran Kiln. They were in the workshop area, the baby in her bouncer placed on the floor, near to the workbench where she could watch her mother. Catrin divided her time between a new piece of ceramic art and caring for her child.

She and Jean had talked about the piece they were making. It was a present, in a sense; Jean had picked out an old design previously unused and made the bisque, the first firing, a blank work surface for Catrin to decorate. After Catrin's part, there would be a subsequent glazing and firing.

Jean had called Catrin with the idea. "It'll please Liz, after my blues at the dinner with Ginny. And it will make Saturday feel normal, having you working away in the back of the Kiln."

Jean and Melanie were in the shop, with Chloe and Lili. Two customers were browsing and asking questions.

It was a typical Saturday lunchtime.

Catrin heard the door chime ping as it opened. There was a sudden yell, a young male voice. "You fucking well saw nothing, d'ya hear?"

An almighty crash of pottery followed.

Catrin literally dropped her brush, slamming the work she was holding on to the table as she spun off her stool and ran to the archway connecting the workshop and the shopfront. As she did so, Mair started crying. Simultaneously, Catrin felt a shard of pottery beneath her shoe. She looked down briefly. There were fragments of dinner plates all over the floor.

There were three big teenage boys in the entrance; young men almost, really. The nearest, clearly the one who shouted, had pushed the pile of plates, now mainly in pieces all over the floor. He was looking hostile, his eyes fixed on Jean as he moved towards a table display with a stack of dinner plates.

As she thought of moving forward, Mair cried again. For an awful moment, Catrin suddenly wondered if a piece of the pottery had hit her daughter, her being nearly at floor level. She stopped in her tracks and turned back to look at her. As she confirmed that Mair appeared unharmed, just frightened by the noise, there was a sound of bone hitting bone.

One of these thugs has hit Jean, she thought, as she turned again to face the aggressor.

But the image was Chloe with her arms out, one on either side of the teen, holding his shoulders. Her head was now moving back. Chloe had moved swiftly across to the door and violently head-butted the youth in a less than lady-like manner. As she turned to face the other two, Catrin shouted, "I'm a police officer; you three are under arrest."

Whether it was her shout of 'police' and 'arrest' or the close-up view of Chloe's headbutt, the two other teens turned and ran in different directions.

It was later they found out that as one got away, the other ran straight into a PC Graham Lowry, on street patrol. He was walking past the other end of the market when he heard the disturbance and threat, shortly followed by a youth running towards him.

"Stop right there," he shouted authoritatively, holding out an arm to intercept him.

Whether in panic or fear, the teenager, a Rasznic Marc, pulled out a knife and swung it at Lowry, catching his stab vest as he tried to move past the police officer. Lowry grabbed the boy's jacket by its hoodie-style collar and hauled hard; enough to lift Rasznic off his feet so he landed on his back, winding him. Lowry roughly turned him over, his knee securing the youth's shoulderblade as he handcuffed his assailant. He then pinned him down with one hand as he called for help on his radio.

A knife assault on a police officer gets priority attention. Lowry heard a siren within thirty seconds.

A short time later, two officers arrived and ran over to him. Lowry told one to go straight to the Cwmbran Kiln. It was a PC Les Riordan who was the first officer to arrive at the pottery.

Both Jean and Melanie stood still, frozen by the shock of the events.

Jean then bent down to pick up Lili, who seemed astonished rather than scared. Catrin quickly picked up Mair and returned to the front shop.

"Melanie, will you, please?"

She passed her daughter, still crying, over to her friend. The two shoppers were now backed away against the wall, similarly frightened and unsure how to react.

Chloe stood hovering over the teen, prepared for any retaliation. He stayed seated on the floor, his hand to his face. As Catrin moved forward she said, "No, Chloe, don't hit him again. Stop right now. Stop."

As Chloe moved back a step and Catrin got closer, she could see that the teen's eyebrow was injured. It was bleeding profusely and the eye beneath it was already swelling and closing.

Chloe just looked at her. "The babies, Catrin. They could have hurt them. I had to do something. With my surgery, I can't play nice, you know. So, I nodded him."

Chloe came from the Liverpool area, Catrin recalled, her accent under stress illustrating the fact. A nod; a headbutt. If Glasgow had been her birthplace, it would have been a kiss; a 'Glasgow kiss'.

Catrin replied carefully, "You certainly did, Chloe. You did that. Now move right away from him. Go over there, by Jean, please."

She grabbed a tea towel, part of a display with a set of kitchen bowls, and folded it before passing it to the youth. He looked angry and shocked.

"Hold it over the eye. It's cleaner than your hand. We'll get you help, but I'm cautioning you now. When other officers arrive, I will get them to arrest you on suspicion of attempted witness intimidation, perverting the course of justice. That's a serious charge, so don't muck me about? My daughter was back there, at floor level."

She glanced at the shards of pottery then leaned in close and whispered, "Anything from you and the other side of your face will be into the floor as hard as her head hit you, I guarantee it."

He looked up at her, comprehending her sincerity on that point, but saying nothing.

She continued in a more normal voice, calming a little, "Sit still. Best not move the eye unnecessarily until it's been checked. What's your name?"

"Jer. Jer Kingsley."

"Jer for Jeremy or Gerald?"

"Jeremy."

After he told her, she stood over him with her hand on his shoulder, reciting the caution statement as she pulled out her phone. In the corner of her eye she noticed a tall police officer running through the market towards the Kiln and further back, two others around another teen.

She called out to the uniformed officer. "This one will need an ambulance. I'm DI Sayer. His name is Jeremy Kingsley. Arrest him on suspicion of witness intimidation and vandalism. I've just cautioned him."

"I know who you are, ma'am. The pottery is on our watchlist these days. My colleague called it in. He has another of them detained."

He looked down at the teen sitting on the floor. "My, oh my; someone's been in the wars. I'll ask for an ambulance right now. He threatened people, did he?"

Catrin succinctly gave a statement of the events. Riordan's head tilted as he turned away, speaking briefly into his microphone. As he turned back, Riordan and Catrin exchanged glances as both looked at Chloe, now looking worried, oblivious to a smear of dried blood on her temple.

"Pity," said Riordan.

One or other of them would have to caution her. While the boy had damaged pottery and made threats, the first violent act against a person was Chloe's headbutt.

Catrin responded, "You. But give me a minute."

Catrin was now looking at her phone, searching for a contact. "Chloe, you will be taken to the police station and possibly charged with assault."

They were in the grey area between an assault and a rightful defense of another person. To navigate it, Cloe needed good legal support.

As she tried to explain her action, Catrin cut her off. "When an officer asks, you give your name and address and tell him or her you are still upset by the events here. And you won't say another word, tell the officer, without your own solicitor present. And then you stay quiet."

The crowd of people outside was growing. Riordan was watching her intently and they could both hear another couple of sirens suddenly cut out near the market entrance. More officers were on the way.

Chloe whispered, "I don't have a solicitor, Catrin. I can't afford one, anyway."

Catrin said emphatically, "Oh, you'll have one, I guarantee."

She asked Riordan, "Which nick, do you think?"

He spoke into his radio. After a terse exchange, he responded, "Probably mine, Bethnal Green."

Catrin wagged her finger at Chloe as Jean, still carrying Lili, moved forward to hug her friend. "Remember, not a word."

Riordan came forward and quietly separated Chloe into the custody of another officer, telling her not to move away; otherwise they would have to restrain her.

Catrin said to Jean, "Let's make some tea."

Turning to the two shoppers who had started to move, she said, "You can't go yet, unfortunately. You'll be witnesses. But would you like tea? And is there anything you want to buy? I think, under the circumstances, you deserve a special discount; don't you, Jean?"

Catrin moved away a few paces. Everyone was watching her now, including her own daughter. She called a number.

"Colin, hi. It's Catrin. No time to talk. What's Tommy Vance's mobile, not the office number on the website?"

After a wait, during which Riordan was talking to other officers, she gave a terse 'thanks' and immediately called another number.

"Mr. Vance, this is DI Catrin Sayer, with the Met. I have a client for you. A possible alleged assault. Bethnal Green police station in about an hour or two. You'd be doing me a favour and I'm paying the bill for a Chloe Keenan. Chloe won't make a statement until you get there."

There was a pause.

"No, I know it's strange, me being a copper. But you'll do it, right? Thanks."

The new officers on the scene entered the Kiln. They would now be sorted out into witnesses and villains. She closed the call, moved back to Melanie, smiled and retrieved Mair.

Twenty-five minutes later, Catrin put her mug of tea down and broke off talking about a vase with one shopper.

She approached a DS Yaqub, the investigating officer.

"See the blood?"

He looked at her, a little surprised, before stating the obvious. "It's his. Yes. The assault victim. Not that I am over the moon about having to write this one up."

Kingsley had been taken away in an ambulance, with a police escort. Chloe left in a police car, in tears, but she held to the advice Catrin had given her.

Catrin said stoically, "It's a crime scene. I want forensics. Specifically, I want the location of every shard of broken pottery photographed. And make sure the witness statements cover the precise location of all people present, including our children."

He looked at her, understanding her intent. "I get it and I sympathize, but it's a simple retaliatory assault, DI Sayer. You know that. I'll get it in the neck calling out the SOCOs and making a meal of this one."

"You'll get worse than that from your boss if you don't make the request. I'll tell Tommy Vance that you refused to collect key evidence necessary for the defense to assess the charge properly. How do you think that'll go down?"

His surprise was evident. Thomas Vance was a well-known defense solicitor in the east end of London.

"Vance? For this? You're joking."

"Do I look like I'm joking? That was my baby in her bouncer on the floor in there. She could have lost an eye with this lot flying around. Lili was in here, even nearer, a little toddler. Call your boss and give him the reason I want it photographed. I called Vance in myself and I am quite prepared to call him again. Tell him that, too."

"You want him to drop any charge, I get it. We'll see what mood he is in when he talks to CPS."

She just gave him a stare that reinforced her statement, then walked off carrying Mair outside into the now taped off area. She saw PC Riordan and smiled as he approached her.

"I was just leaving. Well done, ma'am. That was quick thinking."

He was waving his fingers at Mair, who was smiling at him.

Catrin responded, "More good luck that someone

answered his phone. Is your colleague OK?" she asked.

He smiled, nodded. "Yeah. The vest held the knife. He's a bit sore and will have a bruise, but I've got to go back and do a full report. And you, ma'am? All went OK inside?"

"Yes, I think so."

"Good. I hope your friend comes out the other side of this. That must have been a hell of headbutt. I don't see any worse faces than that, even at the pub fights on Saturday nights."

"It was a knockout, the way he slid down on to his backside. Chloe is passionate about the kids."

"Well, the Limmies will lick their wounds. They've got CCTV of all three of them outside the market, all known, so we'll round up the third. Some of the gang will be out of circulation for a while."

Catrin's mind went back to her discussion with Mark Harper, the unmanageability of it all.

He added, "We'll be putting a special watch on the Cwmbran Kiln now, I expect, as it has been targeted. Your friends inside, the owners, must be worried to death."

Catrin confirmed it. "The knifing of Jemma Kohli - and now this. I'd better go back to be with them. Their world is falling apart."

He was still smiling at Mair. "Yes. Falling into ours, unfortunately. This intimidation could continue until Balogun's trial."

"I know."

Her phone rang. As she checked the number, she saw it was Chris. She smiled and mouthed 'bye' at Riordan and walked away. She told her husband it hadn't been as quiet a morning at the Kiln as she had foreseen..

23 PERSUASION

The following day, Chloe called Catrin late in the afternoon. She wanted to thank her, as she was both excited and grateful that no charges were laid.

"Mr. Vance said how good I was, not saying a thing, just as you said. It meant he had no self-incriminating damage to mop up first."

Apparently, Jeremy Kingsley remained uncooperative during his interview, saying nothing about either the witness intimidation charge or providing information to support a prosecution for the assault against him. He didn't want it going around, he told them, that a woman had floored him, even if she was a 'tranny'.

That didn't exactly help his case of being the injured party.

Chloe had turned up at the Kiln, to talk with Jean and Melanie and help, as they could finally clean up the mess. Paulo, the Brazilian, was also there during the morning. The news of the attack had galvanized their friends.

Chloe stayed on, just in case there was a hint of more trouble. Melanie thought they now had more bodyguards than customers, although the news brought out more of them, too; either to show support or from plain curiosity.

She commented to Jean, "Keep this up; it's good for business. More sales than expected this week, and we can claim the cost of the damages on our insurance."

Jean responded with a stare of rebuttal, then a smile. "No, thank you. Peace and quiet is what I want."

When Chloe rang, Catrin told her, "I'm on my way home from the shops. I'll come over to the Kiln once I've seen Mair."

She knew the outcome already from Vance. He'd called her and said his invoice was on the way.

In the pottery, Catrin held her daughter while she let Chloe explain the Vance-tailored self-defence justification. Jean and Melanie had already heard it.

Another person there, a tall guy called Adrian, one who Catrin hadn't met previously, said hello. "I came to help," he explained, on introduction.

Catrin wondered if he worked as a bouncer, too. It turned out he was a dancer in a West End show.

"Adrian's very fit and strong," said Melanie, later.

Chloe continued her soliloquy. "I was quote, 'protecting myself and others, instinctively' I put in my statement. And I gave a lot of detail about how delicate I am, given the reassignment surgery. He told me to put that in, although I don't normally like talking about that."

Chloe didn't look that delicate as her head came back from delivering the headbutt, thought Catrin.

She smiled. "And how did he position the element of reasonableness? That's crucial to any self-defense claim."

"Kingsley advanced menacingly in a manner that was not open to reason or dialogue. I only hit him once. Young children were at risk. He put it all together nicely, and we wrote it down. He told the officer that he was appalled that they arrested a woman defending friends in the LGBTQ community against a violent drug gang threat. It was heroic."

She paused.

"I didn't like that bit. It wasn't heroic, I told him. It was just stopping Kingsley from doing something that could have hurt the children. Any woman would have done it. I just happened to be the closest."

Melanie said, "Well, Catrin would. I froze. I didn't."

Chloe said earnestly, "Well, you never had the prior experience, I expect. In situations like that, you get in close. Don't give them any room to pull out a knife or gun at more than arm's length or you are history. You either run away fast or get in close."

"Martial arts?" asked Catrin.

"When I was male, well… you learn things. Toxteth is rough."

The area of Liverpool she grew up in, Catrin realised. From Chloe's facial expression, she didn't want to talk about it further.

Jean had been silent, listening and cuddling Lili on her lap. She said to Chloe, "Do you want to hold her?"

It brought a smile. As the girl toddled across to Chloe, beaming at playing a new game, Jean said to Catrin. "And Melanie and I pick up this Vance's bill."

Catrin knew that tone of voice; it was when Jean moved from reasonableness to being immovably stubborn. Adrian proposed a collection among their friends, but Jean said, "No. No way," firmly.

She looked at Catrin for confirmation.

Catrin smiled. "We go halves, for Lili and Mair. And we had better get another piece or two sold through the gallery. Tommy took pleasure in telling me that he didn't give police officers any discounts."

Chloe said, "I don't know what I can do to repay you both, but I will -."

Jean spoke first, interrupting her. "Nothing at all. In fact, we owe you; you stopped it getting far worse."

That's final, her tone said. Catrin just nodded in assent. She and Jean were of one mind on that one.

In fact, the threat from Dogan's crew to the witnesses of Kohli's attack disappeared much sooner than expected.

Ten days later, in HMP Thameside, south of the river, prison officers found Oswald Balogun injured. He was discovered in a shower room in his cell block with two broken ankles.

As soon as he was able, after transfer to hospital, he confessed to the killing of Jemilah Kohli and gave a complete statement about the involvement of other members of the Limmies crew including why it happened.

They were looking for a Bolan gang member whose crew had 'stolen their business', to 'take him out' of the game. They had been through enough run-ins with the competing crew; enough warnings given. Now they wanted the top man out of action; whether injured or dead didn't matter.

Jo-Jo had spotted Kohli and said that the woman was Stevie Jarrett's, one of Bolan's people. Ossie hated Jarrett. Jo-Jo provoked him, saying that Ossie wouldn't have the stomach to take out a Bolan woman in broad daylight. So, he showed them.

Balogun gave them everything, other than the names of the two people who attacked him in prison.

~~

The small piece of copper pipe with a cement core hadn't looked particularly lethal. But Georgie's biceps were large, and it moved fast. As the base of the tibia cracked and Oswald gave a muffled yell of pain, Omar put the phone he was holding to Oswald's ear.

"Ossie, old son. How's life with Burcu? Quite the buccaneer with your penknife with unarmed women, aren't you?"

Oswald recognized the voice. In their world everyone knew Mickey J. Oswald couldn't say anything through the pain and the gag, even if he had the brainwave to ask for leniency.

"Now they will do the other one."

Georgie's arm descended and Oswald's other ankle exploded in pain. This time he threw up. Omar expertly pulled the gag away, and the vomit splattered down Ossie's front and legs. As he took a breath, Georgie's hand squeezed his cheeks together and Omar returned the phone to the ear.

"Now, Oswald Balogun, you will let the screws send you to the hospital. You slipped off a step, tell them. And by tonight you had better have told London's finest what went down when our Jemma was killed. In incriminating detail. My men there now are professionals, see? They don't get off on this, it's just a job. You tell the police everything, or I'll have other people who really enjoy their work take you apart, tendon by bloody tendon. If you know I mean it, give a grunt."

Oswald grunted.

"Good lad. Have a nice day."

Omar and Georgie took the phone and walked out, closing the shower room door firmly behind them. Through the pain and smell, Oswald realised that he would somehow have to get help.

It took him ten minutes to get four feet to the spot where he could reach up, open the door a crack and yell. For some reason, other than Omar and Georgie, no-one else on the block visited the shower room after he entered.

Balogun's trial would now be a formality around sentencing provisions once the court system got around to it. The word on the street was quite clear and spread deliberately; the attack on Ossie had been called by a member of the Bolan gang called Arkady. Mikey Junior backed his man all the way.

~~

"Shall I wait for the flight to leave, sir; just in case?"

Sylvia passed Mr. St. John-Leer's overnight bag from the boot; he held his own briefcase, as always. They had arrived at the Biggin Hill Executive Centre this time.

"No, Alison, I don't expect a problem. You'll collect me at seven tomorrow evening, then?"

"Yes, sir; I'll be here."

He suddenly thought. "You get here early, I expect?"

"I always try to, in case a client's flight arrives early."

"I'll have a word with Hannah on reception and give her your name. If you want to wait in there for me, have complimentary coffee, tea or something inside, you will be more comfortable."

"Thank you, sir; that's much appreciated."

She watched him walk into the flight centre, knowing that within five minutes he would walk out to the jet. She set off south, to join the M25 and head round to Heathrow to collect a Mr. and Mrs. Lytton, regulars at the Ballantine during their UK visits. It would be bonhomie and 'we love your country' all the way into London. After that, she would meet Ian and debrief.

She didn't understand the detail, but the precise information she gave on the trips, the size and observed weight of the briefcase he used each time and the odd snippets of overheard telephone calls were valuable to the Undertow team. Ian said they can get the flight details from other sources, but the rest proved more useful than anything a surveillance team could provide.

But she had told him that she was feeling the stretch of the role now. He was supportive, telling her that they were making progress. Now the insert was in place in the computer in the executive suite, the end was in sight; he couldn't say precisley when, but she just needed to hang in there.

And it could get tougher soon, he said, just for a day or so. He would meet her at King's Cross Station later in her schedule.

24 KING'S CROSS

Ian Underhill watched from a distance as 'Alison' helped the older woman move across to the porter now at the curb, her shopping bag clutched in her hand as she exited the vehicle. Whatever was in it, she wasn't being separated from it.

Her husband had got out on the other side, but he didn't seem in any rush to help his spouse. Ian noticed how his undercover partner looked every bit the chauffeur, even to an exchange of words with one of the station staff, as if he recognized her from previous drop-offs.

King's Cross and St. Pancras train stations were regular trips for the Ballantine chauffeurs.

Sylvia had already taken the cases from the boot of the car to the porter. Her BMW was in the zoned drop-off area and needed to move on, to let other vehicles in, but the couple were taking their own sweet time to leave.

Ian headed into the station concourse and found a table in a restaurant called Le Pain Quotidien. Ten minutes later, carrying a sandwich and a cup of coffee, Alison joined him.

"Twenty pounds, the tip for helping her to the curb, I suspect. Her hubbie is the gambler, she just came with him to go up to Scotland."

It was now a running joke between them. Alison's salary went into police revenues after passing through the Alison Fuller account at the bank. Between Sylvia's own salary and an undercover role allowance, she couldn't hold on to the chauffeur salary.

"What about tips? I'm bound to get them." She had asked the question in the first meeting with Ian, as he laid out the role and terms.

"We don't want to know about them; they will complicate the paperwork."

Since then, she had occasionally mentioned a big tip, just to get Ian to grimace or cover his ears.

As they joked with each other, apart from the casino logo stitched into her lapels, they could have been any travellers or commuters on their way out of London, indistinguishable from others in the crowded station.

But his briefing had no humour in it.

"He'll kill her, I swear. My aunt is forty-four and the neighbour's son is twenty-five at most. I only dropped in on the off-chance and… they tried to make the best of it, but it was obvious. I can't believe it. When Uncle Ralph finds out, he'll… I don't know what he'll do. It will break his heart."

The woman in the seat just behind Sylvia at the next table finished her revelation to her friend. Sylvia refocused hard on Ian. It was the opening sentence about killing that had drawn her attention away. If the next table over were planning a moon landing now, she wouldn't eavesdrop. Ian had changed the subject and now had her complete attention.

"It's a risk, but we want you to record Kryov, if he makes calls on the airport trip, as he did last time."

Their neighbours were talking about domestic infidelity while she and Ian were now focused on trapping a Latvian gang member into revealing secrets.

He passed over the innocuous-looking pen. Its top button released or withdrew the tip into the barrel. Concurrently, it activated and deactivated the recorder. She had used one before.

Training had less to do with electronics and more with understanding recording acoustics, placement and the way to use it naturally.

They had agreed at the outset that the recording of conversations would be on a specific and targeted basis, as authorised by Undertow. Given the limo fleet and assignment of chauffeurs to different vehicles daily, there was no easy way the vehicle she used could be fitted with a recording device. They decided on the pen recorder as an alternative.

"It's mobile and innocuous," Ian had said. "At worst, if it gets you into trouble, we've had the logo of a well-known beverage supplier to the casino applied to the stem. You can say it was a freebee from a person you dropped off and all you do is write with it. It has been modified slightly for us. If you twist the pen clip sideways, it won't break off, but it will erase the recorder memory, to back up your story. A quick twist, and it will be blank and appear unused."

In the event her passenger became suspicious and she was caught with it, he meant.

She checked it out while he watched. Her face had a forced neutrality, trying to mask her apprehension, he surmised.

"I don't like electronics, either; too much can get

screwed up these days. But given the Baltic languages involved, we've no option."

Sylvia replied, "Hopefully we will get something useful from it."

She left it there.

Kryov and a colleague were scheduled for a visit to the casino on the following day and Alison had been booked to return them to Heathrow, for a commercial flight. The Undertow team concluded it was for discussions, not money transfer; Kryov wouldn't risk that through Heathrow. If they had things to resolve in a meeting, though, would Kryov talk about it with his boss on his phone, on the drive to the airport?

As she returned to the BMW to head over to City Airport for her next job, she mused on the task ahead. There was a certain personal risk with recording Kryov, she knew. The most worrying part for both her and Ian was not the physical risk, it was the possibility of revealing the undercover operation before they were ready to arrest St. John-Leer and others. Undertow would then scramble around with their back-up plans while Sylvia would be back in Bedford, in uniform again, with a black cloud hovering over her head.

~~

Kryov's partner on this business trip was younger than him and attentive, she noticed, as she met them in the foyer of the executive suite. He insisted on carrying both overnight bags, not allowing her to do that. It had an overtone of old-fashioned politeness, but 'security' flashed through her mind, the way his head moved taking in the area as Kryov and St. John-Leer said their goodbyes.

If that was his function on this trip, she would need to

be very careful.

As she drove away, she was conscious of the recorder in her inside jacket pocket. She pressed the top, activating it as concurrently she made a call on her headset to Vivian, confirming their departure and checking for any update on the Heathrow pickup scheduled after dropping her passengers.

Neither of them reacted; they were talking to each other in Latvian.

She knew from experience that despite the overlapping voices, Undertow's audio equipment resources could separate the strands of conversations.

After she completed the call, she concentrated on the driving.

As they drove along Half Acre Road heading for the M4, Kryov took out his mobile and made a call. Apparently oblivious to it, Sylvia kept her eyes on the road with glances to the back through the rearview mirror.

When he finished the call, Kryov spoke to his companion, clearly giving him some feedback in the same language.

As something was said, the younger man looked at Sylvia and asked, in English, "Driver, do you speak other languages than English, please?"

It caught her off-guard.

"Some French, sir. I studied it at school."

He switched to the language, asking her if she visited France and if so, where?"

Sylvia also responded in her rusty French.

"Do you know any Italian, perhaps?"

He's checking my linguistic background. Why? She wondered.

"No sir, just some French. That's all and if you don't

mind, the traffic is getting a little hectic. I want to make sure I get you to the airport on schedule."

Let me concentrate, the message said.

"Of course," he replied, sitting back, giving Kryov a look. As Kryov dialled another number, she caught a glimpse of his partner pulling a small yellow device from his briefcase.

An RF detector, she realised, to pick up active microphones. His eyes were now back on her, she saw. She appeared oblivious to the procedure, but her apprehension rose. As she changed lanes, she reached into her jacket and switched off the pen recorder before visibly tugging at her bra strap through her blouse, apparently adjusting it.

Simultaneously, she gave Kryov's companion a hard stare in the mirror, one a woman would give to a man watching her adjust her clothing.

He glanced away, then down at his hands, checking the device. Her recorder was now off; it wouldn't be picked up.

A close thing, she thought.

Kryov, apparently unaware, was speaking in Russian this time, she thought. His companion kept his eye on the device all the time he did so. It must be an important call, the choice of language and the frequency monitoring. It was frustrating, to miss the opportunity.

It was a windfall when, seconds later, Frank Loomis called her. As she took it on her headset and spoke quietly, she reactivated the pen recorder, glancing at Kryov's companion. He had frowned as she took the call; clearly it was registering on his detector. But he didn't react as she activated the pen recorder.

Frank was stuck in a traffic problem at Terminal Five.

"I'm going into Two, though, Frank, and I'm a bit

tight on time to get Mr. Kryov and his colleague there. I have a pickup from Four not long after dropping them."

It was clear that, despite their proximity, she couldn't help him.

She tried to spin out the conversation for as long as she could; all the time it was active, so was the pen recorder.

Sensing that Frank was about to close the call, she reached inside her jacket, switching off the recorder almost simultaneously with her boss telling her he would find another solution, as he closed the line.

Within a minute, Kryov rang off and his companion switched off his device and returned it to his briefcase.

A little later, he asked her about the Resqme tool. He knew its purpose, it appeared. He was interested in why she carried it. Her explanation seemed to satisfy him and made him smile. He spoke in Latvian again to Kryov, who found his remark amusing.

Kryov leaned forward. "You are a tough army driver, I heard, ready to crash a car to protect us! Mr. St. John-Leer should have told us we have been provided wjth such a good driver."

As they left the vehicle at Terminal Two departures, Kryov spoke to her again, thanking her for the safe drive and complementing her on her driving skills.

For a moment she sat there, exhausted, until a short beep on a horn behind her encouraged her to move.

Ten minutes later, parked in the waiting area, DC Rita Tully pulled in, stopping next to her. Driving there, Sylvia felt a wave of 'what if's', as she thought of them, run through her head. If the Latvians had realised they were being recorded? If the pen microphone had been picked up on his scanner? If her movement to switch it off had been spotted? Had the army cover and the Resqme tool made her too visible now?

It was fine. Everything was fine, she told herself.

"How's it going?" Rita asked neutrally. She had completed two earlier pick-ups and drop-offs of the pen with 'Alison' for Ian Underhill over the course of the assignment. She exchanged an identical pen for the one Sylvia now passed over.

"Another day in paradise. I suspect this one is messy, but it has Kryov making a call in Russian, I think. Let them know. One of the passengers had a microphone detector in play for a while, so the recording is bitty, it has stops and starts. I had to cut the recording short, but you'll check, I'm sure."

Rita responded, "Since when did casino executives use security measures in cars? Kryov's in deep, we know that."

She blushed, recalling that it wasn't her job to give the undercover officer any feedback at all. That had to flow through Ian. "Ian said he will give you a call later," she added.

"I'm sure he will."

Sylvia caught the expression on Rita Tully's face, across the width of two car doors. She's checking me out. The tension is visible, and she sees it.

Irritated, she added, "It was a bit iffy, but I made a recording of Kryov speaking in Russian when I received a phone call, so my headset mike masked the recorder from his security guy. Not to mention the bloody M4 traffic I had to deal with at the time. I'm worn out. At least, now I've just got two gamblers from Oregan to pick up."

Her voice had lost its anger as she spoke. She finished calmly with, "It'll be an easier trip back into Chiswick."

In the early hours of the morning, she woke with a start, stifling a cry. Why not cry out? There was no-one else here, she realised, as she became fully awake.

The dream element was intense, still reverberating in her mind. In it, she was driving and Kryov leaned forward, suddenly pulling her seatbelt hard, up to her neck. She was choking, thinking it was insane; he'll kill me but I'll crash and kill him. It's pointless.

She got up and made some tea and checked her email, the surest way she knew to resettle her mind. As she finished the tea, she was reminded of the discussion yesterday evening with Ian.

He understood her tension and told her they were preparing the arrest phase. When precisely that would happen, he couldn't say. Her information throughout had helped them achieve that. It was valued; she was valued.

As she yawned and headed back to bed, she was glad she had flagged her concerns to him. The dream could come back, from past experiences. She didn't need to raise that with him. Not for now, not unless it became worse.

25 DECISION

In New Scotland Yard, Commander Moore, Super-intendent Lauder, Chief Superintendent Dermot Lyall from Serious and Organized Crime Command and Coll-een Barrington, the Deputy Chief of Human Resources, were in a meeting. They were not discussing criminals and crimes, but things equally sensitive, police officers and their roles.

Organisation charts for several units within the Serious and Organized Crime Command umbrella, including Operation Undertow, were spread out on the table.

The senior officers had been at the task of reshuffling personnel for two hours. Some names had been crossed out and new names added. Other boxes had been marked in red ink in Moore's handwriting, as 'leave for now'. The same pen had been used to stroke out three names.

Lauder or Lyall talked, Barrington did most of the writing, except when Moore took out her pen and made her comments and marks on the paper.

Colleen said, "Moving back now to the senior officer

changes in the Undertow team, if we could. We are down to three possible choices in the shortlist, Hutton, Osborne and Sayer. Hutton and Sayer are career 'fast track' officers and Osborne has the profile and relevant experience with the Avon and Somerset Constabulary. He transferred in four years ago and has settled well. The choice here for the team leaders is not so clear-cut, based on performance records, but we need to fill the 'Team A' lead position immediately. Do either of you have more insight or preference, based on the discussions so far?"

Barrington was not privy at all to Undertow files, only to its role and the expectations for its personnel.

There was an unusual moment; a silence, which Moore refused to fill. Lauder exchanged glances with Chief Superintendent Lyall and paused, thinking it through. He looked at Colleen, but knew he was speaking to Moore, her red pen rolling through her fingers.

Who bothers to put a red ink refill in a fancy Parker pen, he suddenly thought. What else does she do with it; mark homework?

"I'm going to go with Sayer. If she waffles about or says no, I'll take Osborne over Roger Hutton. Roger is fast track, but he doesn't resonate with me. He didn't stand out on the Belgravia attack follow-up, a year ago. Hutton may need more time."

Moore looked up, checking with Lyall, who was more familiar with Roger Hutton's performance. Lyall said nothing but gave her a supporting nod.

"Or he may not be going anywhere," added Moore, making a note to herself.

Lauder looked at her. "If Sayer says yes, the next month will show. It will make or break, I suspect, and she could be back in Art and Antiques - or possibly off the fast track if the casino operation falls flat on its face."

"No, she couldn't," responded Barrington, looking at Moore.

Commander Moore said, "We have other plans there, putting Mark Harper back in; he has relevant specialist experience."

Lauder nodded at the logic of it.

Moore sighed. "If it goes belly up, Dermot and I will deal with it, somehow. But I don't think it will. Sayer's ready. Burcu Dogan's mob has done that for us, and it will come back to bite him in the arse."

At this point, Barrington looked lost.

Moore said, pointing her teacher's pen at another box. "Let's move on."

~~

Two days later, Sylvia met with Ian Underhill again.

"We had an evening trip yesterday, to the Royal Horseguards again," she reported.

It was a five-star hotel in central London.

Both officers were used to debriefing sessions. Most of the minute detail was irrelevant to the case and St. John-Leer's illegal activity. But they avoided shortcuts; both of them understood that. You never know when a small item mattered.

Ian stifled a yawn. His younger son had toothache in the night and his wife had taken him to the dentist with an emergency appointment in the morning. Ian had taken most of the shift in the early hours with the child.

"Anyone of note? Any calls?"

"No. It was a pair of executives from the Hawsley Group - to do with casino entertainment contracts. I reported on his meeting with the pair six weeks ago. It is apparently a regular event. He made one call, on the way back to his house after he ran into someone going into the hotel as he came out. They didn't talk or shake hands, though; it seemed a coincidence that they met, a bit of a surprise. St. John-Leer waggled his fingers, the sign to call him, then came across to the car."

Her head was in her notes made after the shift.

"His phone rang as we set off. He said, 'Who would have thought? The same hotel. No, berk, it's not a good time now, either'. He glanced at me."

Ian controlled his response. Dogan's link wasn't part of her briefing. Undercover officers were provided with the information they needed, but a lot more case information was kept from them.

"He called him a berk? Was he a friend? It's not very businesslike!"

Sylvia looked at him, guessing that it may be something of importance.

"Not a 'berk'. Berk or 'berki' or berku'; something like that.

Ian asked, "This other guy; what did he look like?"

Sylvia gave a summary of height, weight, and his suit. She had only seen the man from behind, mainly backlit on the hotel steps. It fitted the description of Burcu Dogan.

Ian didn't push it. He would need his boss's authorisation to go further with her, revealing the link. While this was the first observed contact between Burcu Dogan and Howard St. John-Leer, it was hardly incriminating. But it was useful. After the arrests, they would need to check Dogan and St. John-Leer's phone records for the night in question.

~~

The same day, Sayer was called into her boss's office at 9.30 a.m. DCI Wetherby rose from his chair and said simply, "Our meeting this morning is cancelled, I gather. You and I have been summoned to see Superintendent Harrison. Something must be up; he was supposed to be in Hendon today, but last night he called me. I've been instructed to postpone my monthly meeting with the Stolen Vehicle Recovery Unit this afternoon, too."

Another of the specialist groups he had responsibility for these days.

They are moving you on, was Catrin's first thought. Wetherby had come out of borough policing, and she knew it was where he wanted to return. Perhaps, as she was to attend the meeting, Patterson may ask her to take Wetherby's position and manage another unit as well, not just Art and Antiques.

In Superintendent Patterson's office they found both their boss and Superintendent Lauder waiting.

Around the meeting table and with the office door closed, it was Lauder who kicked off the discussion.

"Sayer, you are being offered a new position within Serious and Organized Crime Command, a Core role in Operation Undertow. Specifically, it is a DCI level role running the team assigned to the casino operation, now called, mundanely, Team A. It's at a critical stage. Undertow is expanding, and in doing so, is forming two teams under direct reports to me. I want you to be one of them."

Catrin looked shocked and glanced at Wetherby, who had equally been caught by surprise. He spoke first, asking politely, "With effect from when, sir… in terms of workload planning. It's not really that long since DI Sayer returned from her extended leave."

Lauder responded, taking both officers into his gaze as

he spoke. "Immediately. By three p.m. today Commander Moore insists I have the detective chief inspector in charge of Team A assigned. We will be announcing the changes within Undertow at nine a.m. tomorrow. If you don't feel the role is for you, Sayer, right now, I will ask another qualified candidate. You are my first choice."

He focused on her. "Team A will retain most of the officers at present; twenty-two of the twenty-eight, to be precise. You will have as direct reports three unit leads each of DI rank. Team B will be small to begin with as it sets up another investigation. Over time, as the casino operation moves through the arrest phase into interviews and preparations for trial, staffing levels will vary as specialist units are moved in support of Team B. Later, as Team A is assigned another case, the flow will swing back again."

He smiled. "It's a job you can do well. I'll support you all the way, but we have an operation running, an under-cover officer on the line and we need to move. So, what do you say?"

Catrin found three older, more senior male officers staring at her, waiting for a response. She recalled the last time she had faced this decision, returning to work foll-owing her miscarriage, after Neville Coltrane had left so suddenly. She had refused a Trident position to stay with art crime.

The brief encounter with Sandra Hunt at St. Paul's Cathedral came to mind, for some inexplicable reason, and Mair's face. In those images, she found her answer.

"Thank you, sir. I am more than surprised but will do the best job I can for you, I promise that. What do I do next?"

"I'm glad to hear that. I'm looking forward to working with you again. Next? You'll get a new warrant card, a security pass for the Lavender Hill suite and, before you do that, give your input as we fill your current position. Arthur?"

Superintendent Patterson spoke. "Congratulations, Sayer. I'll be sorry to lose you. Your replacement? We think Obi isn't ready. He's competent and doing well at present, but we are planning on bringing Mark Harper back to lead the Art and Antiques Unit. He did a good job in the Knife Crime Task Force but has been under a lot of pressure. He was on a stress leave recently. I don't know whether you are aware of that?"

Catrin nodded, "I talked to him, so yes, I understand."

Patterson continued, "He was declared fit for duty several days ago and has been waiting to get back, but we kept him on hold. How would he do in the job?"

Catrin responded instantly. "Technically, very strong; team leadership, good, but in the past, he could be a little weak during confrontational situations. I take it from what you said that the Task Force experience has filled him out a bit there?"

"Oh, yes. A little too much, perhaps."

"Then I can't pick a better candidate."

How fast the change had occurred, she realised, talking about her current role in this manner.

Lauder took over. "Slip off to Personnel and Internal Security. Your changes will be processed this morning; they are prepared. Return to your current role until two p.m.

"Tim, you will call a team meeting for two o'clock, make the announcement of Sayer's promotion and departure and deal with that transition. I expect we will have Harper on board by then. You and Arthur are to talk to him after I leave; he is in the building or should be here shortly. If he accepts, you can announce it and he can start tomorrow. If not, arrange temporary cover."

Wetherby asked, "And after the announcement, sir?"

"Sayer will meet with DI Ed Franklin from my team at 3.00 p.m. somewhere here, to be given the background brief, as I won't be able to do that myself today. Perhaps in her office, if the announcement has been made. He will be the only Undertow officer informed of the appointment until tomorrow morning."

He looked at Catrin. "Turn up for duty at Lavender Hill at 9.00 a.m. sharp."

He stood, shook Catrin's hand, and said, "I'll leave it to you and Tim to organize the transition with Harper, once he accepts."

Then he left; he was a busy man.

As the others stood, Catrin looked at Wetherby, the changes suddenly hitting her. DCI Wetherby had never been a Neville Coltrane, but they had got along well. He had been a good team leader.

It must have been her expression. He said, "Congratulations, Catrin. It is a great opportunity, and in some ways, I must admit, I envy you. Undertow is not visible, but it's about as frontline policing as it gets."

She knew he had not made the choice years ago to leave Camden for his current role; it had been a big adjustment for him. She understood how much he missed borough policing. It was starting to hit her that she was no longer an art crime detective. That felt weird, too.

26 FRANKLIN

The Art and Antiques Unit were 'flabbergasted', to use Isabelle's term, when they were told. They were happy for Catrin's promotion, but worried about themselves until DCI Wetherby announced that Mark Harper was returning to lead the unit. He would begin his duties the following morning.

Strangely enough, it was Aina Jinnah, the person who had worked with Catrin the longest, who remained the most composed. She was the unit's admin officer and had held the same position in the defunct Art Crime Unit of Serious Crimes Command, where Catrin had her first role as a detective.

Aina took a moment to congratulate Catrin privately.

"I will miss you. But I remember you from the first interview for a position in art crime investigation, Catrin, sitting there nervous, waiting to see DCI Worsley. Now, this; I'm not surprised. You'll go far in the Met, and that makes me really happy, to have had the time working with you and see you grow."

Catrin could handle heartier stuff from Obi, Nkrumah

and Howlett, but Aina brought her to tears. It was hard for everyone to get back to work afterwards.

Catrin was still having a hard time with her emotions as they showed DI Franklin into her office and the door closed. She was sorting through files she needed to transfer to Mark at the handover briefing, whenever that would be. Wetherby was organizing the handover, as he wanted to take part.

Edward Franklin was the head of the Digital Intelligence Team within Operation Undertow, she knew, and was DC Bo Digsby's boss.

Given her encounters with Digsby, Catrin somehow expected him to be an academic sort, but Franklin was a physically powerful man and while not tall, he had the build and face of a wrestler or rugby player. Later, she was to find out that her guess wasn't far off the mark. Franklin played scrum-half for one of the Met rugby teams.

He began with, "Congratulations, ma'am. The Superintendent briefed me and sent me to give you the background."

Catrin thanked him and said straight out, "I'm in a bit of a spin on all this. But I am intrigued by the casino case, given my Undertow Focus tasks. So perhaps we'd better begin with that first. Then you can tell me about the rest of my team."

He nodded, happy to get into the task assigned. "Can I ask how well you understand the trade-based aspect of money laundering, ma'am?"

"Well, I'm familiar with its basics, and I had two cases with money laundering associated with stolen art. I received an update at Professor Lister's seminar recently, so let me give you my take on it and you can correct me if I am off-base.

"A legitimate company, A, needs to pay another legitimate company, B, and arranges a bank transfer to do that. Someone at the bank is part of a money laundering system and knows a criminal operation, C, that needs to pay another, D.

"So, the banker arranges the transfer of the payment from Criminal C to Company B. That launders the dirty money from C into a legitimate home. Concurrently, he or she routes the same sum of clean money from A to the criminal operation, D. All the right numbers transfer in the system and payers and recipients are happy. A lot of dirty money has become untraceable."

"Right," Franklin said, "You have the principle clear. The practice, as you inferred, is more complex. There are multiple transactions and a series of recipients. It gets messy. But we have worked out the casino process now. It's not the standard approach of 'buy casino chips with dirty money and cash most of them in for clean currency later in the evening'. Do that consistently and the casino is on to you; it's easier to track these days.

"Think of the casino as the laundering institution, rather than a bank. Gang members, money mules, bring in the dirty money, as players. As they play, that money merges with clean money from regular players. Only the gang accountant and key people at the casino know the numbers involved. Whether the players win or lose, all that matters are the sums that flow into the casino from the money mules, or smurfs as they are sometimes called, or returned to them as winnings. They track all that through the receipts held by the smurfs, not through the casino system.

"We know one or more of the Ballantine casino owners or investors are involved in organized crime. But they aren't in our jurisdiction and, frankly, they will be hard to hit. Somewhere offshore, the cleaned money, now in the casino account, transfers back to Burcu Dogan."

"Dogan?" Catrin showed her surprise.

"Yes, it's his moneyl aundering people who use the Ballantine Casinos. You didn't know?"

"No. I just knew that the tip-off had a Bolan-Connolly link. But it's logical. There is no love lost between Bolan and Dogan."

He nodded, his next sentence making it clear he needed to continue the explanation.

"The key issue here is that the casino management in the UK isn't aware, except for a few key people. The smurfs are just customers to them. The set-up enables Bolan to launder smaller sums, around a couple of thousand pounds at a time, roughly. Annually, however, they process a lot of drug money and other illegal income. Howard St. John-Leer, whom you met, heads up the casino people involved; some in the management struct-ure, some in the cage and vault areas. Those units are the financial heart of any casino. To the rest, including the CEO, nothing is out of whack. OK, so far?"

"Clear, yes."

"A money launderer charges a fee for doing the clean-ing; they make a big profit. Burcu Dogan has to leave fifteen to twenty percent of the money behind as payment for the service. It's a tidy sum. But it leaves an imbalance. St. John-Leer and the other people involved remove their cut from the system separately, to keep the casino's books clean. We have focused on that weak point; it's local and within our jurisdiction.

"We are not sure how they do that internally yet, but the fees are moved as cash, through falsification of chip purchases, transactions made in the cage area, outside their computer system. Once we get into the finance software, we'll pin it down.

"The laundering fee is moved out by St. John-Leer himself. He transfers it to two people, a man and a woman, in different small airports. Just as the smurfs gamble in small amounts, he moves the laundering fees out in larger amounts, once or twice a month. St. John-Leer buries these trips among other meetings with representatives of investors, developers, entertainment managers and their restaurant supply people. His job covers the contract aspects of the full spectrum of casino operations, so he has regular business meetings with many people.

"The cash he transfers to people at the airports is placed in accounts abroad for him and his team, we are sure. We'll also hope to get to those when we make the arrests.

"We have had an officer from the National Crime Agency Interchange Group in place undercover as a casino chauffeur. She has worked her way into being St. John-Leer's personal chauffeur and is known there as Alison. With her help, we now have a route into their computer system, currently latent. She also provided some valuable evidence from calls made from the vehicle by some of St. John-Leer's contacts. She's been at it for over two months already; a long time to be doing this. And we are ready to wrap it up."

Catrin pursed her lips as she processed the new information.

"I'll show my naivety. Couldn't all this money movement be done on-line? Not the smurfing for Dogan; the moving out of the fees?"

Franklin shook his head. "The casino uses a firewalled intranet, sealed off from the internet. It is carefully monitored. Hence the set up involving you for DC Digsby to get sight of one of the dedicated intranet computers. That's what DC Digsby was doing, working out how to access that system. St. John-Leer can't access the internet through that without detection by their security people, even though he has overall managerial responsibility.

"We couldn't break into it, either, without being spotted by the same casino security, but, as I said, we have an access point prepared now. On Thursday, under a warrant, we will break into the system before we make the arrests. We want to intercept a regular transfer of Dogan's money before we deal with St. John-Leer and his laundering fees.

"There is a routine associated with the transfer that Alison has identified. She gets booked for an airport run for the target, as we refer to St. John-Leer, generally to Luton airport. If she goes to the suite a little early, she sees one particular cashier deliver a folio case to the target's office. He is on his computer. We think he makes a transaction online, and the cashier turns the money over to him before he leaves. St. John-Leer then puts it in his briefcase and heads out with the chauffeur.

"St. John-Leer has Alison booked for a trip to Luton at 10.00 a.m. on Thursday. We will activate our access point at 9.30 a.m. The Digital Intelligence team's job is to intercept the transaction and hold a gateway open until we raid the casino and take charge of the computer system. We can do that undetected for long enough, I feel. St. John-Leer will be arrested at the arrival airport with his bag of cash and the other party he is meeting."

Catrin summarised it. "So, our job is to shut down the money laundering operation."

Franklin looked a little uneasy. "The Super told me he

hadn't briefed you at all. Yes, that's our role. Undertow is only one part of a bigger operation within Organized Crime Command but will be crucial to its overall success. Apart from shutting down the money laundering route, we are to get enough information to close down Burcu Dogan and his people, right down to the crew bosses and anyone found with them.

"They will conclude we are after them for drugs. What we will charge the casino people with first, though, is money laundering. Dogan and his people will be arrested the same day. Then we have twenty-four hours to document the details of Dogan's illegal accounts, sufficient to charge him with money laundering also. Chief Superintendent Lyall, Superintendent Lauder and Commander Moore want to take down his organisation completely."

Catrin couldn't help but smile briefly. Payback time. No wonder Commander Moore had made the cryptic comment about Catrin wanting to help with the penetration operation for the casino.

She said, "Bolan's people or someone else will move in and take over the territory."

"But people will get the message. We will go after anyone in the drug business, but will focus on people like Dogan, targeting the kids. Bolan's not stupid."

Catrin paused. "My job is to lead Team A. But it's all underway. What's the true added value of bringing me in at this point? Did Lauder talk about that with you? What is the specific element I am to achieve?"

It was his turn to smile. "He said you might ask that. The biggest contribution, other than managing this operation as it unfolds, is to turn St. John-Leer, so he co-operates with us. If so, we can hold and convict Burcu Dogan and others a lot easier. The Super said he thought you could do that when he mentioned it to me. But he will break it a little more properly when he briefs you directly."

She nodded. "I can only give it my best shot."

She kept her face as neutral as possible. The job change she was going through was sinking in.

When she had phoned Chris to tell him the news, he had been congratulatory, but she heard the unspoken questions in his tone of voice. How would all this play out with them as a family? He hadn't asked that.

After a pause, he had said, "The pay rise will come in useful. We need a new washing machine."

They could afford a new machine. He was just trying to get past his fears, she realised.

~~

Early evening, at home, amid assimilating her new role and talking with Chris, Catrin had a phone call from Melanie. Could she drop by?

"Jean is putting Lili to bed," she began once she arrived. She looked a little stressed. "She's raised the idea of selling up and starting the Kiln afresh in the southwest, Devon perhaps. It's the fear of... well, you know. I understand, but it makes no sense from a business perspective, I told her. We're established here. We have year-round trade with locals and tourists, not just seasonal sales in the summer months. Our friends and community are here. You are here. And the threat thing is over, you said. So did DC Meadows. She has nothing to fear from this Oswald character and his people."

Catrin responded, "Her world has changed." She looked at Chris. "I'll pop over and see her."

He nodded. "I'll give Melanie a glass of that merlot I found. We can plot while you two talk away in Welsh."

"Plot?"

"Well, I'm from Cornwall, Melanie's from Somerset. We'll call my sister in Falmouth and get moving to locate a new studio for the Kiln down there."

She gave him a scornful look as he said to Melanie, "She's just been promoted to Detective Chief Inspector rank this morning. We are staying here."

Melanie's eyebrows raised, in surprise. "Congratulations. I thought you said that there wasn't a higher post in art crime investigation than yours?"

Catrin responded softly, "There isn't. It's a DCI position in Organized Crime. What, I can't say. But I accepted it because I worry about the same things as Jean; about Mair and Lili growing up, I'll tell her."

"You'll miss your art investigation, though, won't you?"

Catrin nodded. "Which is even more reason for me and Jean to stay close; we love working together. And besides, she can't move…"

"Why?

"Liz would veto it. How could she pop down to Devon for an hour, just to complain we need to give her more pieces to sell? Sayer-Hughes art is important stuff!"

It was later when Catrin returned. Melanie had already gone home. The three women had talked together.

"Sorry I was so long."

Chris gave her a hug.

"Don't be. You've had quite a day. How did it go?"

"Good. Jean's better about it, and talking about her fears now, rather than bottling them away. And I had an idea, too."

"And? You've got that look. What am I in for?"

"I want to offer Chloe a job. Let me rephrase that; I want us to offer Chloe job."

27 BOSS

In driving across London to Battersea, Catrin recalled her time as a uniformed officer, stationed less than ten minutes' drive east, at Brixton Police Station.

To be returning to old haunts, places where she had gained experience of the rougher side of policing, but now at the rank of Detective Chief Inspector, made her both happy, intimidated and with a wish to pinch herself to check it was really happening.

She'd driven through Lavender Hill quite a few times over the years, occasionally dropping or picking up another officer at the local police station. The area around it was largely shopping, restaurants and offices. The Undertow team had their own suite at the station, which was next to the local magistrate's court.

Catrin arrived twenty minutes early.

On entering, a duty officer pointed to a set of stairs that led up to a corridor. At the end, there were a set of double doors with a keycard access. It was unmarked and unidentifiable, unlike several other units on the higher floor. She swiped the new pass card and, once inside, went down a small entry corridor into what was evidently the main operations room.

She found a sizeable group of people working and talking. Nearby stood a familiar face, DC Loretta Hills, tall as ever, apparently hovering, looking out for someone; her, no doubt.

Hills came over to her. "Welcome, ma'am. We heard earlier. I'm glad it's you they picked. Do you want to go to your new office?"

Catrin had worked with Loretta Hills during the Ranjani case. Hills had just transferred into Lauder's former team at Trident, a gun crime unit, as a rookie in training.

"Hi Loretta, thank you for that. Before I do any more, you'd better direct me first to Superintendent Lauder's office."

"It's this way, out of the ops room and to the corner office at the end. Lena is his admin assistant. Your office is two along from his. There's been some shuffling."

I'm not surprised, thought Catrin as she followed Loretta, sensing several people watching her now, but saying nothing.

Hills continued, "But that's the thing about Undertow; everything is on the move; it's quite a team."

"You've were in Trident for a couple of years before this, I remember."

"Yes, but Undertow is my favorite job, so far. Here you are."

Lauder smiled as she sat down across from his desk and Loretta closed the door. He looked tired, she thought, although it was the start of the day. He'd been leading this team and its operations since its inception.

"Hills said she would keep an eye out for you. She's

been telling newer people about the Ranjani case. She didn't hit you with our nickname?"

Catrin blinked, then realised the obvious. "No, she didn't; but surely not - the Lavender Hill Mob?"

He grinned. "They use it themselves more than any others do. Forewarned is forearmed, as they say."

Catrin smiled back. "You kept that one back when you offered me the job! Loretta's sounding a lot more experienced than when I first met her. How are the others reacting to my appointment?"

"A mix. Some juniors expected any DCI to come from the existing inspector ranks, but the DI's knew better. They are good, but understand this unit is a steppingstone to other work in Serious Crimes, to gain a broader experience before they could come back here. It's the fact you are from the Specialist Crimes area; that has some of them surprised, but I'll deal with that straightaway. Are you ready to get stuck in?"

Catrin nodded. "As fast as possible. Before I get stage fright."

He suppressed a smile, understanding her tension. "Let's go. Then talk to your direct team leads before you and I meet next. There's no rush on that, today at least. Get settled in first."

That was the initial challenge, she knew.

"Heads up everyone."

Lauder paused a moment, waiting for the room to go quiet.

"You have been told about the restructuring, that a new DCI joins us today. A second officer of that rank will be appointed shortly to lead Team B. Most of you remain on Team A as it enters its arrest phase. That will be led by Detective Chief Inspector Catrin Sayer. Team B remains with me, for the time being. It is in its startup phase, as you know."

He focused on a pair of officers, who looked surprised, then guilty. "For the latecomers, by the time Team B gets to its main phase, I will switch most of you over to support their work and Team A will take the casino investigation through to wind up and prosecution. We are flexible and dynamic; now how often have I told you that?"

There were some murmured comments and a couple of mock groans.

Lauder continued. "DCI Sayer was last with the Art and Antiques Unit, so let's head that one off first. I'm sure you think that it's not a frontline operation, it's a specialist unit. Well, in a sense, so are we, aren't we?"

"Carin Sayer has over twelve years with the Met. Some of you will recall her from the Ranjani investigation. She nearly broke Nirupa Ranjani's silence during the interviews. If Ranjani's lawyer hadn't been so inexperienced she would have, and the woman would still be alive - in prison, but alive."

"DCI Sayer previously spent two years as Assistant Commissioner Sandra Hunt's security aide, seeing the Met from that altitude. She is still an Authorised Firearms Officer, the only AFO in this room, as far as I know, who has used a weapon with lethal force in a face-to-face firefight. Not too many people are told about that one."

Catrin remained impassive but saw that several people's faces showed their surprise.

Lauder continued, "And the scar on her cheek. That came courtesy of an arrest of Colin Cheney, a Connolly gang enforcer in Glasgow a good while ago now. So yes, you'll find your new boss is a wizard at art stuff. We've pulled in an officer with an established reputation as an art crime investigator. But don't let that blind you; she's one of us now and has been around the block. As of today, she will be your new boss. Support her, all the way. DCI Sayer?"

He looked at Catrin. His introduction had surprised her. As Lauder spoke and she thought about being the next person to address this large group, her new team, she had a momentary panic. *What the hell have I done giving up my little art crime team and investigations that I understand?* It sent from her mind the points she had prepared last night and on the drive over this morning.

She moved forward a pace, taking in the people waiting expectantly, eyes on her, assessing her. Some were staring at the scar on her cheek. Many of them were younger or in the same age group as their new boss, she saw, but others were older officers, veterans of organized crime investigation. They had probably been in this work when she was still a probationer.

She threw that last thought out of her mind before it became intimidating.

"Thank you, sir. I felt for a moment part of my life running through my head. I'm glad to be here and to be part of what this operation wants to achieve, and I'll do my level best to help you achieve it, as the casino investigation enters a critical phase. Obviously, I'm totally new to this case other than yesterday's briefing and the two snippets of Undertow Focus activity that involved me previously, the second being with DC Digsby, who I see half-hidden over there. He played the part of an art techie very well, I might add."

There were several laughs and Digsby smiled.

"Some of you I know or recognize, like DC Hills and DS Unwin. I worked with these officers during the Ranjani investigation. Terry Jameson; you were in

Brixton, in Drug Squad work, the day I arrived there and big Gary Day took me under his wing and out on the streets."

The older man smiled at the memory and nodded.

She focused on a young woman. "And you are?"

"DC Tully, ma'am; Rita."

"Rita, you were one of my babysitters in the restaurant at the National Portrait Gallery. Where's your lunch partner?"

The officer looked surprised. "Gavin is off ill; he has the flu. I didn't think we were spotted."

Catrin smiled. "Not by the man I was meeting. You just picked the best surveillance point in the place five minutes after we sat down. That was the telltale. But thank you for being there."

She focused on the group. "As big as this group is here, there is another officer in my team; out there at risk, as I speak, with a partner for a lifeline but no babysitters in sight. She has been in this situation for some time now. So we all need to get on with the job and get her out from her undercover role as soon as we can do so effectively, safely and successfully.

"Apparently, I have an office here, so I'd like to meet my team leads in it in five minutes for an update and briefing. I'll look forward to getting to know each of you better as we get on with the work. Let's get to it."

Keep it simple, she thought.

She turned and looked at Lauder, who just nodded as the group started to move around the room. Then to Loretta, she whispered, "Where's the loo in this place?"

As she walked back, an officer in his early thirties approached her.

"I am DS Ian Underhill. Thank you for focusing on

my undercover partner the way you did."

"You're the liaison, Ian?"

He nodded.

"I'll want to see you later this morning, alone, after my lead team meeting. Will that fit?"

"Unless I get a call that pulls me away. It's 24/7 in this job now, and she's always my priority."

"So she should be. It's good to meet you."

He said "Yes, ma'am" and headed off.

She had been dry-mouthed with apprehension driving across London to Battersea. Now she felt fine, ready to move on. Somehow it was the right decision, and she knew she was up to doing the job. She walked into her office to find two men and a woman waiting, DI Ed Franklin, DI Sarah Wills and DI Andrew Collard.

She began with, "I met Ed yesterday and Sarah and I have been together before on cases. I'm sure you have the best way to bring me up to speed sorted already, so I'm just going to listen and take notes to begin with."

She shook hands and they sat down at the table, her team ready to brief her, building flesh on the skeleton of DI Franklin's briefing yesterday.

An hour and a half later, after they left, Catrin took a few moments before pulling out a blank sheet of paper and writing something. She then stepped out and beckoned Underhill to come in.

Ian closed the door, as instructed. His new boss placed a sheet of paper in an envelope, sealed it and handed to him.

"When do you meet next with Alison?"

"Tonight, after her shift, unless there are any fresh developments."

"Is she doing OK?"

"Getting tired. But she knows we are into the arrest phase, so there is an end in sight. She won't know exactly until we hit. But she's done very well and… she's stretched. I'm glad it's coming to a close."

Sayer said, "Let her read it. Then read it yourself and bring it and the envelope back to me."

As he turned, she said. "No. Open it, I've changed my mind. I want your input first, I just realised. That's the correct procedure. It's been a lot to take in this morning."

He opened the not-yet-dry flap and pulled out the sheet of paper.

Although I've not met you, I know you are crucial to this investigation. I'm new here; everyone knows it; thinks it. And I can't meet you yet.

My first role as a DC years ago put me in undercover work for a short time; a role in which I felt the strangeness of it all but had no risk associated with any discovery. I remember that and think of your own role, your own situation.

Later, I received an injury during an arrest of a person I had to contain, even though the situation got out of hand. I had only a suspicion at the time that another officer was undercover and at risk. It stayed contained.

I tell you these things not to brag but to assure you when I think of my team, you are there, in your challenging role. It's a tricky operation. But I won't let you down. We will do everything in our power both to keep you safe, I promise, and deliver the goods in the process.
Catrin.

As he read it, she asked, "Will it help? If not, let's ditch it. I didn't have much time to plan what to say."

He said slowly, "She will be pleased to read this, yes. It's a lonely job."

She took the note out of his hand, sealed it in a new

envelope and gave it back to him.

"As I said, let her open it and read it first, then bring it back."

He nodded and turned, seeming about to say something as he exited, but didn't. She followed him, her intention now to meet every officer in her command in the area before she went over to see Gerry Lauder. She may lead this new team, but she had her own boss, too.

28 NANNY

It was the following day before she made a change to the casino operation arrest plans, calling DI Sarah Wills into her office.

Wills was five years her senior. Catrin had met her several times around the Met over her career. Years ago, they had been on the same training course and, more recently, had worked together briefly during an art crime investigation. Sarah's specialty was forensic auditing in economic and organized crime.

Catrin said, "I see from reviewing the plan details that you will be with Lennie Fisher from the Drug Squad during the interview sequence with Burcu Dogan? I was surprised. Is there a reason?"

She nodded. "I've interviewed him before, so I know the man. And he knows me; or will remember me, I hope. He didn't enjoy us going through his books three years ago. I'm looking forward to it. He expects subservience from women."

There was a combative tone to her answer.

"Sarah, I'd like you to consider a different approach.

We will have the facts to nail Dogan, hopefully. When he sees you, the interview will be a dogfight to the finish. He'll start out with 'no comments' and make snide remarks about women. Then he'll get angry and it will build."

"That's when the breaks come, when he loses it," countered Sarah.

"Yes. But I'd like you for the first session to stay out and observe, put in DC Chris Roe or another officer of your choice."

"Dogan will have a field day. He'll enjoy riding roughshod over someone like Chris. He's good, but he looks like a university student."

Catrin nodded, smiling. "And then you'll come in just as Dogan realises the interview is not as simple as it seems. His confidence will be on the seventh floor. When he recognizes you, that will tell him the next stop is the basement."

She nodded, understanding the change in approach. "It'll be hard on whoever is conducting the initial interview. Lennie's not a problem, he has experience, but Chris…"

Catrin responded, "It could be. The assignment could also give Roe or someone else their first experience in the deep end, one that will help them develop their interview skills. A lot depends on how well you prepare them. We need to trust that your team is up to the job and will be professional enough to take Dogan's crap."

Sarah pursed her lips, considering the change. From her face she accepted the change in tactic but didn't like it. She looked at Catrin and said candidly, "Then a lot will depend on you and your interview with St. John-Leer. Otherwise Dogan may never get to a stage where we can nail him easily and he will be out on the street again, telling people that our team is a bunch of inexperienced clowns. If you are OK with that possibility, I'll go with it, ma'am."

"It's Catrin. I said I want all my direct reports to call me that, one on one. And I am. So let's do it. You choose the person and let me know."

Sarah gave her an 'on your head, so be it' look and a smile of acquiescence. She would go along with her new boss, give it a go.

As DI Wills walked away, Catrin thought that at least one of the younger officers would get a baptism of fire in a major interview with a gang leader. And the word would get around Operation Undertow that the new DCI was making her mark.

Now she had to meet with Lauder and Commander Moore, to discuss her proposed strategy for the interview of St. John-Leer. It hadn't been what Lauder expected and he wanted Moore's buy-in. If she agreed, that would be another change her team would have to think about.

~~

It was the same evening. Catrin opened the door to their apartment as Chloe arrived right on time. Catrin suspected that she had loitered somewhere close by, to arrive so precisely.

As she entered, Chloe said, "Smells good; someone's cooking."

"That's Chris. His lasagna. Come in, have a seat."

Instead, Chloe went over to the blanket where Mair was on her front, arching her back and babbling away, her focus on a crib toy. Chloe folded down to be close to her.

"She's so sweet."

Then remembering the reason for the visit, Chloe said, "Jean said that you want to talk about babysitting, would I be interested? Is that right?"

Catrin sat down on a chair as she said, "Well, sort of. But Chris and I wanted to talk to you first."

Chloe suddenly looked worried. "I've looked after Lili a few times now and Lili with Mair, once. It's been no problem with feeding or changing her. She likes me."

Chris came through from the kitchen. He said hello, looking at them both.

"Have you asked?"

"Not yet, Chris. No. We were just starting to talk."

Chloe looked even more worried.

Catrin said, "We'd like to know more about you. And whether you are interested in childcare; you seem to be. Would you be interested in becoming a nanny; to look after our little one when Chris goes back to work? It wouldn't be full time all week. We can't afford that, but Jean says you also do part-time work at a pub. We could work out hours and -."

She stopped. Chloe had started crying silently, tears rolling, but with no sound.

"I'd love to. I can't imagine anyone asking me to do that. I'm just overwhelmed."

Chris jumped in, "We'd want you properly registered and do the training courses including the paediatric health one. We'll pay for the course fees, though."

Seeing her looking around and fumbling awkwardly for her pocket, Catrin passed over a box of tissues. Then they waited until Chloe regained her composure.

Chloe had helped Catrin bathe Mair and had declined to join them for dinner.

"I would love to, but I have a late shift at the pub to-night. I take them when I can."

She had sat down and kept glancing at her watch.

"I'm still knocked out by your offer. I really am. I take it Jean told you I left my old job and I work in a pub now."

Catrin smiled. "Yes, we talked with Jean and Melanie about you before we asked. She said your firm had been supportive during the reassignment surgery, but it hadn't worked out. You were uncomfortable there."

Chloe nodded. "I'd been there too long beforehand. Most people were supportive and some found it awkward, but that wasn't the real problem. I chose the name Chloe because the name is linked to a new beginning for me. Finding a new workplace was a big step in that change."

"So, what do you want to do?" asked Chris.

"In life or the job offer? The job opportunity, I've already said yes."

"In life, I meant."

Chloe took a deep breath. "A very ordinary goal, really, now I am feeling healed. I want to meet someone who I can love and who can love me as I am now. To find work I like; achieve financial security. At some point, assuming it gets that far, for my partner and I to adopt children of our own. But that's way off; adoption for anyone isn't easy these days.

"My teens were so rough. I couldn't distinguish between my sexual orientation and my gender issues. That gave me my share of troubles, but nothing that got me any criminal charges. I still see a therapist. You should know that."

She looked apprehensive, as if she had revealed something she would regret.

Catrin said, "So did I at different times; I needed one, too. And I would go back to see him in a heartbeat if I felt the need."

Chloe continued, "I'm getting it together and doing well. And I love children and feel so privileged that you would even consider me."

Catrin said, "We want someone who would fit with us, despite our sometime difficult hours. And who would fit in with our friends. Jean and I have known each other since we were toddlers. We want our kids to have the chance to grow up together, if it works out that way. She and Melanie have had a rough time of late."

Chloe nodded in agreement.

Catrin caught her eye and held the gaze. "What I want is someone who will care well for Mair but above all, will keep her safe. Keep her and Lili safe; to protect them, no matter what."

Catching on, Chloe just said, "I'll do that, I swear, as best as I can."

She looked intently at Catrin. "Is there a problem? Some risk… to do with your job, perhaps? Is that what you mean? Beside Jean's issue of being a witness?"

"Not that I know of, but my job is changing. Being a police officer, one never knows. Does that put you off?"

Chloe shook her head and replied with conviction, "After our discussion just now? No way."

When they were alone again, Chris said, "She was open with us, I felt. My only worry is her past problems. Will they surface again? Could she inadvertently… I don't know, lose it, I suppose?"

Catrin thought for a moment. "With Mair or Lili, or us; no. I have no qualms about that. But if anyone was to threaten her when she's with the children, she would protect them at all costs. Chloe would get them away, as a first choice. If that wasn't possible, she could become aggressive, from what I saw in the Kiln.

"I'm confident it's the right thing now; for us, for Mair - and for Lili, Jean and Melanie. And for Chloe, I feel. She needs the break, the chance. We need someone who will look after Mair well and I think it will be what Jean really needs to settle her.

Chris said, "Then you should tell Jean and Melanie. Pop over, do it in person."

"No, you tell them, seeing as it was a joint decision," Catrin replied. "I'll stay with Mair. And relaxe a little. I have a long day tomorrow."

29 ARRESTS

As Sylvia Johnston made her brief journey at 8.45 a.m. from her apartment off Ealing Common to the casino, Catrin Sayer had been on the road for some time. First, she drove from her home to Lavender Hill, to lead the early morning briefing of the assembled Undertow team, although her team leads, in turn, had the major items to address.

Fortunately, other than a couple of late changes to team assignments, it was smooth going. There were no sudden surprises, which was fortunate. They knew they were in for a long day.

Both Lauder and Commander Moore had also attended the briefing but said nothing.

The weather played a significant part in the timeline review, one of several critical factors. Events included a flight of a charter jet taking Howard St. John-Leer to his planned meeting in Humberside, as they wanted to arrest his contact there.

It turned out to be a nice day for flying.

Sylvia packed her cases before leaving the flat, not that

she planned to leave just then. The exit plan called for her to continue for several days, at least, after the arrests. But one never knew, so she was ready to collect the bags and leave at a moment's notice.

The new DCI's note yesterday had picked her up visibly; Ian observed that as she read it.

"DCI Sayer sounds very experienced. Tell her I really appreciate it," she said as she returned the note and envelope to him.

He responded, "Looking at her, at first you wouldn't think so. But she is, you can tell when she speaks. There are no airs and graces about her, but she's a team player and decision-maker."

"I'm glad. It'll help you all during the next phase. Superintendent Lauder was already overstretched, you said."

Implicit in her response was that she wouldn't be there and would probably never even meet the new boss.

She met Superintendent Lauder at the beginning of the assignment. It was only for a half-hour in the assigned apartment during a visit he made with Ian. His job, he said, was primarily to thank her for joining the team. The meeting was a little too formal and stilted to be comfortable for her, but she appreciated him making the effort.

Sayer travelled with several team members from Lavender Hill, heading north across the river, not to Chiswick but to Kew, a couple of miles from the casino. The two officers were less than a mile from each other, but Sylvia wasn't to know that.

Alison arrived early for her first trip today, Frank Loomis noted. She had settled in well and was a regular part of the team now, he reflected.

"Can't stay away? You've got well over an hour before Mr. St. John-Leer's run. I'm not sure he is even in the building at present."

She gave him a small half-smile and said, "My dad called early this morning. My mum saw the doctor yesterday and will be going in for surgery very soon; they are waiting for news of an available slot. In the end, I got moving and came in here. It felt better, somehow, to take my mind off it."

Her boss made the right noises of sympathy, checking with her. No, she was fine. Work would help keep her busy. She'd just walk round a bit and grab a coffee in the café bar upstairs. She'd treat herself to one of their lattés.

He thought that was a good idea.

Sylvia's instructions from Ian were to remain in the signal range for the implant placed in the executive computer. In her shoulder bag was a small paper bag containing a case twice the size of a mobile phone, one with an array of electronics installed.

It was now the responsibility of the computer people in the Undertow team to make the link and, in doing so, not get her surrounded by casino security staff trying to stop her breaking into the executive network.

In an unremarkable van in the car park, DI Franklin, DC Digsby and another member of the Digital Intelligence Team were waiting to break into the system. Laptops at the ready, they sat in the two rear seat rows of the vehicle, focused on their screens. Whatever they were doing mystified Loretta Hills, who was the sole visible occupant, sitting in the driver's seat.

They would start the penetration when advised that St. John-Leer had entered the building. Loretta, with others, was keeping watch.

She saw St. John-Leer arrive, dropped off by a chauffeur car. She knew it wasn't Alison driving; that had been part of the briefing. As he entered the building, Ian Underhill followed him in.

Inside, as St. John-Leer headed up the private staircase, Underhill went up the public one, heading for the café bar. As he bought a coffee, Sylvia finished her latte and picked up her bag, heading away to start her workday.

To onlookers, it would be coincidence that the man carrying the coffee chose the table just vacated, as he pulled out his mobile. Peripherally, he took in the small paper bag left on an adjacent seat, mainly hidden underneath the table.

"We're active," said Franklin, several minutes later.

His team members just nodded as they started typing at their keyboards.

To Loretta, the scene in the van was the epitome of inactivity, other than the keyboarding. A minute later the call came over her earpiece that Target Two and Target One were on the floor. Alison and St. John-Leer were now both in the executive area, in common parlance.

Loretta took a deep breath and let it out slowly. Her first assigned role in today's events was approaching.

Digsby and his colleagues worked in silence, with the odd meaningless word to each other as the minutes passed. All Franklin asked at one point was, "Are we still stable?"

Digsby just nodded.

Ten long minutes later, they got the call that Target Three was on the Executive Floor. It meant that a staff member, Greg Mulholland from the treasury cage, was delivering the money package to St. John-Leer.

Suddenly there was the sound of success from the back of the van; an indecipherable exclamation from someone, followed by a 'Yes!' from Digsby.

The call came through the radio that St. John-Leer and his chauffeur were leaving. A couple of minutes later, Loretta could see the man in the distance getting into the limo parked at the front of the building. As the chauffeur walked to the driver's door, Hills thought that she had the only sighting she would get of Alison, their undercover officer.

She was wrong on that one.

Digsby just said under his breath, "Show time, Loretta."

Not an approved command in the plan, but that followed in seconds, over the radio from DI Collard.

Andrew Collard, Catrin's third team leader, ran the Surveillance and Logistics Team. Ian Underhill reported to him. During the arrest phase, Collard was responsible for the implementation plan and its coordination.

Hills left the vehicle and entered the casino, walking initially to the money exchange area apparently to buy chips. She took her time, loitering there fiddling with her wallet, extracting some cash and her credit card while eyeing an ATM machine until she saw Mulholland finally return from upstairs. As another Undertow team member joined her and before the staff member could re-enter the money exchange, she walked up to him, pulled out her warrant card and handcuffs and said, "Gregory Mulholland. Metropolitan Police. You are under arrest."

As she handcuffed the startled man and recited the litany of the official caution, the laughter between two customers passing by died away, to be replaced by silence and surprise.

But not for long; the two officers were leading Mulholland out of the building as a large group of plain-clothes officers and others in uniform, some armed, came through the door. Several of them focused on the security people, to gain their co-operation, while others fanned out inside.

Each officer had an assigned purpose. The weapons were not for the primary targets; they were prepared for clients in the casino possibly being armed or getting out of hand. One never knows.

Within ten minutes, the casino doors were closed. New arrivals were refused entry by uniformed officers. A team was now in the executive centre, and Digsby and his colleague were working away on the computer system in St. John-Leer's office.

Collard was now waiting on feedback from Alison.

~~

On arrival at Luton forty minutes after their departure, St. John-Leer said, "Thanks, Alison. I'll be back around four this afternoon, weather and flight times permitting. But you will check, as usual."

Mr. St. John-Leer was his semi-formal, luke-warm self.

"Of course, sir. Then we'll get you home as soon as we can."

She spoke warmly, lying fluently. He would be back before then, in handcuffs in a helicopter, Ian said. He hadn't explained further, but she knew they would arrest him with others, on arrival at the money transfer point.

All went well on the journey from the casino to the airport. This trip was as boring as usual. He received no calls on his phone and showed no alarm. Mostly, he had just read the newspaper.

Behind her, at an appropriate distance, was an unmarked police car with other officers. If needed, they would stop them and make the arrest at the side of the road or at the departure airport. But their inaction meant that all the money laundering ring members had been arrested in place, as planned. No-one had found the opportunity to phone or text St. John-Leer.

As he entered the building, she called Ian and updated him, giving a brief wave to the car with Undertow staff now turning around, heading off to their next task.

Sylvia had her own role to play. She called into the office to confirm the delivery to Luton. There was no answer; it went to voicemail. That end was on schedule too, it seemed, if Vivian wasn't at the desk.

Her next stop was her flat, to meet Ian, monitor developments and await further orders. They would adjust her exit plan accordingly, based on today's developments. During the initial interviews, if anyone revealed she was compromised in any way, it would be an immediate exit, a 'thank you for your help' and straight home.

She changed from being in the vanguard of the action to a waiting role at the rear of the battlefront now and wasn't at all unhappy about that.

~~

DCI Catrin Sayer was not at the casino; Lauder said he would oversee that phase himself. Instead, she was with three of her team members in two cars near the home of Lorenzo Suarez, the Ballantine's chief executive officer. He lived in Kew Foot Road, overlooking the famous gardens.

They knew that Suarez had attended a formal dinner in Central London the previous evening. He planned to be later than usual arriving at the casino today. His work habits were well understood now.

They monitored developments and when the word came through, they drove the last few hundred yards, parked and knocked on the door.

"Howard St. John-Leer? Are you sure?" Suarez asked in disbelief.

Catrin had just informed him that the casino was closed. Some employees were under arrest.

His face revealed his shock when told the Metropolitan Police were closing down a major money laundering operation centred on the casino, one run by his vice-president of finance.

Casino guests were being processed and would be released shortly.

"When is 'shortly'? These are my clients, my staff!"

Sayer looked at a DC Faulk, who was monitoring the Undertow communications traffic.

"He's in the air, they say; with twenty minutes to arrival."

"Once Mr. St. John-Leer's arrives at Humberside airport, we will arrest him there, with others involved. They will be returned to London for questioning."

Suarez was looking at the warrants now served on him as CEO, aware that people were already in his own office.

Catrin said, to help him. "You will need to speak with your legal people, of course. And I will caution you, purely as a routine matter, so anything you say will be admissible in court. Our next step is to secure the evidence we need from your building, your people and your computer system and let you get the casino re-opened as quickly as possible."

He would talk to his lawyers but that last comment

was a goal he could support.

She added, "News is leaking out on the internet now. Guests leaving the casino are spreading the impression the arrests are linked to criminals gambling there today. All we are telling customers is that the extra officers are there for their security, given the increasing violence in London these days. They are drawing their own conclusions."

Her expression told him she knew this would be significant. Suarez could see a glimmer of this turning out not as badly as it otherwise could have, aside from the ramifications of St. John-Leers activities. Damn the fool if they are true. But he was the senior executive.

"Who's in charge, so we can get moving on this?"

He liked to work with other top people, one on one.

DS Lee, an older officer who knew Catrin from Brixton days, said brightly, while nodding at her, "DCI Sayer, sir, it's her operation. That's why we are here."

Suarez looked at the younger woman afresh. "Perhaps, you and I should talk together with my legal advisor; for you to brief him directly."

30 ARKADY

Concurrent with the casino raid, officers from Serious and Organized Crime Command went to Burcu Dogan's large home near the Royal Blackheath Golf Course in Eltham. They took him into the local police station for questioning.

Dogan had heard that the building was earmarked for closure; he had never been there before. The insistence by the police that Dogan should 'assist their enquiries' in an interview there didn't raise any particular alarm, but it irritated him. However, it wasn't the first time he had been taken to a police station for questioning. Police interviews came with the territory of any drug dealer.

Burcu Dogan came from Antalya in southern Turkey. His father had been a train conductor and worked hard. Burcu decided early on that he wanted a lot more money than his father earned and not to work as hard or at all to get it, if he could avoid it.

He was naturally an aggressive man, in his stance, his features and his demeanor. As violent as his people were, and as much as he encouraged them to think of being united and strong against a world of losers, his intimidation came in the form of words rather than physical actions.

He had people working for him who would hurt others if he wanted.

Naturally, he refused to speak with the police officers until his solicitor arrived. He understood the procedure, his eyes said; he would keep them waiting around for a while. His solicitor was based in Central London, so it was easy for Dogan to make the local yokels wait. They should have taken him to an inner London police station if they had thought about it. A man like him would not use a high street family law firm.

On arrival, the solicitor insisted on a preliminary briefing about the questioning and any potential charges.

Once alone with Dogan, the solicitor explained the background.

"It's the aftermath of Oswald Balogun's confession to the murder of Jemilah Kohli. One detective is from Organized Crime and the other is from the Drug Squad. They are fishing, I believe, with questions about known links between you and the Limmies."

What would worry most people didn't perturb Dogan. No one was talking. Ossie had confessed only because some bastard called Arkady got to him through Mikey J. That gave him another reason to retaliate against Bolan, one that Burcu Dogan would seek satisfaction over, in time.

He had expected his instruction to decommission one of Bolan's lot would have been inflicted on one of two dealers they had identified in the Spitalfields area. It had been Ossie who caused the problem, showing flair at an opportunity to hit someone linked to Dolan's money people. Ossie had a long-standing grudge against Steve Jarrett and hadn't thought twice about knifing one of his women. Well, when you fire up the troops, blood will flow, Dogan mused.

But he felt that he was still on safe ground.

Lennie Fisher with the Drug Squad was a seasoned detective sergeant, unlike young DC Roe. Chris Roe, small in stature for a copper, showed a zeal and performance that moved him into plainclothes work at a relatively early age. He grew up locally, in Avery Hill.

When they entered the interview room, Dogan saw that he was going to be questioned by a regular copper from the Drug Squad and a kid who looked his daughter's age. He immediately typecast Roe as an inexperienced copper with a superman complex.

DI Wills had summarised Roe's task well. "Chris, you and Lennie will take your own sweet time with him, listen to all the 'no comment' responses and get him to the stage where he is so confident, he is trashing you both and making jokes at the Met's expense. He thinks he'll be out of there at the end of it. He won't. Don't react, but if you see the chance to give him a left jab, metaphorically, take it. Wind him up and take the crap he throws back."

The key objective was to isolate him for several hours.

Once Dogan and his lawyer began the interview, a much larger team from New Scotland Yard and the boroughs began arresting his gang members and crew leads, taking them to separate police stations around the Met.

~~

They had left Kew for the short drive to the Chiswick

casino, with Catrin and Suarez in the back of the first car and DS Lee driving, as a call came in to Catrin from a DC Stillwell, back in Lavender Hill.

Pauline Stillwell had shaken hands once with her new boss, three days ago. She worked at the bottom end of the totem pole in Team A, newly transferred in after only six months in a plainclothes role in West Norwood. Her assigned role in this whole exercise was to be an HQ data gopher for the Digital Intelligence Unit staff, while they were out at the casino.

Catrin recalled that Stillwell had a nice smile and seemed personable. She wondered how long the young woman hardly out of uniform would stand the computer screen world of Franklin, Digsby and Co. before wangling a move.

"Ma'am, sorry to bother you, but I just saw something in the data coming in. I wondered if you and others had already discussed it. A Mrs. Cadwallader. On the casino personnel lists."

Keeping her response cryptic and hiding her initial irritation, she said, "Yes, she's on the list. We knew that."

"Roberta Cadwallader. R. CADwalladEr, phonetically could be ARKADY. Me and my crosswords. It just struck me and... it's a strange coincidence as I know we are also looking for an Arkady tied to the Bolan gang. Perhaps Arkady isn't a Russian."

From the change in her tone of voice, Catrin recalled suddenly from her own past that Stillwell's next phrase would probably be, 'sorry to bother you now, if it's nothing'.

"Hold on," she interjected.

Catrin assessed the implications. It may be irrelevant, but Bolan and Connolly were each a different breed than Dogan. She wouldn't put it past either man to insert a person into an enemy drug operation. If so, they knew a great deal, including the name that John Dalton had given her at the National Portrait Gallery.

That did it for her.

"Ask DI Collard to seek any extensions to existing warrants needed to cover the person's home. On my authority, tell him to send a search team to enter anyway, with probable cause, while the person is still confined. Collard can take the search team from the casino customer processing unit, tell him. You join the house search. And, before you ask, whatever Digsby is having you do, sort out how to get that done, too. I have to go."

She closed the call. Lorenzo Suarez looked at her but said nothing. He saw that this Welsh police officer was lost in thought. Every management operation had hiccups that the top people were there to sort out.

When Catrin met up with Lauder at the casino and introduced Suarez, the executive seemed in balance. His first words were, "I have spoken to my solicitor and also to the Chairman of the Board. We are to cooperate fully. From the brief explanation that DCI Sayer has provided, we are shocked. I am insisting, independent of your enquiry, to bring in our auditors. What do you need from me?"

Lauder responded, "In due course, organize key people from your staff and auditors to assist our finance and system specialists. Help us build a clear picture of the transaction history of this laundered money. This fraud has been going on for quite a while; at least through two years of annual audit review without being detected.

"We need to know how that happened. So please make sure that your auditors send experts without any prior involvement with your operation. We'll require verification of that before any of them are given access.

"For now, please be available to answer any questions that arise. Can you also instruct other employees to help us? They will be informed that no-one other than our own people will touch the casino computer system until after Mr. St. John-Leer has been interviewed."

Catrin's challenge was far greater than a routine interview of St. John-Leer. If she convinced him to cooperate, it could short-circuit a lot of hard work.

As Suarez was passed along to DI Franklin and his team, Sayer brought her boss up to speed about the possible discovery of the Bolan gang member, Arkady. He nodded slowly, in agreement, as she explained her rationale for follow-up action - until she suggested that, if Cadwallader was Arkady, they should try to turn her against not only St. John-Leer but also Mikey J.

Then he shook his head. "CPS wouldn't agree. The lead provided by Bolan has delivered for us. We couldn't act on your suggestion without it screwing up Bolan's parole opportunity, and we have an agreement in place on that.

"What do you think about the timing of the interview with the woman? Wait on the home search first?"

"I'll have a go at her. She's Welsh, I'm Welsh; that could help but I'm not sure how at present."

Then they waited for St. John-Leer to arrive at Lavender Hill and for any news from the search team now on their way to Roberta Cadwallader's home.

31 INTERVIEWS

The three members of the administrative team working on the casino executive floor had been taken to Paddington Green Police Station, near Regent's Park. It was the nearest Met location to the casino.

On arrival, they kept them together as a group in one of the informal meeting rooms. These rooms provided a friendlier environment than bare interview rooms. They were places where police officers spoke to visitors, the parents of missing children, or broke the news to relatives that a family member was being charged with a criminal act.

For the last forty minutes, DC Loretta Hills had done a sterling job of gently taking their statements, one by one, in an adjacent room. She did that without hurry and a lot of sympathy for detaining them. It's just procedure, she repeated. No, she couldn't say why, but a more senior manager was now under arrest. Who, she couldn't say.

They only worked there, each one said, and didn't understand at all why they had been brought into a police station. Then Loretta arranged for a friendly, uniformed constable to bring them a tray with coffee and two teas before she left them chatting.

Twenty minutes later, Catrin entered with a big smile on her face accompanied by Loretta and two uniformed constables.

"Ladies, I am Detective Chief Inspector Sayer. I am sorry to keep you so long, but there has been a lot going on, as you can imagine. We believe certain people in your casino, including a senior executive in your work area, have been assisting organized gang crime. There will be charges laid.

"I read your statements and we have just a few minor questions, then we will arrange a ride back to the casino for your vehicles, or get you home, one way or another."

"Now, Eve Kennedy, please go with Constable Jacks; Florence Innes, go with Constable Patel and Roberta Cadwallader, stay here with DC Hills. We'll wrap it up in a jiffy."

It made the women smile; the wait was finally over. As they made noises of gratitude or surprise about the news, two of them picked up their bags and were led out by their assigned officer. Once alone with Loretta and Cadwallader, Catrin closed the door.

The woman seemed surprised that Catrin stayed, rather than leave them after her explanation, but she said nothing.

Catrin began, "Mrs. Cadwallader, I'm trying to place your accent?"

She already knew from the background check.

"I'm from Aberaeron. You are valley Welsh, though; I can tell."

Catrin said seriously and quickly, "Right. We aren't releasing you, Roberta. There is no need for other staff to hear that.

"You are more than just aware of the money laundering activity by your boss and Burcu Dogan; they involved you in it. Now before you protest and demand a solicitor, I have a bigger, more immediate problem. You'll need legal counsel before being interviewed formally and, I gather from Mr. Suarez, the casino will provide legal support initially for any staff member detained."

She paused, letting it sink in a moment. "Before we formally interview you, do you want a solicitor of your own choice?"

Catrin could see the woman look contemplative rather than shocked.

"Why; why that question?"

"Because we also know you are Arkady, aren't you? R. Cadwallader; Arkady. You are one of Michael Bolan's people. And I haven't cautioned you yet, so note that."

Catrin was indicating that this conversation stayed off the record, that it couldn't be used in court.

Cadwallader looked away but didn't answer. Loretta had expected her to deny it or ask what she meant; she didn't understand.

Catrin pressed on, "We have a team working through your home at present, with your husband protesting loudly, I'm told. Never mind. You don't trust computers, do you? There'll be nothing on your home system. But we found an interesting notebook and a burner phone. We are examining those."

The truth was the search team found book and phone thirty minutes earlier, but neither was yet being analysed. It had been the trigger for the plan to separate the commiserating trio. DI Collard had argued for doing the analysis before the next step. Catrin said no.

"We need as much time as possible to prepare DI

Wills for the confrontation with Dogan. Any help Cadwallader may give us could also assist my interview with St. John-Leer. We interview her now. Let's push up the pressure and give her only one way out."

That decision had resulted from a three-way call with Moore and Lauder, five minutes earlier. Lauder was supportive but a little doubtful of the outcome. Moore jumped right on it.

"Sounds good to me. It's not as if she gets to walk, right?"

Catrin pressed on, sounding self-assured. "So, you've been giving the details of Burcu Dogan's money flows to Mikey J. From those, he can work out a lot about the supplies and the sales. Read the business results and know your enemy, right?"

Roberta Cadwallader just stared at Sayer, revealing nothing, thinking. Loretta had seen the woman go from an anxious admin staffer to a cool and uncooperative customer in a matter of minutes.

Catrin said, "Here's our deal; one time, right now. We go after you for complicit involvement in St. John-Leer's criminal activity. You can claim it was minimal, done under duress, whatever. Give nothing away there during the interview unless you want to plead a deal.

"We'll put any involvement with Michael Bolan's business off the table. That's a huge 'give' from us, con-sidering what we can prove. Nor will we pick away at you with questions about Mikey J. and a pair of broken ankles attributed to someone called Arkady. That name will never surface from us. And that's involvement in a grievous bodily harm charge.

"The likelihood is that CPS will go for a two-year sentence for you on the casino money laundering, as you have no priors. With our support they won't object to a one-year stint in open prison. You'll be out on parole in six months. Personally, I think with the right lawyer and judge on the right day you may get more lenient terms, but not a suspended sentence. Your record is clean, true, but it's a serious crime, money laundering. But all that is speculation."

"We'll keep you here overnight pending a bail hearing, we'll say. You start now, give us everything on St. John-Leer and Burcu Dogan that you have. We already have St. John-Leer's computer files, and he is ankle deep already and sinking fast on that score. You flesh out our case with what you know - until the wee small hours, if need be - and we have a deal."

She paused again, long enough that Cadwallader asked, "That's it? Have you finished your spiel, or what? I don't understand what the hell you are going on about!"

Catrin read the woman's face and body language. Cadwallader wasn't buying it and playing the innocent, but her eyes had given a lot away as she listened.

She reiterated, "It's a big offer from us, staying quiet about Arkady, concentrating only on your links to St. John-Leer."

She switched to Welsh. "Satisfy us there, please. Don't, and we go after everything and, personally, I'd really rather not do that with you."

The last comment seemed to shock Cadwallader.

She responded in the same language. "Why; the last bit? Not because we are Welsh?"

She sounded ironic, disbelieving.

"Because Burcu Dogan, when he finds out what you've been doing, if he does, will arrange for someone put a knife in your chest for similar reasons he had Oswald Balogun fired up enough to kill Jemma Kohli. My friend Jean was the woman who gave Jemma first aid, so I saw that through her eyes as well as being a police officer. And now you've spoken in Welsh, I recognize the voice from Jemma's funeral. You were there, weren't you? We can always check CCTV records. I'd hate to follow up on that one. But I will if you leave me no choice. One time, as I said. Right now."

The recognition of the Jemma Kohli aftermath seemed to hit Cadwallader; she swallowed and turned her head away. Then it spun back.

She spoke in English, angrily, "God almighty! You are one strange copper, I tell you!"

Loretta looked nonplussed at the sudden outburst in English. Her boss, breaking regulations it seemed, had just used another language with a suspect without an official interpreter present.

She glanced at Catrin, registering her concern. But the head of Team A just waited, weighing Cadwallader's response before responding in English, too.

"The street noise was that an Arkady called for Oswald's ankles to be broken and Mikey J. agreed. We want Dogan and his entire operation. That's the focus of this investigation. I want your help with that."

It must have rung true with Cadwallader.

She blurted, "I want to make my phone call now, alone. When I have a solicitor, I'd like to talk with you again. With you specifically, even if others are present, before my formal interview. You won't be doing that, I hope?"

"No, someone on my team will; it will be part of the regular routine. We'll give you that call now. Take your time. We'll assume you are calling a solicitor, of course."

Cadwallader gave Catrin a long stare, then spoke again in Welsh. "I know something that even you and CPS would give me a suspended sentence to access. But I want to speak to a lawyer first."

"Let's get moving, then." Catrin had responded in the same language and then looked at her mystified colleague. "Give her the call," she said in English.

Loretta dialed an outside line on the desk phone, passing the handset to Cadwallader before both police officers left the room and shut the door. On the way out, without a word, Hills picked up Cadwallader's purse and placed it inside a large evidence bag. Cadwallader wasn't going to be using that for a while, whatever it contained.

Inside the operations area, Hills said, "I think she bought it, boss. That was good. What was the last bit?"

"We may have opened up something we didn't even think of, it seems."

While the call was private, the number she called wasn't. Cadwallader hadn't called anyone linked to Burcu Dogan. She had reached out to Michael Bolan's solicitor, Donald Killam, on his direct line.

~~

Burcu Dogan was annoyed now. It seemed as if the two police officers interviewing him had dried up on questions. He had expected to be released.

They left him and his solicitor in the interview room for fifteen minutes. Burcu was about to insist on leaving when the nasty boy, as he thought of DC Roe now, came in and told him they had further questions, but were giving them a statutory break.

Burcu responded quietly, menacingly really, as he stood. "We're going now, son, unless you fucking well arrest me. And I'll remember you, I guarantee it."

His solicitor winced.

Roe stood his ground. "Move from this room and I will arrest you."

"What the hell for?"

"Threatening and abusive behaviour to a legally appointed peace officer."

Roe started to recite the relevant section of the law as the solicitor intervened, grabbing his client's arm. "There is a misunderstanding. My client is happy to stay and assist your enquiries."

His tone of voice made it clear that Dogan had better sit back down and shut up. Burcu wondered what was next. And with that he perspired; he couldn't help it. Anger and clammy armpits went together for him, big time.

They gave him lunch in the interview room. His solicitor, though, ate in a pub around the corner. He talked with his secretary to readjust his schedule and arrange coverage for his afternoon appointments. His cash register rang every quarter-hour, billing it to Dogan.

In the afternoon session, Burcu started to worry. His solicitor had insisted on being briefed again, as it was a separate session. Thank God for the detention clock, Burcu thought. They had nothing to charge him with, as far as he could see, so the extent of this police interference in his life would be twenty-four hours at most. At least it gave him a story to share with his people; how he handled the coppers.

In the time allowed together before the second interview began, Burcu's solicitor told him that other gang members had been taken into custody; how many, he wasn't sure. He had no idea if it was coincidental or linked.

Burcu's face gave nothing away as he started to worry

more. He needed to be wary and assume the worst.

But in the interview, the questions now came from Fisher, not Roe, and were no longer about Ossie's crew. The subject was drug lines into East Anglia, which DS Fisher hammered away at while the nasty boy sat there, staring at him. Burcu entered a new 'no comment' phase and 'why are you asking me that?' response. Fisher suddenly seemed to know a lot about his county line drug routes.

And then the boy took over the questioning again, pressing him about money he had given in broad daylight to people in the White Crown pub in Herne Hill. He owned the damn place, nearly; at least he owned its pub manager. How the hell they got an undercover officer or snitch in there, which they must have done, would need to be sorted out.

All this for a few hundred quid handed out to some kids; it was unbelievable.

Burcu returned to 'no comment' and silences. And perspiring a lot more. This interview wasn't a routine 'rough up Dogan' exercise at all, he concluded.

32 BRIEFING

"That's a turn up," said DCI Owen Armstrong from New Scotland Yard, in charge of the Dogan gang arrests. He was connected to Lauder and Sayer over a video link. "If Mikey J. knows Dogan's money flows, he probably knows his business inside out."

Lauder posed the question. "We still go after Dogan; still try to turn St. John-Leer. What is the impact on the current operation? The clock's running. St. John-Leer will be arriving at Lavender Hill in ten minutes."

Catrin responded, "We'll only find the full value when and if Cadwallader gives us her prize piece of information. It strikes me, though, that she's at the Ballantine West casino dealing with Dogan's money yet also involved in Bolan's money laundering. Won't that turn up in the accounts as we go through the books?

She looked at Lauder. It was delicate ground. How many people knew that the tip-off about St. John-Leer arose from a Connolly-Bolan source? Did DCI Owens know?"

Her boss suddenly asked, "Jemilah Kohli; which

casinos did she use. Owen, do you recall?"

"No. But hang on."

He disappeared from view for a minute and reappeared with a junior officer looking a little apprehensive at being pulled in.

"You worked up the profile for Jemilah Kohli, the stabbing death. Where was she active?"

The officer recited the casinos.

"But not either of the Ballantine casinos?"

"No, not that I recall. I'll check. We got the impression she was busy enough with the ones we found. Steve Jarrett worked her hard, it seems, and she had a full-time day job as well."

Lauder spoke up. "Thank you. But don't do that. Leave it alone for now."

DCI Armstrong said, the note of resignation in his voice, "So the Ballantine casinos weren't being used by Bolan because it was Dogan's money being processed there. Michael Bolan kept it separate; neat and tidy. He uses others."

Lauder shook his head. "If Bolan gave us one casino operation, you can bet he has already moved away from that scheme himself. And probably Dominic Connolly has, as well, so we don't give it to Eileen Strachan."

DCS Strachan was an experienced senior investigator of organized crime in Police Scotland. Years ago, she had led Operation Finisterre, the drug bust that put Connolly in prison.

There was a knock on the door. As Sayer opened it, she found Loretta Hills standing there.

Hills took in that a video link was open and hesitated to speak. Lauder just asked, "Where's Cadwallader at now, Loretta?"

Hills responded, "She has a lawyer on the way here,

someone that came out of her call to Donald Killam. And she has asked to speak with DCI Sayer again, right now she suggested."

Sayer frowned. She was in a time crunch. Shortly, the plan called for her to be in Lavender Hill police station, interviewing Howard St. John-Leer. He had already arranged for his solicitor, a Jerome Norman, to meet him there. Ideally, they needed results from that interview while Burcu Dogan was still being questioned.

Lauder simply asked, "What do you want to do, Catrin?"

Cadwallader spoke in Welsh. "Are we still off the record?"

Catrin nodded. "At present, yes."

The woman looked uneasy, but she continued, "I said I would wait on my lawyer and a formal interview, but at this stage, I am advised to give you one piece of information. My gemstone, so to speak, and I trust that the Met will honour the value of it. I'll take the charge of involvement with Mr. St. John-Leer. If I didn't get char-ged, it would raise flags, wouldn't it? But I want a suspended sentence and my gemstone is worth it. I'll see whether you are as good as your word earlier."

Catrin sensibly said nothing, waiting her out.

Cadwallader took a breath, then reluctantly shared the piece of information.

At the end, she asked, "So what do you think?"

Catrin said, "You are right, it could be useful. I'll pass on your expectation, and honestly, I'll give it my support. But it's not my decision alone."

Cadwallader was assessing her closely.

"Please tell Superintendent Lauder that Mr. Killam is aware of my situation."

We got that from the phone number you called, thought Catrin, but made no response. Catrin could tell Cadwallader wasn't happy with taking the risk, but presumably Killam ordered her to do it.

She wrapped up with, "Well, thank you for the information. I'll brief Superintendent Lauder, as you request. I'll hold to my part, giving it support, but I have to go."

As she turned to leave, Cadwallader turned away, staring out of the window.

Two hours later, accompanied by a solicitor unconnected with either Michael Bolan or Burcu Dogan, Roberta Cadwallader was interviewed. The focus was on her involvement in the criminal affairs of Howard St. John-Leer.

She didn't answer questions.

They charged her and she was detained overnight then released on police bail the following morning.

Her husband met her. She looked exhausted. He took it his wife hadn't slept very well in a cell.

The reason for her release, noted in the log should anyone be suspicious and snoop, was logistics. She was a minor player, and they needed the cell space for the influx after another series of arrests. Based on information from Operation Undertow, the Met made a further series of arrests in East London of members of a drug gang and three of its crews.

~~

As Loretta drove Catrin's car from Paddington Green police station back to the Undertow headquarters in Battersea, Catrin tried to get her mind straight for the crucial interview to come.

They drove in silence and, for some reason, as they parked back at Lavender Hill, Catrin thought of Commander Moore and, on occasion, former Assistant Commissioner Hunt.

Earlier that morning, Commander Moore appeared at Lavender Hill while Lauder and Sayer gave the final briefing to Team A. Then Moore returned to New Scotland Yard. Some officers who knew her thought she would stay around the operational areas. She hadn't spoken, just been there to show support for the team leaders.

The days when she would make 'helpful comments' and occasional threats, generally about interviewing a suspect herself, were over. Catrin expected that Moore would return to her office to monitor events.

Still, she would have been surprised to hear the conversation between Moore and Commander Roscoe, DCI Armstrong's ultimate boss, sitting in Moore's office.

A videolink connected the senior officers to the still-empty meeting room chosen for the critical meeting with Howard St. John-Leer and his solicitor.

The screen came to life with the entry of DI Franklin and a surprisingly smart looking DC Digsby. They settled at a table at the back, both officers with laptops. Digsby activated the display screen on the wall and connected to it, testing one or two of the presentation slides to be displayed. He picked up a laser pointer and tested it before placing it on a coffee table between four easy chairs. Then he returned to his seat.

Two minutes later, Sayer and the Crown Prosecution Service representative, Lionel Aspel, entered.

Sayer moved across to her team, talking to Franklin and Digsby.

Moore said, "Sayer insisted on the room layout. The

easy chair positioning is the same as in St. John-Leer's office, I gather."

Roscoe said, "I'm more impressed that she got Digsby to look smart."

As the uniformed officer brought in St. John-Leer and his solicitor, Catrin and Aspel stood, as if in welcome. It was Jerome Norman, the defense solicitor, who was more surprised. They were in a lounge, with a worktable set up near the rear wall.

Two plainclothes officers sat at the table, with laptops open.

Catrin began with, "Mr. St. John-Leer, have a seat, please. And Mr. Norman. This is Mr. Lionel Aspel, a Senior Crown Prosecutor, and at the back are DI Franklin and DC Digsby. Digsby and I have met your client once before, Mr. Norman. I am Detective Chief Inspector Sayer. I'm the SIO on this investigation."

The Senior Investigation Officer.

As the others seated themselves, Sayer continued standing. "How often, Mr. Norman, has the first meeting between a client under caution and the police involved the SIO and a senior legal counsel in CPS? Could you say, based on your experience?"

Norman responded carefully, "This is a first for me. I expected from the pre-interview briefing that this would be a formal interview, on record."

Catrin responded, "That's my next point. This is on record, I must advise you, but it is a briefing session for you both, prior the interview. That will follow immediately afterwards, I assure you."

Her hand moved, revealing a screen pointer, as the wall screen lit up showing a diagram. The laser dot on the screen started moving.

33 QUESTION

"This will be a synopsis of the the investigation we are now conducting. But before that, I have only one question for Mr. St. John-Leer, one that is not in any way incriminating. It's rhetorical. The answer will matter more to him than to anyone else here."

The screen changed to an image taken of St. John-Leer's desk, of a close-up of a photo frame showing his family with happy, smiling faces. Catrin had noticed it on the man's desk during her visit to examine the painting. In the photo, he was standing by his wife with his older and younger daughters, both in their teens, in front.

"Your daughter Emma is in her last year in the sixth form. She plans to study medicine at university, we understand, to become Dr. St. John-Leer; a physician, a healer. Assuming she is successful in her chosen course of studies, do you want to attend her graduation?"

St. John-Leer's face was a mix of bewilderment and anxiety as the screen changed back to the former diagram.

Sayer moved the pointer as she continued speaking, not waiting for or expecting an answer. Several faceshots appeared.

"We have arrested and charged your accomplices already. They are being interviewed now. This one, Cadwallader, isn't saying anything at present, nor is Johan Kryov, now in custody in Grimsby, not on his way back to Latvia. The other two are talking away. They all will, in due course, I suspect. They will want sentencing deals. It's just a matter of time."

Back as Scotland Yard, Roscoe murmured, "She sounds convincing; she's good."

Moore gave no response. Her focus was entirely on the meeting itself. I know that, she thought.

The pointer moved to St. John-Leer's image on the diagram. "My financial analysis team is well into your system now. We have had access from early this morning, but we now also have the support of Mr. Suarez and company expertise. We are focusing on the completion of this stage of our analysis in time for the casino to open tomorrow, which he appreciates. But take it as a given that your money laundering tracks in the system are as clear as boot prints in snow. We'll show you proof of that during the interview."

She moved the pointer right, to another series of boxes on the diagram displayed on the screen.

"We waited to arrest you in Humberside to make sure we could get to this man, Kryov. Not so much for him, he's a bit player in an expensive suit, but to tie in his boss, Peteris Martinov, who gave you the painting. Now Peteris' own boss, Ivan Costic, has a company that holds the lease on the Embraer jet that brought in Kryov.

"The money was in the plane when we made the arrest, so our colleagues have seized the aircraft. It is valued at four million US dollars and is now impounded, unlikely to be released in a month of Sundays. Let's call it a 'proceed of crime'. Costic will see that loss as linked to some foul-up by Kryov, Martinov and you; and possibly by Burcu Dogan or his people. Like Mr. Dogan, his temperament is not one of his best features, we understand."

The pointer moved back to his name.

"Finally, your transaction this morning didn't go quite as planned. Our digital intelligence team was able to stop £352,164 from transfering to Kerzinsky Enterprises. It was paid instead into an account we own, a seizure under the money laundering regulations.

"Again, these are proceeds of crime and become Mr. Costic's loss, as well as the loss incurred by you and your colleagues."

She changed tone, a little more upbeat. "So, we are inviting you to cooperate with us, aren't we, Mr. Aspel?"

The defense solicitor jumped straight in, interrupting before the CPS officer spoke.

"I would want to speak first with my client -."

He stopped. Sayer was shaking her head and had raised her hand, signaling him to stop.

"This isn't the interview, Mr. Norman. That is to come. Lionel?"

The CPS lawyer spoke up. "This is as unusual for me as for you, Mr. Norman. I'll tell you now, though, to forget about any plea bargain that involves dropping charges; Mr. St. John-Leer is far too senior a figure in this crime ring. The best you will get, I assure you, is a third off the median guideline sentencing provisions and a guarantee of a Category C prison. An easy ride, comparatively."

The defense lawyer was now shaking his head. "That's hardly anything."

Catrin said firmly in rebuttal. "It's everything; and will be everything. Remember my original question? As you go into your interview, Howard, I will meet your wife to explain what's happening. How I approach that discussion could mean everything in your world in the years to come."

St. John-Leer looked at bursting point, lost in his thoughts.

Norman said, "Now look here, Chief Inspector; that sounds somewhat beyond the boundaries of interview persuasion. It's coercion. I'll -."

St. John-Leer gave vent to his anger. "No. Nothing. They will kill me. Nothing."

Round two, thought Catrin.

She moved her pointer, clicked a button and said to no-one in the room, "Let's have coffee, tea or something, shall we? It sounds as if your mouth is a little dry, Howard."

The image of Jemilah Kohli lying on the ground flashed on to the screen. It was an image taken by an onlooker who gave it to the investigation team. Jemma's chest was leaking blood and two people were kneeling by her. In the corner, like a photo bomb, was the face of a baby, smiling apparently at an older woman, whose back was to the camera. Jean and the medical student's backs were visible, but Jean's head had turned to glance at Mair, the strain on her face clear.

Catrin said nothing as a constable entered the room with a tray containing a mix of refreshments. Mr. Aspel took a coffee; St. John-Leer gulped at an apple juice. The defense lawyer ignored the offer and took out a notebook into which he started making notes, presumably about this strange meeting with the Met. He was looking cynical, noting points he could use to his future advantage.

Lauder had cautioned Catrin. "Tread carefully on the issue of breaking the news to his wife. The solicitor will use that as an attempt to coerce him by blackmail. And the Kohli image will only antagonize the lawyer further."

Sayer sat stock still, staring at the screen until Norman had finished writing his notes. He was now glaring at her. Her boss was probably right on the mark.

The pointer moved. "That's my daughter in the stroller, Howard. She was five months old then and I'm grateful that my friend Jean had the presence of mind to turn her away as Jemilah Kohli lay dying, as Jean and the medical student tried to help her. I remember your comment when I came to see you in the casino. You said, 'A sad affair', I recall.

As she pressed the button, the image from Spitalfields was replaced by a blank screen with a passport-sized photo of Jemilah in one corner. Lines started flowing from it as Catrin continued talking, linking to similar sized images as they appeared.

"We can trace from Jemma, through her self-confessed killer, Oswald Balogun, to his crew boss, to a third rank with Dogan, a Kes Laird, on to Dogan's right-hand man and finally to him. And now to you."

As the image of Kohli at one end appeared bolder, so did the image of Howard St. John-Leer at the other. The line linking them became bolder, more solid.

St. John-Leer said hotly, "You can't make me the -."

To be stopped by Sayer's voice, loud and abrasive. "I can. I have. And I haven't started on the list of dead addicts and broken families yet."

She moderated her tone, controlling herself, and stared at him intently. "Burcu Dogan and most of his key people are in custody. Through parallel operations to those conducted at the casino, we have all tier one and most of tier two gang members in cells now, held for interview. We will lay charges built from undercover work, inform- ants and, in the last few hours, people who have co- operated with us. It will close the Dogan operation."

The image changed to a map of south-east England.

"With the cooperation of other police service and the National Crime Agency, we've taken out both of Dogan's county drug lines into Suffolk and Cambridgeshire today.

"The youngest dealers we have arrested so far are eleven and twelve, respectively; children. But the picture will fill out. And courtesy of your excellent records, we can charge Dogan for money laundering associated with that as well."

St. John-Leer's shock at this was evident. His lawyer was looking concerned.

"Burcu Dogan's power is based on money to control people and pay them to carry out his wishes. As of today, he has no UK legal or illegal assets available. He has no people to instruct. He'll be in a prison with no other person he knows well; we will make sure of that. The only financial assets he could use to exert his control and induce people to kill you in retribution, as you stated earlier, are overseas. I want them. After that he will have nothing."

Finally, St. John-Leer could see what this meeting was all about. Catrin saw the recognition in his eyes. He understood.

She pressed on. "A Turkish national, with nothing going for him in prison and without his people to support him, will be cut down if he swaggers around there as he is currently doing verbally, I may add, with other police officers. He thinks he will be out in twenty-four hours. Neither of you will see the outside for quite some time. With you, it's the quality of daylight you want to see. We are giving you that choice right now."

She stared at St. John-Leer. "Well?"

He said, "What exactly do you want?"

This was the truly treacherous point, Catrin knew.

"Burcu Dogan is hands-off on everything; it's his mantra, part of his ability to survive all prior arrests. That includes his overseas accounts. He didn't set them up; you did, my people tell me. They see your handwriting on them. And they have convinced me you must have access to them other than as a depositor. We think you are the person who does all the international money movements for Dogan, not only the deposits of the laundered income."

He replied softly, "That's a long stretch by your people and totally without foundation."

"I believe my people; not you. You either give us that or we walk out and do it the long way round. And when we prove it, we'll hit you with another set of charges while you are in prison, which will generate a whole new sentence, because it will be documented that we asked for co-operation and gave you the chance to deal with this right now. After that, the only trips you'll make are to a courtroom, not to a graduation ceremony; for Emma, or even for your younger daughter, Penelope, I suspect."

It was also Cadwallader's gemstone that she had traded, but she would not reveal that to him. They looked at each other in silence.

His lawyer interjected. "I'd like some time with my client."

St. John-Leer simply said, "Stop it, Jerome. Can't you see? Even the chairs. The whole thing. This is DCI Sayer's casino; it's her table, her game, her bet."

He stared at her in silence as his lawyer stopped talking.

In Commander Moore's office, as in the Lavender Hill operations room where Lauder was watching the screen with several other officers, there was silence.

They had no more cards to play.

Lauder thought Sayer had delivered the agreed plan elements well, but it was now all on Howard St. John-Leer and how accurately Sayer had assessed the man, based on one previous meeting and a case profile.

34 FAMILY

"What else do I get?"

St. John-Leer sounded resigned now.

Catrin answered softly. "What Mr. Aspel said earlier; a sentence reduction and a Category C prison environment. You give me the accounts and access codes and you'll have a chance to save your marriage and your family relationship. You will serve your sentence in a place where your wife and kids will be able to visit you without fear. Think about that; you will get to see your children regularly."

As Jerome Norman seemed to come back to life, she spoke directly to St. John-Leer, moving forward, focusing on him.

"All prisoners are initially classified as Category B status. We could legitimately push for Category A for you, the most restrictive level, given the size of the drug deals in which you are involved financially. Agreement by us to a Category C rating is a big step.

"I don't remember us ever doing that with people at your level of a drug organisation. From a Category C prison, the next step is an open prison environment, Category D, and the prospect of day parole. Start at A and it will take years to work your way to an open prison status, if ever.

"With Category C rating, perhaps you will see your older daughter graduate. You'll never do so if we go for Category A. Mr. Norman knows all about that, so talk with him, if you want. There's nothing else."

She put the pointer on the table, waiting to see if he would ask for time alone with his solicitor now. St. John-Leer was sitting with his eyes closed.

Moore wasn't watching St. John-Leer anymore, as probably all others were. She was watching Sayer's face. Now remote, it appeared almost disinterested. It was resolute. There was no indication that her heart was in her mouth, as it must be.

St. John-Leer suddenly said, "Who will speak to my wife?"

"Yes!" said Moore, "She's got the bastard."

Commander Roscoe said, "Hold on, Karen. Let's wait and see."

But Moore knew.

Sayer said, "I will inform her personally. No one likes this task, I tell you. It's almost as bad as breaking the news to a mother that her child has died from an overdose. And I've done that more times than I would like in my career."

"What'll you tell her?"

"The truth. The bare facts, but the truth. Your solicitor will have more to say on that with your family, in time. If I say you are under arrest but have agreed to assist us in our enquiries, it will have a big effect on the family. If they are completely blindsided, that is. Mr. Norman, am I correct?"

He said, "Well, yes, that's true, but it's premature to jump to conclusions. Mr. St. John-Leer hasn't been charged yet. I have nothing specific to advise him about at present. It's unclear to me whether it is truly in his best interest to cooperate or not!"

Catrin said forcefully, "Fine, I can do that now. I was leaving it until after the formal interview."

She spoke to the air, to someone watching. "Can someone bring in the current charge sheet for Mr. St. John-Leer, please? He was cautioned on arrest, so have the arresting officer here with me, too."

Norman tried one more delaying tactic. "You mentioned various Eastern Europeans – who will continue to have assets and their freedom. I am concerned for the safety of Mr. St. John-Leer."

Catrin responded. "I was very specific; all I am after now is Burcu Dogan's accounts and information to close his operation down. In doing so, it will remove his capability to threaten anyone. Category C and a reduced sentence for that alone."

St. John-Leer suddenly stood, surprising everyone. As he moved, both Norman and Catrin also stood, and the uniformed officer near the door moved to intercept him. But he walked across the room towards the table, addressing Franklin and Digsby.

"You hacked our system."

A statement, not a question, directed at Digsby who, thankfully, stayed unresponsive.

St. John-Leer continued, "Are you in it now?"

Catrin nodded at DI Franklin. He replied, "With a warrant and Mr. Suarez's agreement; yes. We are live and secure."

The executive reamed off the name of several accounts and a file folder. It was meaningless to Catrin.

After a minute, DI Franklin nodded at Digsby and said to Catrin, "We have four banks, five accounts offshore. Are these all full access, no withdrawal limits?"

St. John-Leer replied, "Completely for four. The fifth, the Swiss one, is US$250,000 max per transaction per day without a physical verification at the bank."

Digsby nodded.

Franklin continued, "We will need passwords and additional key codes, I think, for the Cayman Islands accounts. Do you need access to other files to give us these?"

St. John-Leer shook his head. "All in here." He tapped his forehead and walked over, looking at the screen. Catrin moved next to him, ready to thwart any stupid lunge forward, but the man spoke directly to her.

"I have one condition. I see my wife today, alone, after you've broken the news. If she'll see me; I hope she will. She'll want an explanation. Without that, we can't move forward at all."

Catrin nodded slowly. "I'll arrange it; at least, I will offer her that opportunity. You can meet her in this room, alone in private. It's more comfortable. I'll set up childcare coverage for your daughters and a family liaison officer afterwards, to help them deal with this blow."

He breathed out, a half-sigh, half-surrender.

She added, "It's why we didn't search your home yet, which we will. We'll be as considerate to them as we can, under the circumstances. The passwords?"

She motioned for the uniformed officer to bring a desk chair over for St. John-Leer, to be behind Franklin and Digsby as they worked.

At one point DI Franklin asked, "The Swiss account, ma'am; we are on to that now. Leave it untouched for the follow-up or take the maximum limit?"

Catrin had no hesitation. "Take it now. If it puts the Swiss in a snit, we'll sort it out later."

Only one person smiled; Howard St. John-Leer.

Forty minutes later, they had $14.3 million dollars of Burcu Dogan's money in a seizure account in the UK.

DI Franklin headed out, to follow up with the Swiss authorities and freeze the access to the remaining 2.1 million dollars held there. Bo Digsby sat motionless, supposedly closing out the system on the two computers.

As St. John-Leer returned to sit with his lawyer, who wanted a private word with his client now, Catrin looked at Digsby. She leaned forward and whispered, "Not just this, now, but you have done a bloody good job today, and throughout this investigation, I suspect. Well done."

She turned round and looked at the camera, saying, "We are finished here," apparently to nobody.

Commander Roscoe sat still, deciding what to say to Moore. He looked serious, but after a moment he smiled. "You stuck by her, giving her free rein, Karen. I think you see a bit of you in her."

Moore raised her eyebrows. "What do you think?"

"You were lucky on the windfall from Cadwallader. Otherwise, this was premised on Sayer's leverage based on her read of St. John-Leer as a family man. He may well have given up smaller stuff for the deal we offered, but kept the big monies for trading later, for a better sentencing deal."

She smiled. "I'll give you that. But there was no way he will get released on bail. He couldn't exactly run for the

Cayman Islands and use the stuff himself, despite having access to the account there. And the account information could have been a liability, anyway."

Roscoe's brow furrowed for a second before he grasped her meaning. But Moore wanted to play the card anyway, so she continued.

"We didn't know that he had full access to the account, no. But he had the account numbers. Sayer intended to point out that people who had that information when a gang boss gets arrested have a habit of dying or disappearing. She would talk about Nirupa Rajani with him, dead on her living room floor because she knew too much."

"Then his solicitor would certainly have a field day. That is more problematic than playing on his family ties."

She nodded. "I told her that. She said she still wanted to do it, if necessary. I quote 'I can always make more money as an artist than I do in this job, ma'am', if you have to kick me out."

Moore looked pleased, as if she had just played her trump card.

Roscoe tried to conceal his smile. "She has more than a bit of you in her then, Karen. God help us all."

~~

DI Wills of Undertow and DI Fisher of the Drug Squad received the instruction that they were to move on to stage three of the apparently pointless interview with Burcu Dogan.

As they prepared to enter the interview room, Burcu Dogan's solicitor was at the point of pressing them to allow his client to go home and, if they insisted, they would return tomorrow for further questioning. Both were tired and his client clearly needed rest, a shower and a fresh set of clothes.

As Wills entered and DC Roe stood, Dogan gave her a glare, remembering the woman from a past meeting. She had been a detective sergeant at the time, he recalled, an accountant of some sort.

"What now?" he asked bluntly.

Wills said, "Now we charge you."

A custody sergeant in uniform and another uniformed constable entered. DC Roe had moved back to the wall as Wills joined Fisher at the table.

She formally charged Burcu Stefan Dogan with offences involving money laundering, tax evasion, and sundry related charges. There was not a mention of drugs.

His lawyer called for a full briefing. If they were going to question Dogan further, he also requested a post-ponement of that interview. It would be more approp-riate to hold that at a future date.

Dogan was blinking, whether holding back tears or in anger, they weren't sure, but he suddenly said, "He'll pay. They'll all pay."

He didn't say St. John-Leer, but they knew who he meant. Neither officer spoke for a moment. Then DI Wills responded, "Payments in general, of any sort, may be an issue for you. Your accounts in the UK are now emb-argoed; they are subject to a court order, to disting-uish the earnings truly associated with your legitimate businesses from those derived from proceeds of crime."

She opened a file and passed copies of the court order to Dogan and his solicitor.

Dogan stared, impassive. He still had money to make his threat materialize, he knew. But he would bide his time, savour his revenge.

Wills continued. "And this afternoon we seized or

froze your overseas assets. All of them."

She had decided not to itemize the list, just leave him to stew on the news. Dogan blinked, but otherwise remained silent.

Wills added, "We will hold you here overnight, Mr. Dogan. Tomorrow morning you will be transfered to the jurisdiction of the Norfolk and Suffolk Police. Their Joint Major Investigation team, in conjunction with the Cambridgeshire Police, will interview you in Ipswich.

"They will probably detain you for further questioning, I might add, there or in Norfolk. Your solicitor may wish to make arrangements with them."

She nodded at Fisher. He took a business card of an officer in the Suffolk JMI from his folder and passed it to the solicitor.

The man looked surprised. "Surely the charges you have made must be addressed first?"

DI Wills looked serene when she responded. "We'll get around to those as expeditiously as possible. But the Crown Prosecution Service has agreed that the East Anglia drug line charges are a priority. Children as young as eleven and twelve have been pulled into drug distribution, so these are serious matters."

She stopped. It took great discipline on her part not to lay it on harder with Dogan. Her older child was ten now.

She was happy that the interview had gone on as long and as well as it did. Chris Roe had done well. Her own task had been far easier today. Her boss's call on the interview strategy had been right.

For the first time in several years, Burcu Dogan experienced a deep twinge of fear, not anger. The prospect of imprisonment far away from his family and his people seemed to be the foretaste of more problems to come.

35 RING

Shortly before Burcu Dogan envisioned his new horizon, Catrin Sayer was preparing for the next phase of her operation.

She had sat down again with St. John-Leer and his solicitor. The casino executive suddenly looked older and exhausted by the stress.

She said, "Howard, we will give you a break now. You can have a meal if you want one, but I can understand if you don't feel hungry. Afterwards, DI Collard and DS Singh in my team will formally charge you and begin the interview. I can see the set of events has taken it out of you, so we won't prolong that stage today, but there are several critical questions we need to get on record.

"They will first prepare Mr. Norman, as required by law, although he has a good idea already, I'm sure, from our meeting.

"We will hold you in Lavender Hill Police Station tonight and interview you further here tomorrow. At some point, there will be a remand hearing and we will oppose bail. If remanded, my team will hold further interviews on subsequent days, as needed."

He nodded, taking it in. "I'm not saying anything about Peteris or his people."

She replied evenly, "Mr. Norman will guide you regarding your interviews. I'm heading off to talk with your wife now, and I'll stick with our agreement there. If she's willing, we'll bring her here and you can have time alone together, as I promised. But I want you to understand that she may not be ready for it. It will be an enormous shock.

"As soon as she agrees to see you, though, we'll arrange the meeting. I just can't guarantee that it will take place in the next few hours."

She picked up the file she had brought in at the beginning of the session and hadn't even opened. It was mainly for show; she'd had everything memorized.

St. John-Leer responded, "You left that image of the link from Jemma Kohli to me on the screen for a very long time."

She nodded. "I thought of how any normal person - and take that as a compliment, please - would deal with that image. You routinely shut out the dirty end of the business; never considering that it linked to you, I suspect."

He looked blank, too tired to rebut the assertion.

"Me, I've had to think about a lot of links like that in my job over the years, even when I was dealing with art crime. It hits me every time the same way it hit you earlier."

She stood up, walked out and closed the door.

Fourteen million pounds of illegal funds recovered already. That should get the people complaining about Operation Undertow's running costs off Commander Moore's back for a while.

Then her mind moved to Cadwallader's last comment made earlier in Welsh. Her gem had led exactly where she said it would. Arkady's solicitor would get her off with a suspended sentence or minimal prison time, she expected.

As she re-entered the busy operations room, people stopped and gave her a brief round of applause, which surprised her.

"Good work, boss," said a DC Cormack, someone she hadn't spoken to yet.

She smiled. "Is the search team for St. John-Leer's place ready? And we'll need a car to transport his wife here and back home, if she's willing. Who's the FLO again?"

The Family Liaison Officer.

Lena, Superintendent Lauder's assistant, replied. "DC Keaton, ma'am, Iris. She's with the search team waiting near the home, prepped in case you couldn't do the family contact yourself."

"I'm ready. Give me a minute, though. Where's Loretta?"

"In the washroom, I think."

As she got her update, she checked the time again.

Lena continued, "Superintendent Lauder has just gone into the videoconference with the East Anglia JMI now. He's looking happy, ma'am."

"Right. Then I'm off to St. John-Leer's home."

She saw the tall officer hovering; Hills had reappeared, as planned. Then she saw DC Stillwell.

She raised her voice. "Everyone; a moment, please. Stillwell, come over here."

As people paid attention and the young officer looked surprised before responding and walking over, Catrin looked at her and whispered, "You did well. I'll talk to you tomorrow."

Then she said loudly, "You congratulated me as I came in just now. I want the same for Pauline here. She took a risk with an idea, one which turned up trumps. It made our work today a great deal easier. She deserves it."

As she moved away slightly to face the younger officer and join in the applause, she saw her blush heavily. There was something about Stillwell; she had what it takes to get on in this job. She needed watching. Then Catrin realised she was thinking like Karen Moore or Sandra Hunt, when they first spoke to her, years ago.

As that little exercise finished, Stillwell murmured, "Thank you, ma'am."

Catrin looked across at Loretta and nodded. They were off to deliver the news that would break another woman's heart and change her life and that of her family, forever.

They were half-way there when Commander Moore called. Catrin answered on the speaker phone.

"Catrin, good job. Who's with you? Anyone?"

"DC Hills, ma'am."

"Loretta, how are you doing? About time you put your nose to the grindstone and finished your sergeant's course, if you ask me."

Hill's eyes widened visibly as Moore turned her attention to her, Catrin saw. She had seen Moore work on Loretta this way in the past, during the Ranjani case.

"I'm almost done, ma'am, but it's been too busy of late for courses. My new boss is working me to death." She smiled as she gave the response.

"Anyway, well done your team, Catrin. So far, so good. I know you are off to do the difficult deed now, but keep on going. We have an excellent news story for the media. We were all talking about sentencing deals for Mr. double-barrel and you read your man, didn't you? Straight to the heart of it; his family. Caught him right between the eyes. I'm glad Gerry put you in the job."

Catrin couldn't resist it. "That money laundering course that you sent me on. It was totally unrelated?"

She smiled at the momentary silence on the line.

"Just covering all my bases. Gerry wasn't pushed, I assure you. Keep it up, both of you."

The line went dead.

Loretta said, "I feel like she is always there, hovering, pushing away at me. It's been like that ever since I joined Trident, before coming to this job."

St. John-Leer and his family lived in Hampton, near to the village centre and Hampton Court. Their road had a glimpse of the Thames at the lower end and comprised expensive detached properties. As they turned into it, two other vehicles joined them, a car and a van. Loretta had been coordinating with the search team as they approached.

"His wife got back from shopping about twenty minutes ago, they say. She's there alone. She'll be going to collect the girls from school soon."

Catrin said nothing. She pulled her car into the second parking space and led the way to the front door. She rang the bell.

As the well-dressed woman opened it, Catrin said, "Mrs. St. John-Leer, we are police officers. May we come in, please?"

Catrin and Loretta automatically held their warrant badges up for the woman to read them, as her face changed.

Forty minutes later, the same pair of officers, looking sombre, left the St. John-Leer home, now being searched. Catrin had stood by her word and explained to Yvonne St. John-Leer the seriousness of the charge but added that her husband had owned up to his involvement and was now assisting their enquiries. They would take it into account, she was sure.

All his wife could focus on, though, between the tears, was the connection to illegal drugs. That her husband was involved in such activities. After all his talk about how the casino kept standards high, even his spiel on how they tried to ensure that gambling addicts were dealt with sensitively.

And now this. She couldn't handle it.

At an appropriate point, Catrin signaled to Iris Keaton, the FLO, to take the lead, to let her and Loretta make their exit. In the back of her mind, she was playing out how Mrs. St. John-Leer would have reacted if she had given her the other story; if he hadn't been cooperative, revealing himself to be an organized crime hardcase.

The Met had sent a car to collect the children from school. It reappeared as Sayer and Hills got into Catrin's vehicle. Both officers were glad to be out of the domestic scene unfolding. Each had witnessed previously the sort of pain and shock the family would now be going through.

Sayer phoned DI Collard.

"As we thought might happen, Mrs. St. John-Leer is in no state of mind to visit and see her husband at present. She said she needs to be with the children now. They need to absorb it all. The offer still stands, of course. Keaton is staying with them now and will report in. Anything new?"

"Yes. Burcu Dogan isn't talking now. He's nonresponsive verbally. They're having him assessed medically, just to be on the safe side. But the hot air and confidence has evaporated. Superintendent Lauder is heading to the Yard to be with Commander Moore for the press briefing, as planned. Everyone's busy with their roles. I checked with Underhill, as you asked. It would be OK anytime now, he said."

After the call, Sayer said nothing at first, then sent a text.

"Let's do something a little more positive, Loretta. You are not to talk about the meeting we are going to now with anyone else. Anyone at all."

Hills looked surprised.

Before she asked, Catrin said, "We are popping over to see Alison, to thank her for the good work she did."

~~

Sylvia had driven from Luton Airport to her apartment in Ealing to debrief with Ian Underhill. An hour after leaving the airport, she called Frank Loomis, but Vivian in reception answered.

"They are all out, Alison, with the mess here at present. The casino is closed, but we are trying to sort out the VIPs a bit. Mr. Suarez asked Frank to help, and we are doing what we can. What about you?"

"Well, we got to the airport and after I was sure Mr. St. John-Leer had left, I locked the car and headed for the loo. When I got back, there were police officers waiting for me, asking questions. They were interested in the trips to airports with him. They've been checking my logbook, my phone and the car while I've just been waiting, unable to do anything. Anyway, I'm free to go now and they gave me back my phone and the Merc keys but taken the iPad with the logbook programme as evidence, they said. I have a receipt. I drove back home to get myself sorted out until I could make contact with you. I'll head back into the casino now unless the boss says different."

"I'll check with him. We could use the help. Stay put and I'll call you."

They were into her exit plan. It was important now that her departure should not raise any suspicions with people there. Easier said than done, she knew; rumours and misinformation spread like wildfire.

It was ten minutes later that Viv called her back.

"Frank says, can you hold on to the Merc for now? There are two VIPs coming into Heathrow about five p.m. and, as we are closed, we are being paid to do a courtesy service to another casino of their choice instead; a goodwill gesture to keep their business when we reopen. They have elected to go to ours in Brighton, thank goodness. But until then Frank says that you should take a break, as it's a long drive to Brighton and back.

"Mr. St. John-Leer is under arrest, Frank heard. He thinks it must have been a shock to have police asking a lot of questions, with you being his chauffeur these days. They've been all over the place here, and some coppers are working up in the executive offices. Have a break and a rest."

After closing off the call, she told Ian. "I've got most of the afternoon off."

All that remained for Sylvia now was to answer questions arising from the array of interviews, if she had any knowledge of the item.

Ian told her, "It's busy as hell at Lavender Hill at present. I'm heading back over there. Relax for a while. I'll call you if I need your help on anything."

Mid-afternoon, Sylvia had just packed a sandwich and an orange into a small travel bag, to eat in Brighton after dropping the VIP pickups from Heathrow, when Ian called her.

"Heads up! The DCI is on her way over. She wants to see you and has a DC Loretta Hills with her."

Sylvia responded, "I'm about to leave the flat, to get to Heathrow in time for my pickup."

"I thought so. She's almost there. It won't take long. The DCI is medium height and a dark blonde and Hills is a tall ethnic Caribbean woman."

"Right. If you say. Well, if she does, I guess."

It was unexpected.

Ian continued, "And she did an outstanding job on the target, I tell you. It made all our work worthwhile."

On impulse, Sylvia said, "Tell her I'll be at the bench right across from the end of Grange Park, right behind the sign that says The Common."

If the DCI couldn't find that spot, it didn't say much for her as a police officer.

He confirmed the location and rang off. Sylvia reminded herself it wasn't over yet.

For some reason, Sylvia stood as the two women got closer. She had seen them park and checked their description before heading to the bench she had mentioned. Better safe than sorry.

"I'm Catrin, hello."

The smaller woman spoke first, holding out her hand. The taller officer looked a little wary as she similarly extended her arm and said, "Loretta". Sylvia had seen that before in officers unfamiliar with undercover work.

The bench would hold two, not three. Sensing it, Loretta said, "I'll stand, ma'am."

Sayer and Sylvia sat down, automatically angling towards each other.

"Thank you for that message, ma'am, on the day you started. It was a big boost. I don't know how you knew I needed it, but it helped a lot."

For some reason, the night after reading it had been the first night's sleep without the Kryov dream lurking in her thoughts as she awoke.

Catrin smiled. "I'm glad it did. I wanted to meet you in person, though, to give you our thanks from the rest of the team. You were crucial to this operation. It looks like we are having some early success. You leave soon for the airport, I gather, the start of the phaseout?"

"Yes, ma'am."

"And you are OK? Not deflated by the wind-down? It happens, I know."

Sylvia smiled, "No. it's not the first time for me, and this has been a long one. I'm good, ready to go home."

Loretta Hills was silent, watching them, but totally focused on this police officer in a light grey suit with motifs at each lapel.

Catrin pressed on. "Can I ask something? Something outside protocol. Say nothing if it is out of line. Why did you insist on wearing the engagement ring? I saw the note in the original transfer file when I did my catch up."

Sylvia couldn't stop herself. "You must read everything that crosses your desk!"

It made Hills laugh.

Sylvia continued, "Why do I do undercover work is the normal question I get, yet you picked up on the ring specifically. You must be a mind-reader. It's not mine. My partner is in the job, but we aren't the marrying sort. He's tactical. I, well, I have this stranger life than him, really. But it works for us.

"My brother bought the ring for his fiancée. He did physics at Lancaster University and was engaged, but it fell through. One of those things. Some friends took him for a night out, a pick-me-up from his depression. He had his first sample of Ecstasy, they said. With the booze in him, he overdosed unintentionally and didn't make it."

She looked at the finger, twisting the ring now. "His ex-fiancée couldn't keep the ring, she said. I found I could. It's a comfort and a reminder."

She looked up, directly at Catrin. "And that also answers the other question you didn't ask, doesn't it?"

She glanced across at Loretta and squinted a little; the angle of the sun through the branches was now a problem.

"It's my way of doing my bit. The people who run this program know I want to work on drug crime ops if I get the chance. In my regular job, I am a fleet driver. So this one was a great fit."

Loretta replied, "I'm privileged to be here and have met 'Alison'. Your name has been part of our team briefing for months now."

Sylvia smiled. "And soon to fade from any team."

She looked at Sayer. "Ian has been first class. I couldn't have worked with a more professional colleague. He was always there for me; always got the answers I needed, and he gave me clear direction. He is very good at his job."

Sayer nodded and smiled at the positive feedback for Underhill, but Sylvia pressed on. "Seeing as I'm not from the Met, I can say that he just told me you are, too, despite your note saying that you are new. But I'd better head out, ma'am, and get to Heathrow for a pickup. I still have to stay in the role."

Catrin smiled, standing to close the meeting.

As Sylvia stood, the Welshwoman said, "I'm glad we made the time for this. Safe journey to Brighton, Alison, and soon, safe travels back home. Your people will be hearing about the good work you've done."

They left, heading in different directions.

Sylvia noted that the DCI had parted with a similar comment to the one made by Captain Hollingsworth, after the training on the Wolf. Both officers had a sense of mission orientation around people at risk. Fleetingly, she wondered what experiences in DCI Sayer's life had caused that.

She started the Mercedes, ready to head over to Heathrow. In two days, she would tell Frank Loomis that there was more bad news from home about her mother. She hated to do it, she would tell him, because she liked this job, but she was quitting and going home. She'd work through the busy weekend runs, but would leave on Tuesday.

Sorry about that.

As they drove back to Lavender Hill, Loretta was silent; unusually so.

Catrin was feeling tired, but still had the group wrap-up on the day, a meeting with Lauder and any late developments to deal with. She had no illusions that it would be plain sailing. The big job now would be to transition her team into the post-arrest phase.

She had quick calls from Franklin and Wills, giving status updates. One of the casino employees off-duty they wanted to arrest had tried to escape by vaulting a wire fence behind his home, but his foot had caught in the wire and he landed on his head. It left a nasty scalp wound.

Collard said, "His older brother is filing a complaint.

There are witnesses and we have statements, so we are prepared. No-one rushed him or provoked the incident, but as he made a run for it, we've arrested him. The brother watches too much television if he thinks that a com-plaint will help."

They caught the BBC news on the radio. It included an item on a series of arrests linked to a large drug gang operation in London and East Anglia. Superintendent Lauder was quoted.

As she switched the radio off, Catrin said, "You are unusually quiet, if I can say that. You are one of the few who gives Commander Moore as good as she gives."

Loretta said, "I was thinking about what Alison said, that's all. I'm in awe of you, to be frank. The interviews; the meeting just now; the way you dealt with Mrs. St. John-Leer. You have so much experience... and are still so young. It blows me away. You've been our boss for just a few days, but it feels right, you know?"

"Thank you. I'll take that as a compliment and tell you I was really nervous, but now I am okay. And I'll remind you of it when you grimace about me pushing you to finish your sergeant's prep and take the exam. I'm not buying that 'too busy' malarkey you gave Karen Moore. I had that for long enough from John Obi in my last team. I shouldn't have put up with it for as long as I did."

Loretta looked at her, smiling truculently. "No wonder, boss, that you and Commander Moore get along."

The conversation improved during the rest of the journey back.

It was six forty-five when Catrin finished with Lauder. Her team leads were still there, as were many of her team members. She grabbed her coat and purse and headed out with a wave and a goodbye. She was going home to see her husband and daughter. Tomorrow would be another day.

But she was reminded of what both Alison and Loretta had said. She'd arrived in her new job.

36 GUIDANCE

In the week following the arrests, Catrin kept busy, but was not away from home at all hours. She held to regular workdays.

Her time was spent in 'lead team' meetings, to receive feedback and give her staff directions for action, or in working with Lauder on the analysis of the information arising from the various interviews. Between them, they made decisions on the growing list of charges and any further arrests associated with the complex money laundering chain.

Taking stock of her team members' individual performances during the operation occupied much of the rest of her time.

DI Collard took on the brunt of the liaison work with the Crown Prosecution Service, to collate the evidence files for each set of charges.

For a week, the Digital Intelligence team and the Financial Analysis team buried themselves in the Ballantine computer system and its accounts, working for part of the time with the company auditors.

DI Wills made a two-day trip to Switzerland, to deal with the request to close out Burcu Dogan's account. While the Met didn't get the money this time, neither would Dogan. The authorities arrested a bank employee there for breach of procedures.

As those aspects wrapped up, the Digital Intelligence and Finance units were the first people to be reassigned in support of Team B, under a newly appointed DCI Ken Osborne. Team B was assigned to infiltrate and dismantle a migrant-trafficking syndicate centered in South London.

It was a surprise when Catrin had a request from Bo Digsby for a personal meeting, without his boss. It came two days after Franklin's team took on their new case. She wondered if some dissension was appearing in the team, a complaint brewing.

With the door closed, at first it was unclear whether Digsby would speak at all.

He eventually began with, "When we met, you know, in Commander Moore's office, you said your husband is Chris Treneer."

She smiled. "Well, you did ask, but yes."

He sat silent for a moment before responding.

"I've worked with him on a couple of things together. He's very good at his job."

"Well, thank you. I think he is, from all accounts, and coming from you, that is a compliment."

Digsby's self-consciousness was steadily increasing, she saw. He spat out suddenly, "Can I ask, is it okay to ask, how you two met, ma'am?"

She sat back, surprised, then looked at him a little askance.

"I was a detective sergeant sent to Cornwall on a case. He was the local e-crime support person assigned to the investigation, led by a DI in the Devon and Cornwall mob. I was to assist on the art elements and traveled to Falmouth several times during the investigation. We liked each other."

A glimmer of the reason for the meeting started forming, but she wasn't sure if she was on the right track. "What's this about, Bo? Not work, obviously."

He gave a short laugh. "Work's fine; I lose myself in that. It's just that everyone treats me like the nerdy computer guy and they are friendly and… I'm not good at relationships."

He tailed off. She was right; the issue was personal, not work. Bo Digsby was raising with her his apparent awkwardness and difficulty with interpersonal relationships.

She said, "They say perception is everything. Are you in a relationship already, can I ask?"

He smiled. "I wish! No. I play at a squash club in my free time. Like here, I get on with people in a group, but I am not at ease one-on-one. But I want to be. I wondered how Chris was able to be successful as a technical expert, but still end up with a partner like you. I'm sorry, I am too intrusive, I apol -."

She stopped him with, "Hold it there. Are you feeling the stress from the case? Do you need counseling support, perhaps?"

He was the one to look surprised now. "No, it's not the work; I love the job."

She gave a big sigh. "When I met Chris, I knew he was a computer nerd, as you put it. We had a drink together once, then a lunch, after which we worked together closely for a few days. By chance, his sister invited me to join her one evening for dinner with her partner and Chris, and I saw that he fancied me. I liked him, but I worked for the Met in London, he worked for the Devon and Cornwall Constabulary, based in Exeter. He liked me more than I did him, I rationalised. It would go nowhere.

"I invited him for dinner near the end of the assignment; it was my turn to pay, anyway. As we met up at the table, I told him nicely that we were only having dinner, that anything more between us wasn't practical, so let's be friends and not push it. I was telling him to back off. I'd be gone in a couple of days, I told him. He stood up, said he couldn't do that, and left."

Digsby looked astonished, "He walked out?"

"Yes. He was really upset. It took me by surprise, I tell you. I ran after him and he said he had fallen for me. My proposal was an ironic joke, the complete opposite of his own plans for the dinner. Under the circumstances, he found it too hard and it was best if we just went our separate ways right then.

"And in those seconds, I suddenly realised what a fool I was, pushing the guy away. That's how our relationship began."

He sat back, thinking, attentive as she continued her explanation.

"He didn't treat me at that point as a colleague or aquaintance; analytically, carefully. He spoke like a man who knew his mind, prepared to embarrass himself by expressing his feelings. I could have thought to myself, 'lucky escape' and gone on my merry way. That would have been the last of it. But he got through to me.

"So stop perceiving yourself as a computer geek. You are a police officer as much as any other here. Take risks in being more open with people you like. If you are attracted to them, at some point tell them, but recognize that it may not work out. Be open but don't push it, not too hard, at least; respect people's own opinion. Police work is not the easiest environment to meet partners, for a range of reasons. You know that."

He was nodding as he stood. "Thank you, ma'am. It's not a work issue, I realise, but... it helps me."

As he reached the door, she said, "Bo, if you breathe a word of what I told you, I'll pour scalding hot coffee into your laptop, when it's sitting on your lap."

He laughed as he left.

She sat back. My God, she thought. I'll be playing marriage guidance counsellor next.

~~

Burcu Dogan spent ten days in custody in East Anglia, in Ipswich, being interviewed by officers of the Norfolk, Suffolk and Cambridgeshire constabularies.

A doctor assessed him medically twice, regarding his hypertension and behavioral issues, the latter related to non-responsiveness.

When he returned to London, on remand at HMP Thameside, some of the former life and behaviour re-appeared once he surrounded himself with several of his former entourage, now also facing charges. But even they could see the change in the man; he appeared deflated and depressed, with none of the former drive.

In the same period, three assaults took place on former Dogan crew members still on the streets and one knifing of a Bolan dealer. Bolan's people had moved in fast, the Drug Squad said, and were starving out the residues of the Dogan crews; making sure that they had no supplies. In succeeding weeks, the pattern stayed the same, thankfully without another knifing.

Bolan had prepared carefully to retake this part of his patch. To make a point, the people beaten up were found in areas around schools noted for their drug problems. The Drug Squad were not seeing any replacement dealers so far, and they now faced a new set of problems as addicted teenagers started searching further afield for supplies. But it was early days, they said.

In HMP Thameside, Georgie and Omar walked together along the corridor to the agreed place; the shower area on Level Three.

As they approached, they saw four people; Burcu Dogan with two of his gang members and a scared-looking big teen from the Limmies, barely old enough to be held there. The two Bolan men didn't break stride until they stopped six feet in front of Dogan; the unspoken line, the point at which his entourage would move in front of him.

His followers said nothing but one, a hard-looking blond man, gestured at Georgie, at his hands and pockets.

Georgie gave a dismissive sneer. "We aren't carrying. We're here to talk."

"You two did for Ossie," hissed the man.

Georgie moved his hands away from his sides, inviting someone to pat him down.

Burcu Dogan sighed. "Leave them. And what does Mikey J. have to say?"

Omar moved a pace forward. "Mr. Bolan wants to pass on some advice, Mr. Dogan."

Burcu caught the intonation. "Do you mean Mikey, or his father?"

"Mr. Bolan senior."

That surprised Burcu. "What advice does Michael Bolan want to give me?"

Omar recited the message verbatim. "Mr. Bolan has the impression that people from Turkey are very enterprising. That impresses him. All the business initiative they show around industries like handmade carpets and high quality genuine fake watches."

The laughter from the two crew members interrupted his flow. One said, "Genuine fakes, what a joke."

They were stopped by Dogan's expression. His look told them fake watches were no joke. In fact, high quality fakes were a sizeable business.

Omar continued. "Mr. Bolan, out of respect and wanting the best for everyone involved, suggests that you find a new line of business."

He stopped; they had delivered the message.

The other Dogan gang member stepped forward to confront Omar, but Georgie leaned in and put his hand out, touching the younger man's chest. Whether it was the gesture, or the size of the arm and its pressure, the man stopped and Georgie murmured, "Easy! We admire loyalty, but we are just doing our job, what they pay us for."

His eyes showed that he understood that the people with Dogan probably weren't being paid, at present.

Dogan stood stock still. His people expected a response, probably a torrent of invective and rebuttal.

He replied in neutral tones and his face was unreadable. "Please thank Mr. Bolan for the message. I will give it careful consideration."

The teenager from the Limmies looked puzzled, then disappointed. The others stared, their faces looking hard. Omar didn't take his eyes off Dogan until, several seconds later, the man turned away. It was in the final few milliseconds that Omar caught the fleeting look of resignation.

The two Bolan men backed off, moving into the corridor and walking away. Omar checked with Georgie, just a question in his eyes.

"Yes, I saw it. He's finished. We'll watch him, but if that's right, our job is easier."

For the two of them, he meant. The alternative in the days and months ahead would be to beat the hell out of Dogan's toughs, who fooled themselves that they could take on the world of hard men in prison.

37 HEARING

"The primary issue for this board hearing is whether your release presents any risk to society, Mr. Bolan."

The chairperson's voice was even, neutral and clear. She was an experienced, older woman, a university criminologist by profession.

They were in a brightly lit room in a modern high-rise block on the South Colonnade, part of the Canary Wharf Development of what was once the West India Docks.

At least it's not a stuffy basement in a block in Whitehall, thought Catrin. Stories of parole hearings held in those had been recounted by DCI Jane Worsley, embellished by a glass or two of merlot and a wicked skill in parody.

Most people in the room knew or had every reason to suspect that Michael Bolan was still heading up a London drug operation. Unfortunately, no-one could prove anything other than the stupid act that put Bolan in prison years ago.

He had been in a road accident near the Dartford Tunnel while driving a hearse, of all things. A sharp-eyed traffic officer spotted that a supposedly heavy coffin wasn't so heavy, after all; it moved too much during the collision. Someone had neglected to clamp the coffin properly.

It contained bags of drugs, mainly cocaine, not a body.

Later, Lauder found out it was the first time in years that Michael Bolan had been 'hands on' during a drug shipment. Driving the Daimler hearse was supposedly a 'lark', he claimed.

His defense at trial was that he was unaware of the contents of the coffin. The jury didn't believe him.

It was Catrin's first parole hearing. Previously, Neville Coltrane or Jane Worsley, her former bosses at the level of DCI, attended any hearings linked to cases involving her. If Tim Wetherby attended any, he never said. She had asked Jane about it once, a case Worsley worked on long before she became Catrin's boss. At the time, Catrin had recently returned from the ordeal of being treated as a hostile witness at a trial in Scotland.

Jane responded blithely, "They are like being a witness in court, except you are never quite sure whether it's the person convicted or you in the dock. It depends on the panel."

After the Glasgow experience, Catrin was happy it was not part of her job. With her promotion, now it became so, and DCS Lauder prepared her accordingly.

Catrin, on behalf of the Met, was the next intervenor. The panel had just heard Bolan's case officer speak about his record in prison. The man used the words 'impeccable attitude' at one point.

"Mr. Bolan treats staff and other inmates with respect and courtesy, always. He seems to have a stabilizing effect on others, raising the standard of behaviour."

Catrin suspected that Bolan paid people in prison with him to lower that standard considerably whenever he wanted. Mikey J. certainly accessed them, given Oswald Balogun's fractures leading to his confession.

Checking her list, the chairperson said, "And now the Metropolitan Police. Detective Chief Inspector Sayer, I believe. Have a seat, please."

After she moved from the row of chairs for inter-venors and observers, to sit at the table with the panel, the chairperson said, "For the record, we understand that the Met is appearing today because you opposed parole at the last hearing,. Is that correct?"

"Yes, ma'am. That is so."

"Let me first ask, are there any additional comments to that last intervention that you wish to make?"

"No."

"Does the Metropolitan Police have any new, evid-ence-based concerns about Mr. Bolan being released into long-term parole?"

Thousands, thought Catrin. He's a major drug gang leader. She hesitated only a second.

"No."

The chairperson looked a little surprised but concealed it well.

"Then do you have any input regarding potential parole conditions you wish to place on record?"

It was the only other area that they would ask the arresting authority to address, Lauder told her. He had briefed her on that aspect as well and she had a message to deliver.

"Yes, ma'am. We wish to see the usual provisions that stipulate Mr. Bolan should have no contact with people with prior convictions or links to organized crime. Just as young addicts must avoid contact with their former dealers, to avoid being drawn back into the spiral of addiction, we expect Mr. Bolan to be aware of the need for him to act similarly."

Picking up on the glowing remarks of the last intervenor, she added, "Given the comments by his case officer a moment ago, perhaps he can also become a role model for others in his sphere, if he so chooses."

The three members of the panel exchanged glances. The chairperson asked them if they had questions of the Metropolitan Police. There was a muttering from one panel member to the chair regarding the word 'sphere'; should they seek clarification from the police officer.

The chair gave a silent but firm shake of her head. She didn't want Detective Chief Inspector Sayer unleashing a list of Bolan gang names and recounting tales of Mikey J. and his ilk.

The other panel members remained silent.

The chairperson summarised the situation for the record. "So, we will record that the Metropolitan Police have no specific objections to a release on parole, providing appropriate conditions are applied. Thank you."

She glanced down at the intervenor list.

Catrin stood and turned. In doing so, she came face-to-face with Michael Bolan and Donald Killam, sitting next to each other, client and lawyer, looking impassive.

She had delivered; DCS Lauder had fulfilled the conditions of the unwritten agreement for the tip-off leading to the demolition of Burcu Dogan's gang. It was now on record, along with the oblique reference that they expected Bolan to deal with the young addict issue.

It wasn't lost on Bolan, whom she hadn't seen in person before the hearing. As they made eye contact, he gave her a single nod. Catrin walked past him and left the room.

Michael Bolan brought back memories of Dominic Connolly. He projected the same presence, a feeling of intimidation with no obvious signs of physical threat. But in the single glance, she now understood that she was on his radar.

38 LI

"I would love to visit Asia, and see places like Hong Kong," said Chloe.

She was busy with Lili and a toy as Catrin returned to the living room from settling Mair.

Jian Li Yeung from Hong Kong just smiled. "One day, perhaps you will; who knows?"

Li and Catrin had been friends for over a decade, ever since they met in Wales. Catrin had been a new detective constable. Jian Li had spent a year studying at Bangor University during the search for her missing brother, later found murdered there. It had been Catrin's first assignment as a plainclothes officer.

A month earlier, in the height of the casino operation, Li had called Catrin with the news that her employer, a Hong Kong shipping company, was transfering her to Stockholm for a year, an assignment to see if the maritime lawyer would transition into business management or continue in a legal department career track. Li would visit them in London once she had settled in Sweden, she had said.

Chloe and Li had just met. Li responded, "I went to Liverpool for a weekend once, while I studied at Bangor University. You make me think of that visit, with your lovely accent."

Chloe laughed. "Lovely; it isn't usually described that way; but thank you."

Lili, feeling a little left out now, focused on regaining Chloe's attention.

Chris and Catrin, Jean and Melanie and Li were going to dinner. Li had arrived from Stockholm that afternoon.

In the French restaurant on Brick Lane, Li said, after they ordered, "It's still early in the assignment. So far, I am settling in and doing OK. My boss, the head of LinTan Shipping for Denmark and Sweden, seems happy with me. It's the local person handling legal issues who is more tentative."

Catrin asked, "Why's that? Because you know more about maritime law, or what?"

"I'm not sure yet. It may be that she is insecure, thinking if I stay, will they combine roles and make her job unnecessary, but we have no plan to do that. I want to go back to Hong Kong when this assignment finishes. Besides, it is colder there!"

Li focused on Chris. "And how is Catrin doing in her new role? You'll tell me the truth, I'm sure."

The dig made Catrin smile. "Say nothing, Chris. Tell her you are covered by the Official Secrets Act."

Chris smiled. "Catrin is doing well. She has a bigger team to manage, yet she is home, if anything, earlier and more consistently than when she was in Art and Antiques. It's Mair exerting her control; she's the boss around here."

They were finishing the main course when Catrin answered a call on her mobile. From Chris's expression, Li saw that it was her work phone. Catrin listened, then stood and moved away from the table.

When she returned, they could all see she was disturbed, but trying to cover it up. It was Jean who, as Catrin tried to pick up the conversation, said, "If you can't tell us the details, tell us how you are feeling. Don't say it's a work issue. I know when something hurts you personally."

Catrin looked around the table, seeing similar expressions on her husband and friends.

"A man I arrested recently will now receive compassionate release from prison, I just discovered. He underwent a medical check in custody after a sudden collapse there. He has terminal heart problems, and it's too late for any restorative surgery."

There must be more to it, Li thought.

Catrin added, "He has asked to see me. I failed him, he claims, on a promise I made."

Jean asked, "What did you promise him? You told me police officers didn't make those."

"Well I did. I promised to give his family support, as they had no idea about the crimes which led to his arrest. It hit them really hard. He says they aren't getting it and he has little time left to deal with it."

Melanie said, "It's that Burcu Dogan, isn't it? His family can't claim -."

"Not him. Someone else. Look, I need to make a quick call, then I will be back. Properly back, interrogating Li on what she is really up to in Stockholm while her husband is a thousand miles away!"

She was away for fifteen minutes but, true to promise, on her return you couldn't tell that anything was wrong -

unless, of course, you knew her well and were prepared to go along with her efforts to cover her emotions.

Over the evening, as they enjoyed each other's company, things returned to normal, thank goodness.

39 LIGHTS

Catrin, DI Andy Collard and the family liaison officer, DC Iris Keaton, entered the private room at St. Mary's Hospital near Paddington Station, bracing for the meeting with both Howard St. John-Leer and his family.

He had undergone surgery for a tiny rupture of an aortic aneurysm the previous evening. The repair of the small leak had been successful, but the surgeon's prognosis, having seen the state of the rest of the major artery, was clear. It was fragile and could fail within hours or days. On the optimistic side, it could last weeks, perhaps a year at the outside, if properly managed.

The officers were advised that he was on medication to lower his blood pressure dramatically. The side effects were fatigue, difficulty to concentrate and dizziness. Under no circumstances could their presence exacerbate his condition. They had ten minutes maximum, only because St. John-Leer's anxiety was tied to his wish to talk to them.

A continuing prison existence or the stress of a forth-coming trial would kill him much sooner, both the surgeon and St. John-Leer's solicitor now argued.

It was unlikely that the new development justified the costly preparations for trial by either the Crown or the defendant, given the news. This morning, CPS had agreed in principle to the solcitor's request and now they needed to start the process for a formal compassionate release.

And while St. John-Leer had enemies now, he also had influential friends built up over his career. He was unlikely to return from hospital to prison.

Catrin spoke first. "We were very sorry to hear the news yesterday. All we can do is to offer our best wishes for a steady improvement to your condition."

In the back of her mind was the thought from yesterday evening; he could have dropped dead in custody at Lavender Hill after the arrest. Her comment was as good as she could make it. She still had St. John-Leer firmly linked in her mind to the lives and deaths of young addicts.

Yvonne St. John-Leer nodded vigorously. "That's what I told Howard. We have to be positive, to take every day as a gift."

"We have to be realistic, too." St. John-Leer still sounded like a senior executive.

"Thank you for the wishes. Strangely enough, I ought to thank you, I was thinking. What if you hadn't caught me, and this aneurysm had been fatal? Then you come along afterwards and expose it all. How would Yvonne and my daughters have coped then? Now, at least, we can talk about it."

He paused, resting a moment. They just waited. The nurse hovered at the periphery but didn't intervene.

"Chief Inspector Sayer, you told me you would offer family support at a critical time during our discussions.

There is an agreement of sorts, as I understand it. Penny, please tell the police officer about the bullying."

The younger daughter looked torn; afraid to speak and afraid not to do so. Catrin could see that, with all the news of the last few weeks, the girl was under tremendous pressure. Both the daughters were tense and looked sleep deprived.

"It's school. They can't do anything. I'm called names. Other kids damage my locker. I get notes calling me a slag and worse. There's a group from my year, they just gossip about me and tell awful things, lies."

"Such as?" Catrin asked.

"Dad's a criminal and so is all the family. That I have free drugs because my dad knows the top people. That we are filthy rich because we stole money. It goes on and on. And now this, the news about dad. Yesterday someone texted me, 'It served me right. God's justice on us is revealed'. The girl, Geraldine, doesn't even go to church, the hypocrite. She's not the first I have had to block."

Catrin was listening, but her eyes were glancing at the monitoring screen by the bed, seeing St. John-Leer's vital sign's change.

She said, "OK, Penny. Thank you. I get it. You spoke to Constable Keaton, and she spoke to the headmaster, as you know."

It was the girl's expression as she looked at Iris Keaton.

"Yes, Miss Keaton talked with the headmaster. My form teacher at the beginning spoke to the class, but that wasn't really any help. She's clever, but not very effective at controling things.

"But each time Constable Keaton or my mother raises the issue, we are told that the school has to collect facts before they can act. Who said what? When? Were others present who saw what happened? They are building files. They can't raise issues with parents until they have substantiated any allegation. It goes on, but for me, it just builds up. I hate going to school these days."

The girl had summarised well the feedback Catrin had received earlier from the liaison officer. Howard St. John-Leer just looked at her, waiting.

After a moment, Catrin said, "Iris, contact the headmaster now, please. Get me five minutes with Penny's class this afternoon. And Penny, I would like you to be present. A police car will bring you back to your dad afterwards, but let's try to turn this around for you, if I can."

She stood looking at St. John-Leer. "I meant what I said."

He nodded. "Thank you."

The FLO gave her a look and said carefully, "I don't think the school will take well to a police officer talking about bullying, ma'am, if I may say so. That's my read."

Catrin responded, "Who said I want to talk about bullying?"

Outside, as Keaton called the school, DI Collard said he would head back to the station. He had other commitments.Catrin responded, "I'll wait on Iris, to see how that goes with the school. I've got other calls to make, anyway."

As he turned to go, he said, "You are seeing Pauline Stillwell this afternoon, she said. Shall I tell her it's postponed?"

Catrin shook her head. "That's one of my calls. She can meet me here and come with me to the school. I'll bring her back. We can talk on the way."

~~

"Before the afternoon classes, a member of the Metropolitan Police will speak to you briefly."

When the headmaster entered, accompanied by Penny St. John-Leer and three women, the youngest one, DC Stillwell, found the boys looking her over, checking her out. The oldest woman stood close to Penny, now looking anxious.

The headmaster spoke clearly, but his tone of voice conveyed that this interruption would be brief. They had a schedule to follow, and Catrin's request did not sit well with him.

It was her statement that she would not dwell on the issue of bullying and take less than five minutes that swayed him.

Catrin moved to the centre, at the front of the classroom, and gave Penny a smile before addressing in the class, now seated.

"I am Detective Chief Inspector Sayer. With me are two members of my team, Detective Constables Keaton and Stillwell. DC Keaton is a Family Liaison Officer, currently assigned to duties that include support for the St. John-Leer family, which is why she is standing beside Penny."

She paused, giving it time to sink in.

"Police officers aren't heroes. Each of us has training, true, but we don't possess special capabilities to take on criminals or terrorists. We aren't any more comfortable than you around people who would kill or injure someone without a second thought.

"What we have, though, is something truly valuable; we support each other through thick and thin. From that bond, each of us finds the strength to do our job and, at times, keep doing it under incredibly difficult circumstances. That's when the media calls some of us heroes.

"So, I never look for heroes to work with, I choose people who can be strong team players. Particularly when the odds are against me, or another person. People who will do the right thing. And that's what I am trying to do now.

"Some of you will have noticed the scar on my cheek. I was injured years ago while making an arrest in Scotland. I remember being driven home, still partly sedated after recovering from surgery, with my face bruised and ballooned out with dressings.

"All the way down the motorways, police cars would flash their lights at our vehicle. You see, the word was out on the police radios that an injured officer was on her way home. People whom I didn't know at all took the time to find us. Some of them were highway or traffic officers working on our route, and others detoured just to say they were there for me. Those lights, that journey has stayed with me and bolstered me for a long time."

She paused. Eyes were on her face now, on her scar.

"I'm told by your headmaster that this is a good school, that you can rise to a challenge. I am giving you one now.

"Several weeks ago, my team arrested people involved in a criminal operation. We laid charges against them and under our law, they remain innocent until a jury reaches a verdict of guilty. Penny St. John-Leer's father was one of those arrested, and you all are aware of that. As you are also aware, he is now very ill.

"The family didn't know about any of this. You may have heard that they did, but I can say, because I was there, that is a malicious rumour. They have been devastated by this development. Their biggest challenge now is to support each other through some tough times."

She turned and looked across at Penny. "So, I am here

simply to flash my lights at Penny, to let her know I support her. My challenge is, will you do the same?"

As several students rose to move forward, Catrin raised her hands, stopping them. "Not now. Later, in person or in whatever way you communicate. DC Keaton is taking Penny back to the hospital to see her father now. This isn't a witch hunt to find those who won't come forward and stay in their seats."

She paused.

"Just realise that if you support each other, no-one, and I mean no-one at all, can pick on a member of a strong team."

She looked at the headmaster. In the silence that followed, she said to him, "Headmaster, thank you for the time with the class this afternoon."

As she walked back to join Pauline Stillwell and Iris Keaton, Penny said 'thank you' to her. Someone started clapping and the room burst with applause. Catrin ignored it as they all left through the door, leaving the form teacher and students to get on with their day.

In the corridor, the headmaster made a complimentary remark, but Catrin just grimaced as she turned and stopped to face him. Penny was now thanking Iris for the support.

She said quietly, "My assessment of the class as I spoke is that two girls in row three and a boy further back are probably among the ringleaders in this bullying. I don't know who they are, but you probably have information of that nature. You have processes to follow in the school and the education authority, but so do we. I was watching Penny's father in the hospital this morning, as she talked about the bullying she is receiving; it really stressed him. Be aware that if he dies soon and questions arise about any link to the stress on his children, I will speak to the coroner and go on the witness stand, if needed."

It won't reflect well on the school she was intimating.

The headmaster looked nonplussed. "I detest and don't tolerate bullying, Chief Inspector, but Penny's stress is far more related to her father's actions, to be frank about this."

Catrin gave no ground. "Mr. St. John-Leer will have an administrative release. He will never go to trial; never be found guilty. Right or wrong, that's the law. I suggest you be cognizant of that implication and act in the best interests of the school - and Penny, I might add."

She held out her hand. "Thank you for your time."

They were in Catrin's car starting the return journey to Lavender Hill, her driving. Stillwell had just responded to a general question from her boss.

"The talk went well, ma'am; but I wonder why you asked me to come over and accompany you?"

Catrin said, "We had a meeting booked for this afternoon and I didn't want to miss it or postpone it. It's been four months since you joined Undertow, How are you feeling about it? Are you happy working in Digital Intelligence or do other areas catch your interest?"

Stillwell felt that she was under scrutiny. She had done nothing wrong, she thought. In fact, she had that recognition from Sayer during all the arrests.

She frowned. "I'm a little surprised, ma'am, by the question."

"Why?"

"DC Digsby and I only reported to DI Franklin yesterday that we are seeing each other, so we don't fall foul of the regulations. And now you are asking me that question about moving within Undertow."

Catrin burst out laughing. "I had no idea about that! It is a complete coincidence. Nothing has been said to me, nor does it need to be. You informed your direct superior, that's enough. No, I'm just interested in where you think you are going in the Met?"

As Stillwell talked earnestly about her job and interests, Catrin focused on her answers and the road.

It was only later, as they walked into the Lavender Hill Police Station, that she allowed herself the indulgence of a private smile that Bo Digsby had plucked up courage to approach Pauline Stillwell.

40 GOATS

In the glorious weather of high summer, Dominic Connolly took his wife and kids back to The Fonab Castle for a few days. Being outside his home area, he needed the authorisation of his parole officer to do so. The officer had no issues with the request; Connolly had been a model citizen so far, while on parole. How could he turn down a request for a long weekend away?

Dominic had remembered the people he knew in Shotts. He wasn't allowed to visit there, of course, but he sent things they wanted through official routes. Books for someone's study course. Art supplies and reading materials. Subscriptions to magazines on an allowed list. Two of his former gang members (or, as he put it now, people from his former life) had been sent to university on his coin.

Whatever he sent them via unofficial routes wasn't put down to him.

The Connolly couple had opened a new business in Joan's name, a high-end hair stylist in the centre of Glasgow called 'New Luck', employing male and female ex-prisoners trained as stylists. It made no secret of the past lives of the owner's husband and her staff and it was popular.

He also bought into a funeral business, ironically in Edinburgh, still the home base of the Milne brothers, Steve and Frankie, now sworn enemies of Connolly after the Operation Finisterre debacle that put Connolly away. That piece of news led to a conversation between Lauder, Catrin and Chief Superintendent Eileen Strachan of Police Scotland.

Strachan said, "With the link between Connolly and Bolan, keep an eye on any moves by Michael Bolan involving the funeral business; they could be up to something."

Lauder smiled as he responded, "What? After Bolan did time for driving a hearse loaded with Class A drugs?"

Catrin said, "Just because he doesn't like the driving seat anymore, doesn't mean he doesn't like the vehicle; the hearse or the delivery route."

Strachan laughed.

Police Scotland carried out a routine check on the guest list for the Fonab Castle during the period Dominic Connolly was staying there. No-one with criminal links was on it and they didn't bother to arrange for a surveill-ance car. If they had, it wouldn't have turned up anything incriminating, anyway.

Once Dominic and Joan had settled into the suite, there was a knock at the door. A hotel staff member delivered a package left for them by a guest staying the week before. In it was a vase.

When Dominic reached Michael Bolan, it was the Londoner's second day of freedom. He was home. After congratulating Michael on his release, Dominic said, "Of all the things; something by Sayer and her partner. You could have left whisky. It would be better appreciated."

Michael chuckled. "No, that would have been too easy. We had one of Mo's friends buy this at the gallery. I'm watching Sayer's lot like a hawk these days, for the first signs that they are coming after me. I'm a bit fey on that. Cadwallader told me that Sayer was heavily involved in the process of putting Dogan away. Then, of course, I can't forget her working on Nirupa Ranjani, making her talk."

"She is persistent, I'll give her that."

"She's more than that, Dom. In talking with Roberta, Sayer had her stitched into an 'only way out' deal within a couple of hours of picking up that I planted her on the casino. And Roberta is no fool. When she made the call to Killam, he told her to take Sayer's offer to leave any involvement with me out of the charges. Cadwallader will be out in a month; like us, on parole."

"What'll you do with her?"

"Keep her clean, at least until her sentence is complete, in a job in a travel agency running the call operators. She's good at managing people. When she's free and clear, we'll see... But it'll remind me to keep Sayer out of my life."

Connolly said, "That's a bit more difficult for you, given her new job. I don't need the Met and Sayer to worry about; I have Police Scotland and bloody Strachan watching me. By the way, any more on Dogan?"

"He's back in London, in Thameside. A couple of his guys are looking after him, not for the money, either. He has none of the piss and vinegar left in him, I hear. We'll leave him alone to enjoy the misery and he still has his trial to go through. If we see any of the former 'Dog' coming back, I'll sort him out."

"And the territory?"

"Tony Hewitt moved in on some of the Southwell patch. We are leaving that for now. I had Mikey talk to him. If he goes after the juvie business there, we'll take him out hard. The kids are desperate for sources, but most are getting supplied through their older friends or family. No-one of mine is selling to them on the streets or around their schools, and we are shutting down any serious freelancers. I want Lauder to see I'm keeping my side of the understanding, at least through my parole. I want these years on the outside, thank you, and if Mikey has to break a few more ankles to do that, so be it."

The bell at the suite door rang.

Connolly said, "Hang on; there's someone at the door, Joanie is just opening it."

"No, I'll go; enjoy the holiday. We'll talk later."

As Bolan disconnected, Joan appeared from the entryway with a young bellman carrying a floral arrangement and an older man in a suit that Dominic recalled seeing here previously.

Joan said, "Some flowers from the hotel, Dom, welcoming us back. Remember Gordon? He has been so helpful over the years."

The older man was saying some welcoming words to them that Connolly partly missed, still thinking about the conversation with Michael. But he responded quite jovially, "Good to see you again, Gordon, and nice to be back here. I'm looking forward to dinner!"

The bellman had been checking with Joan on where she wanted the flowers. She was deciding between the placements of the vase and the flower arrangement. The bellman waited and Gordon said, as conversation filler, "An interesting piece of art, sir? That was the box we sent up earlier, I believe?"

"Yes," said Joan, "A present. A work by a pair of artists called Sayer and Hughes."

She gave Dominic a smile; it was an inside joke.

"Sayer?" said Gordon. "That sounds like a Welsh name."

Dom thought that the man's voice reflected something between surprise and alarm.

"Yes," he responded with a smile. "Created by someone we know."

The concierge was looking particularly peaky now, Dom thought. He hoped it wasn't a bug or something catching.

~~

Jean asked Catrin, "What will happen now, around here, I mean? The Limmies are as good as gone, Paulo says."

Catrin was in the Kiln, finishing a platter design. Paulo had popped in earlier in the day and passed on some street talk picked up in his job as door security at the Crimson Goat. Jean had repeated it and Catrin had admitted that it was reasonably accurate.

She shrugged. "I don't know. Their crew boss and his wife are both awaiting trial, with him held on remand. She is only on bail because of the kids. Paulo's sources are right; the Bolan gang is reasserting some territory control in the east of London. It's likely to get a little messier still before it stabilizes, we suspect. Burcu Dogan's drug crews are seeing big changes and some damage. As to Michael Bolan being old-fashioned and Paulo saying that his business is for grown-ups, not kids, I can't speak to that. Time will tell."

Melanie asked, "Paulo also said that you were involved

directly in the case. Is he right? You said you are working in organized crime investigation now. Is this the sort of thing you are going to continue with; not go back to art crime?"

"Yes, I'm sticking with my new job. And I was part of it, but there were lots of other people involved. I don't know what I'll be doing next; it may or may not be a case to do with drugs. Mark Harper has my old job. He's happy in it, he told me."

Jean said suddenly, "I went last week to see Jeremy's mum; to talk to her. She had sent me a card."

Catrin suddenly recalled the youth, on the floor in the doorway, 'Jer' Kingsley.

That surprised her. "How did it go?"

"Well, I think. She heard how I've been, and I heard what it was like for her with Jeremy and his life. It was his latest arrest, she told me. He had others."

Catrin just grimaced. "I know."

Jean pressed on, wanting to get it out. "I'm going with her to see him next week in his detention centre. We are going to talk to him together, we decided, to see if he is ready to change his life or not. His mum's hopeful, but not betting on it. I feel I should support her."

Catrin smiled. "Are you ready for this, though? You still have the memory of the crew coming in here."

"I have to face it, to see him as a boy, not a gang bully, and ask him to find a better way to live. We are staying here, not moving the Kiln, so I need to get over my fear, but do it my way. I talked to someone at St. Stephens about it."

St. Stephen's was an Anglican church with a strong 'rainbow' message. Jean and Melanie had been attending the services there for a long time.

She looked a little defensive.

Looking at Melanie, Catrin could see that she wasn't completely on board with this plan. And Chloe was looking skeptical.

Chloe added, "I asked Mr. Vance whether I should go with her. 'No way', he said. It might give him and his family grounds for a civil lawsuit; it's too risky."

Lawyers and priests; they see the world differently, thought Catrin.

"Each of you has to do what you feel to be right," she said.

She walked over and put her arms out, giving Jean a hug, holding her tight. Over Jean's shoulder, she said to Melanie, "It's like our schooldays. I was the one in the arguments with others, while Jean was pulling us together, wanting us all to be friends."

She squeezed her friend. "You have the best heart of all of us, you know that? I'm so glad we are still friends."

Jean had tears in her eyes. "We'll always be that. It's being together; so our kids can grow up like we did. That was the hardest part of thinking of leaving."

"For me, too. I think it was why I felt I had to do something more as a police officer. Art crime wasn't doing it for me anymore."

Jean paused. "I have an idea for a piece for us to do together, if you are up to it."

Catrin smiled and looked at Mair and then at Melanie and Chloe.

Chloe reached over, picking up Mair and fussing her as Melanie called to Lili.

"Lili, let's take Mair to the park, shall we? Your mum and Aunty Catrin want to work together here for a bit. We can go play ourselves with Chloe."

Jean was mum; Melanie was mummy.

Lili squealed something indecipherable. As Melanie

looked perplexed, Lili ran up and bumped her head into Melanie's thigh. It was clear what she meant. Chloe put her hand to her mouth, remembering Lili's astonished look as she turned back to face the people in the shop after head-butting Kingsley. She bent down.

"No Lili, we don't want you hurting your head, my lovely; not play at being goats. It wasn't a good game. There are better ones we can play now."

~~

Her duty sergeant in the Bedfordshire Police head-quarters had looked hard into Sylvia's eyes as she approached him; a knowing, concerned stare. It was her first day back on normal duty.

"Okay?"

Sylvia nodded. "All well; yes, sarge."

"And the holiday? You have a nice tan, I see."

"Aidan and I went to Italy again. We like it there."

There was no discussion of her real absence before her holiday leave, time accrued while she was undercover and the special leave thereafter. It was best that way; they both knew.

He sighed. "Well, back to the grind for you. I have you lined up for a 2.00 p.m. departure, a drop-off of the deputy chief constable at Heathrow by 4.00 p.m. Then you are free until 5.15 p.m. there, a collection of a couple to go to the Mercure Hotel in Bedford. They are Americans coming in for victim support and to make statements, I gather. DCI Houghton wants them met."

Sylvia was writing down the instructions. Standard stuff.

"This morning, I've got you with DC Freyer, taking a Mrs. Cumberland to see her son at his hearing. You know

319

Linda Freyer, Family Liaison?

"Not well, but I know her, yes."

"She has sprained her ankle badly and can't drive, but she wants to stick with Mrs. Cumberland during her son's appearance in court. It won't be long, so you can hang around then bring her back."

Sylvia had stayed in the role of Alison with the Ballantine Casino for four days, not two. She had talked with Frank Loomis, picking up on the fabrication that her mother's surgery and the situation at home were such that she had to go back to help. The casino seemed to be back to normal by then in most ways. Several people had been detained but, for the chauffeurs, the obvious holes were Mrs. Cadwallader and Mr. St. John-Leer.

Sylvia agreed to work the extra two days, to allow Frank to find a substitute. It was on her last day when she went to collect a visitor from the executive floor. The painting of the dice had disappeared. Eve noticed Sylvia staring at the space.

"Mr. Suarez had it taken down and returned to the family; he thought it was for the best. Mr. St. John-Leer is no longer with the company."

They were on the A428, driving through rain. Sylvia was only half-listening to the mother talking with the FLO in the back. Freyer was doing a good job of bolstering the older woman. Sylvia suspected that Cumberland was a perennial whiner.

"If his dad were alive, he would have had none of this, I tell you. None of Neil's antics and friends."

The glance exchanged between the two police officers via the rearview mirror confirmed for Sylvia that this was old ground being reworked between Cumberland and

Freyer.

Cumberland continued her monologue. "I should never have listened to him; marijuana is like beer, not like hard drugs. The Dutch legalized it and the Canadians are talking about it. It was all together for him, the weed, the pills and the other things. And now this."

Linda Freyer responded mechanically. "They won't be asking him his opinions, Phyllis, just the facts. He's agreed to testify, as we discussed."

"Well I hope he doesn't try the 'justification' stuff he put me through. I love him, but he's wrong on this one. He shouldn't be pleading 'not guilty'."

"We just sit there and watch; not comment. You can't speak. You have to leave everything to his legal counsel."

Sylvia suppressed a smile as she exchanged glances again with the liaison officer. It was not a job she would want.

Phyllis Cumberland sighed. "How did it come to this? All these drug gangs, all these people driving our kids into this sort of hell. It seems to me that we can't cope with the people who do this."

Driving along, Sylvia thought back to the note from DCI Sayer and the short meeting with her after the arrests. Some of us are trying, she thought. Some of us are taking them on.

Unconsciously, she twisted the engagement ring on her left hand and her thoughts turned to her brother.

EPILOGUE

The retirement send-off for DC Isabelle Howlett of the Art and Antiques Unit, held at the Lord Moon Pub on the Mall, was a gathering and a half. Current and former colleagues turned up, with only a core of them staying the course. Others came in at different times and stayed for a while or left after bidding her farewell.

One surprise participant was FBI Senior Agent David Klintz, who travelled the Atlantic on his own dime to be there, as much for his former colleague Morley Kerswell as for Isabelle. He was heading on holiday thereafter, into Europe, but he didn't say where. Morley had traveled over to London from Paris for the last week of Howlett's time working at the Met.

Detective Sergeant John Obi, as Isabelle's direct boss, took on the job of orchestrating the melee and choosing the best time, given the comings and goings of people, to invite DI Mark Harper to address the group. Mark spoke both flatteringly and humorously about Isabelle and gave her the department farewell gift.

She had already been presented with her formal

retirement plaque and a watch at lunch, hosted by Superintendent Harrison. The early evening gathering was noisier and more chaotic.

As John called for order after Mark said his piece, Isabelle tried to keep her focus on him, but her eyes kept checking the door. Inevitably, she stood up to respond; to speak to a group of fellow officers yet again today, give a second farewell speech.

She made Morley come and stand by her this time.

"It's been a hell of a day, finishing up. I've experienced nothing like it before. Normally I am sitting over there, having a drink, watching the person on his or her way out. And now it's me."

She looked around at the smiling faces, now quiet, attentive.

"I will not talk about the past *ad nauseam*. In twenty-five years, I've had my share of difficulties and good people to work with - and some less than that. Other than one boss, who is dead now, and you don't speak ill of the dead, they've all been good to me in their own way. Some of them are here, so I will not show favoritism. All I'll say is that I resisted every one of you wanting me to be promoted. Why? Because I liked the work I did; particularly so when I moved into Art and Antiques. It's a job I have loved and hated and laughed about and cried over and…"

She stopped, suddenly looking at the two people who had just entered, Catrin Sayer and Neville Coltrane.

"You made it," she continued, smiling.

"His train was late," Catrin called out, in response. "But go on, it's your show."

"I was saying I'm not going to favour any one boss I had, they've all been good except one - and only Neville could say who that one was; he knew him and took me into Art and Antiques; saved my bacon, in a sense."

Coltrane smiled and nodded.

She pressed on with her remarks. "Art and art crime have fascinated me. I thought at one time I would do art conservation as a career, but I can now say I'm glad I did what I did.

"Morley and I are going to live in Paris, as you know, and the first day we met was there. We found we both liked and admired Rose Valland, the woman who worked to save French masterpieces from the Nazi pillages. In my own way, in much easier and peaceful times, I've done my bit to keep art where it rightfully belongs and bring to justice people who would abuse it. I'm proud of that. And proud and happy to have worked with you all here, at different times."

There were some murmurs and applause, but she waved her hands; she wasn't finished.

"There's only one person I wanted to single out tonight, and it's Catrin. Not because of her as a boss, but for sending me to Paris. When I went to the Art Crime Task Force for the first time, it should really have been Mark who attended; he was more logical to send and had the background. It was quite scary to do that for me, but she made me do it, deliberately breaking the traditional roles. Morley and Agent Klintz looked after me there. That's how we met and without Catrin seeing more in me than I saw in myself, I wouldn't be the lucky woman I am tonight.

"Thank you Catrin for that, especially. Thank you all for being my colleagues and being here tonight. And I'm not saying any more other than enjoy the evening."

In the applause, she sat down, head focusing on the floor to hide her tears. Morley smiled but said nothing as John Obi stood and said, "Right. Enough speeches. A toast to Isabelle and Morley."

As they raised their glasses, Catrin smiled and felt happy for her former team member. People would come up to the couple in dribs and drabs, sharing anecdotes or memories, then making their farewells, she knew. She and Neville went over to say hello and talk with her and Morley before that started.

It was later, in a quieter corner of the pub, that Neville, David Klintz and Catrin got together after seeing Morley and Isabelle off home. In two weeks, they would be settled in Sevres, near Paris.

Neville was talking about the Masud case. "I'm glad Jon Masud got what was coming to him, but sorry you had to be a witness, Catrin. David told me about it afterwards."

She smiled. "I wasn't recalled; the defense lawyer never got to the difficult bit."

She was referring to the collusion between the two men sitting with her now, to make sure Klintz made the arrest. She gave the pair a look as they both feigned innocence. Neville changed the subject.

"It was nice to see so many former colleagues. Mark seems to be doing well leading the Art and Antiques Unit. And Laura Bainbridge; still at it! A consultant on rare stamp thefts, in and out of the USA these days, she says."

David Klintz smiled. "There are a lot of wealthy American philatelists, that's for sure. I talked with her a bit, earlier. She was quite open about it; a lifelong spinster, no family living now; her work is her life, and she is enjoying it thoroughly. Being let go from the Met on early retirement was a wake-up call, she said."

He turned to Catrin. "You are looking well - and very formal if I may say so. I like the jacket."

She knew that Klintz was a careful dresser, even when on holiday, it seemed. Neville was in a suit still, as he had been in Paris during the day, at a UN meeting. She was more somberly dressed than usual, too. They had all stood out a bit in the gathering, she realised.

"Well, thank you!"

She explained, "I was at a funeral this morning. Someone I arrested during the Ballantine Casino case. He never went to trial as he had an undiagnosed heart problem."

Coltrane arched his eyebrows. "A DCI, checking out which of his cronies turned up?"

It was normally a job for the lower ranks, he inferred; a classic police procedure, checking out weddings and funerals of criminal gang members.

She shook her head. "No, to support the family, actually. I said to him I'd do that, and I thought it was fitting to attend for some closure."

But there was someone at St. John-Leer's funeral I didn't expect, she thought.

None of the people who had been in executive flight centres around the UK, taking money packages, had appeared at Howard St. John-Leer's funeral. They were overseas and one, at least, was in prison. Nor did anyone from the casino turn up other than Roberta Cadwallader, who was similarly regarded as *persona non grata* by the Ballantine Group.

Cadwallader approached Catrin after the funeral service. All she said was, "It wasn't that I didn't enjoy working with him, you see? I just used him. We never spoke after our arrests, so I came to the funeral, instead."

"And life on parole? How's that going?"

They were watching the funeral cortege preparing to

leave for the cemetery. Catrin didn't plan to go to there, as she had to get back to work.

"It's okay. I have a job in a travel agency now. In fact, I have to go, get back to work."

She smiled and turned, walking off without another word.

Catrin hadn't noticed Penny St. John-Leer, who had slipped away from the family group, until she turned around. She was standing several feet away, watching.

"Hello, Penny."

She had offered her condolences to the family earlier.

The girl asked shyly, "That woman; did she work with my father or is she a police officer?"

Catrin smiled. "She is a former colleague of your father, yes. How are you doing at school these days?"

She recalled the close-out report from Iris Keaton.

Penny replied, "It's a school and there are camps. But that's why I came over, partly. It's OK now. I am stronger about it all. It was a bad time, so thank you for flashing your lights, then and today."

Catrin nodded and smiled.

The girl glanced over at the gathering and saw her sister beckon. "And thank you for the last weeks. Our dad had always been away, so distant, always at work. I feel that I got to know him better. Despite his failings and his illness, I got to be closer to my dad for a while."

She nodded, as if happy that she had expressed what she had wanted to say. She walked back before Catrin could say anything in response.

Klintz asked, "And you, Catrin; how is your life balancing out now, in your new job?"

Catrin pondered the question. "Most weeks, very well; according to plan, one could say. Home regularly, plenty of time with Mair and my husband. I leave a lot to my team leads. They get the longer hours these days. But at times it goes to hell in a hand basket.

"Chris and I have a person who helps at home; she is now pretty much a nanny full-time, between Jean and Melanie and Chris and me. So Mair is well cared for. But I hate being late home these days."

"And the pressures? Organized crime versus art crime?" added Neville.

Catrin laughed. "The two have been pretty well mixed in together. We all know that and have those case experiences."

She paused.

"I was talking with Vittorio a couple of days ago, calling him to pick his brains on a lead for a contact in the Carabinieri, not to talk about any art case. We chatted a bit as well and he suddenly asked me something that tied back to a comment Sandra Hunt made, just as I was coming back after my maternity leave. He asked, 'In my new job, did I feel happy that I had grown into it?' I told him I do."

Coltrane exchanged a knowing glance with the FBI man and then responded to her. "Then that's a good thing. It's all that matters really, don't you think?"

She smiled. "I think so. I hope things will settle down for a while."

Then she saw Klintz and Coltrane exchange knowing looks.

"So, what do you know that I don't?"

"Nothing!"

Coltrane was too emphatic, so much so that Klintz just laughed. "The UN is a gossip shop, Catrin. Neville tries to stay above it all but occasionally plunges in head-first."

With that, her former boss had no option but to share the latest rumour.

"I heard, from a reliable person, that the Met is likely to appoint a new commissioner soon. You know, checking the normal rotation through that position, some noises in diplomatic circles, it will not be too long and... you know what that means!"

Catrin grimaced. "They stir the pudding bowl again. There are shuffles and new titles and..."

Klintz, amused, added, "Organisational reorganisation, *ad infinitum*."

Catrin smiled. "All I can do is keep working at the job I've got, take care of my family and enjoy life."

"And ceramics!" added Coltrane, causing Catrin to nod and smile in acknowledgement.

"Sounds like a toast to me," added David Klintz, raising his glass.

NOTES

Every novel starts with a blank page. For some, it holds the terrors of writer's block. For others, it is the moment when scraps of ideas are sifted, a sentence or two is written and the story begins to grow.

I had decided to take time off from the Catrin Sayer Mysteries to write a quite separate novel, *Canons*. As I finished book seven in the series, *The Thornham Copyist*, I made notes with some preliminary ideas to develop the career and life of Catrin Sayer, for when I returned to it.

In March 2019, totally immersed in writing *Canons*, I read the news about seventeen-year-old Jodie Chesney being murdered in a senseless knife attack tied to drug

330

crime in a park in Harold Hill, Romford. It was not that far from Rainham, Essex, where I lived for a decade. I knew immediately that some elements of this awful crime would feature in the next Catrin Sayer novel.

This is not, of course, a rendering of Jodie's sad story. In developing *The Chiswick Chauffeur* though, the aftermath of the senseless murder, the reactions, the arrests and the trial of the people accused of the crime, stayed with me.

I have always endeavored to make my villains real; more amoral, greedy and selfish at times, rather than psychopathically evil. Perhaps in writing *The Chiswick Chauffeur*, I have voiced the faint hope that there are people in the world of organized crime who won't exploit and ruin the lives of our children. I know very well that such a premise is ill-founded and rose-tinted, but it is my novel, and I can be allowed to dream a little.

As stated in previous novels in this series, the Metropolitan Police in London does have an Art and Antiques Unit within its Specialist Crime Command that was established back in 1969. However, the people, structure and activities described herein are entirely my own creation. The same caveat applies to other Metropolitan Police units mentioned.

My wife Gill and my friends Jack Soule and Fred Grigsby read drafts of the work at various stages, which contributed significantly to the development of the story.

ABOUT THE AUTHOR

Allan Jones lives in Ontario, Canada. He was born and grew up in Merseyside, England. By profession an industrial chemist, he worked for many years as a consultant on international chemical regulation. He has lived in or travelled to most of the regions featured in the Catrin Sayer novels.